I0699555

Sienna Cogsworth

&

The Legend of the Sparrows

Aditi Bagul

Text copyright © 2024 Aditi Bagul
All rights reserved. This book or parts thereof may not be reproduced in any form, stored in any retrieval system, or transmitted in any form by any means such as electronic, mechanical, photocopy, recording, or otherwise; without prior written permission of the publisher.

Cover art: Magic Studio

This is a work of fiction. Names, characters, places, and incidents either are the product of the author's imagination or are used fictitiously and any resemblance to actual persons, living or dead, business establishments, events, or locales is entirely coincidental.
Published 12/15/2024

ISBN: 979-8-218-56776-7

To my mom, dad, and little sister, for being
the real stars.

Table of Contents

Prologue

A few star-years ago in Philoxenia

The streets of Edmonia were filled with townspeople sweeping their porches and decorating each building with pastel thread. It was the annual Blaze Festival—a day where local Edmonians would throw powder into purple fires and make two wishes each year.

A fourteen-year-old girl name Mazie Polaris stood on the balcony, her braid wavering in the air. She had pockets full of magical powder in her versatile dress. But she never made her wishes. And she never did anything with her powder.

"What are you doing up here? We've been looking for you." A boy called, and he was running out of breath as he ran up the stairs. His face was covered in powder.

Mazie shrugged, "Oh, I don't know." She took out her powder and handed it to him, "Here, take it to the Blaze Fest. You can have it"

He frowned as he grabbed the bags from her hands, "Why aren't you ever with us?"

She shrugged again, her finger tracing the imprints on the balcony rails, she didn't answer.

He tried breaking the silence, "Look, it's going to be fun, c'mon." He stretched out his hand, but she didn't take it. "Look on the bright side, you get two wishes."

"They never come true."

He knitted his eyebrows in surprise, "Sure they do."

"Prove it."

He laughed, he glanced down the balcony. The purple fires were lit and they changed colors every few seconds. The warm colors up lifted the town and the clashing of vibrant fires muddled with the girl's thoughts.

She admitted, "If wishes weren't true, I wouldn't be friends with you right now." He bit his lip, hoping the vibrant fires down below would cover his blush.

She arose, her lips couldn't help but curl into a smile. But her grin faded, "Are all the things they said about you true? About your father, Macladez Zecron?"

He dismissed her idea with a gesture, "I don't even know who made those rumors."

She slumped over the balcony again, "And you're sure they're not going to judge me from what happened?"

He held out his hand again, "I promise."

She gave a small sigh and took his hand, "Okay…I trust you, Campbell."

Musical notes floated in the air and touched the hearts of many at Mazie Polaris's tent.

In front of thirteen-year-old Mazie sat several little children with their legs folded, awestruck by her melodic performance.

Her friend from the other end of the hall initiated the applause, with all of the little children following him.

"Wasn't she wonderful?" He exclaimed, and the applause grew louder.

She bowed while holding her peculiar instrument, with strings stretched between an irregular crossbar, "Thank you, thank you."

A small boy holding a smaller version of her instrument stood from the crowd and ran towards her, "Can you tune my instrument?" He asked from the bottom of the stage.

Her eyes illuminated, "Of course, I'd be happy too." But as she reached to grab his instrument from his arms, he vanished in the blink of an eye.

"Where did he go?" Mazie screamed in distress, "Where did he go?"

Campbell began pacing around the room, "Did anyone see him?" He asked the children.

Parents standing around their children grabbed their hands and backed away, whispering in their ears.

"Wait! I'm not sure what happened, please!" Mazie begged. "Come back!" She set her instrument down and ran backstage.

Another eight-year-old girl, Disha Raj, walked into the tent, approaching the girl's friend, "Excuse me sir, I have a folk-song from Honeyville from the Tech World that I would love for her to play–"

"Don't you see we're busy?" The boy yelled, "She doesn't have time for this!"

Tears streamed down the little girl's eyes, "But Mazie always has time to--"

"Go away!"

Disha, stunned, ran away from the halls, with the boy running backstage, calling for his friend.

"Hey! It's going to be alright."

Mazie was sobbing behind the curtains, "I don't know what happened, Campbell. One minute he was there and the next he–" she couldn't finish her sentence

Her friend patted her back, "We'll find him, don't worry." He took out a small contraption from his pocket, "If you ever need it, it's a time machine."

The girl paused, reaching her hand out for the little innovation. Her tears didn't stop streaming, but curiosity added to them.

"It only goes back to 1901. Use it when you need to." He gave a small wink.

Chapter One

Is It Just Me, Or Are Those Purple Stars?

Looking into my telescope at night from the old circus caravan always left me with more questions than answers. Don't ask me why. That's another question.

But every unresolved doubt left a small void that I couldn't quench easily.

Maybe I am looking for something. Something very special. And hopefully that something special helps me be as great as my Aunt Katelyn.

I mean, I always spent most of my time observing the stars when the sky is dark. All that time has to pay off someday. At some point.

And tonight, I saw something magnificent, something beautiful, yet something uncanny. The clear and convenient autumn breeze clasped onto six purple stars–allowing them to embrace the dominance of the sky this time.

Purple.

I shoved my rolling chair back and peeked my head out of the window of the caravan. Four of them could make a triangle, and the other two were on opposite sides of the triangle. One in the front. And one in the back.

I squinted my eyes and focused deeper. Between these large stars were smaller ones. It was like you were playing a game of connect-the-dots, instead it was in real life. The stars formed a dome in the front. A *head.*

The triangles were the wings.

And the two stars were the tail and beak.

It was a *bird.*

I laid back, titling the chair a little, and puzzled with myself. Did I see a new constellation?

Wait.

Humans can't see purple or green stars. Can they? So, I glanced at the constellation again, only for the stars to show me that the color purple was its prime attribute. I stretched my neck out of the caravan, letting the breeze ruffle my red hair. Maybe I debunked that theory, maybe I *did* prove science wrong.

I rushed to the other end of the circus caravan where the square window was. Aunt Katelyn parked the caravan right outside our home so that the caravan's window was parallel to the kitchen window in our one-story house. This way, we could always talk when she was cooking and I was stargazing. If the kitchen window was ever unlocked, I would cross through the caravan window and the kitchen window to get in the house—when she wasn't looking, of course.

Aunt Katelyn was in her room across from the hall inside the house, braiding her brunette hair at her vanity. Her eyes widened and her lips curled into a smile as I walked in.

"Hi my little *beanie*," she said, using her favorite nickname and tying the end of her hair with a bow. "Always, always, braid your hair before you sleep. Here, Sienna, I'll do it for you."

I sat down next to her and she separated and combed my ginger hair into three parts.

"The secret to beautiful hair, Sienna, is not taking any stress." She said, stroking my hair, "You see my skin?"

I nodded.

"It's almost as soft as yours. Why? Because stress isn't a word in our dictionary."

I picked out a soft bow and handed it to her behind me as she finished braiding my hair, "And words like courage, bliss, and zeal are." I replied.

Aunt Katelyn triumphantly wrapped her arm around me, cuddling me into her warm hug, "I raised you so well."

I sat there for a moment, letting all my worries slip away like water trickling from stormy clouds. All the rain piled up was set free by her. And I always try not to let it back in...

…It was two years ago, maybe three, when Aunt Katelyn let the word stress appear in her dictionary.

"It's so nice of you to give these children gymnastic classes," said the activity coordinator of the local foster care center as she scribbled down notes on large sheets of paper.

Aunt Katelyn smiled, "Well…it's one way to help them out. You can't force them to do anything, you have to take what they gravitate toward and start from there." She turned her over from the lobby to find a couple of kids chasing each other around the pillars.

The woman nodded and clicked her pen from behind the front desk. As she leaned over her desk, she whispered, "Katie, you had so much potential, and yet you paused it all for taking care of that young girl."

Paused her potential? Even if the woman's words were let out soft, it didn't hide the fact that they had sharp edges. The activity coordinator pushed her glasses up the bridge of her small nose and tilted her head--waiting for an answer.

My aunt giggled, and rubbed my shoulder, "Sienna? She's my niece, her success *is* my success." I grasped onto her hand and squeezed it tight.

Her success is my success.

The woman stepped aside from her desk, "Katelyn, you know how far you could've gone with your contortion skills. You used to be in the Harrison Circus, everyone *only* came to see you."

Aunt Katelyn tensed, her knuckles whitened as she tried to grasp her feelings into a fist and her heart was pounding in her throbbing throat. It was probably anger. Or guilt. I couldn't really tell.

"She's all I have…"

"Of your brother? I know."

Aunt Katelyn's eyes began to glimmer and she led my hand out of the doorway. Not saying her cheery goodbye, or leaving with a remarkable exit like she always did. She simply walked away.

I pulled my hand back from hers on the sidewalk outside of the center, "You're not going to send me to foster care, are you?"

She let out a melancholy breath and picked me up. I wiped away a bit of her tears, but only more and more streamed down her cheeks. "No, my little beanie. You're my world, Sienna, don't you ever think that."

We walked home in silence. I couldn't help but think what Aunt Katelyn's life would've been like if she took that woman's advice. If she would've been a growing sensation in that circus, or if her talents took her somewhere else. Somewhere other than raising a stable life for a little girl— like her father wanted.

Nights after that, I would lay in bed, pretending to be asleep so I could watch Aunt Katelyn pretend too. That was the only thing she wasn't the best at. Pretending…

…"Auntie," I called, "I wanted to show you something I saw today in the old circus caravan."

Her eyes lit up, she set down her hairbrush and stood up, reaching out a hand, "What are you waiting for? Show me!"

My lips curled into a smile, and I grabbed her hand, dragging her to the backyard.

In the backyard, I opened the latch, over the sign painted on the front of the caravan: *The Harrison Circus* and pushed open the wooden door. I indicated my hand to the telescope, "Look."

The purple bird constellation still dominated the sky with each star individually gleaming. Aunt Katelyn squinted her eyes and peeked through the telescope, "What is it that I'm looking at?"

"Well, it's a purple constellation. See it?"

Aunt Katelyn gasped, "Purple?" She then looked again peeking through the telescope and adjusted the lens, pivoting it around the window. With each turn, more and more confusion grew on her face.

I set the telescope aside and pointed directly into the sky, you didn't even need an instrument to see it. But Aunt Katelyn kept searching for it. "Sienna, where–"

I frowned, it was *right* there. I blinked several times, and the purple stars were the first thing my eyes saw when they opened each time. How could she not see it?

"Auntie it's right there–"

She glanced at me and her face lowered a little. When she saw the concern in my eyes, she searched out into space, looking for it again. And her eyes lowered again before she knitted her eyebrows to find the stars once more. She placed her arm around me. "Can you point to it again?"

I raised both hands this time, letting my fingers draw the outline of the bird. Aunt Katelyn dropped her jaw and stood up. "Oh, I see! It's one of your clever games, isn't it? Well, Sienna, you have a beautiful imagination for making new constellations. Let me try to find it—but be warned, my imagination isn't as bright as yours." She scrunched her eyes and looked around through the window, using her finger to trace random stars in the sky together. "I think I found it. It's beautiful, isn't it? Looks like a little bird on a branch…"

But the bird I saw was *flying*.

This wasn't a game of finding the shapes in the clouds, where people see different shapes in the same cloud. Or in this case, find different shapes out of the same batch of stars. This was a bright, purple constellation we're looking at. How could she miss it?

Aunt Katelyn swayed me back and forth, "My little girl created a new constellation. *An eleven-year-old astronomer changes the course of the stars.* That headline has a nice ring to it."

I smiled, "I think I'll name it after you…and then you can be in all the interviews with me…and maybe we can open our own observatory.

"There's no limit, beanie, remember that." she said, rubbing my shoulder. I looked in her eyes, they were still searching into the sky, *trying* to believe me, trying to hope that I didn't go crazy. And then she softened, concluding that my imagination is simply beyond her understanding. "Now c'mon, it's time for bed."

She stepped over to the large window that was back-to-back with the house. She opened the kitchen window and stepped through, "You coming?"

My jaw dropped, "I thought you'd–"

She laughed, "Think smarter not harder, Sienna."

I followed her into the house and she fluffed up the pillows on our bed. Aunt Katelyn's phone received a notification. The illumination of her lockscreen was like that purple star amongst the house at night.

She turned to look at it, and shook her head in laughter, "Look at this." It had to be something special. She only received notifications regarding her jobs as a gymnastic instructor. Rescheduling, shipping of new equipment, and those were always super, super dull.

Instead, it was an email detailing the Harrison Circus' past escapades and requesting kids to participate in their new circus camp. For the whole week of fall break, they would teach children basic gymnastics, swinging and performances.

Auntie slapped her hand on her forehead, "That's so silly, the circuses doesn't even exist anymore."

A brilliant idea popped into my mind, "But what if we signed up? Then maybe, you could re-live your days as an acrobat…how it used to be for you."

She shook her head, "Sienna, if I'm being honest, I don't want to go back to that circus, I'd much rather work at the gymnasium. It has forever scarred me."

"Scarred you?"

"When your father needed me to take care of you, the circus said I had to go. They were very, very, cruel in nature."

My heart dropped and my veins ran cold. I tried to swallow the knot that tightened in my throat so I could speak. But the knot won.

She shook her head and put her phone back onto the kitchen counter, "The Harrison Circus doesn't exist anymore. It's probably a Trojan Horse." She lifted me up into a piggyback, "Now, it's time to sleep before our journey tomorrow." Aunt Katelyn stroked a pose like a captain leading the ship on a voyage.

I giggled as she carried me into her bedroom.

Aunt Katelyn always left the curtains of the window open. She made the stars my night-light ever since I was a small child, and tonight, the room ignited that hazy purple color.

I laid awake, trying to let the soft cushion lull me to sleep, but the feeling that Aunt Katelyn faked being proud wasn't doing me any favors. She's a terrible liar, so she can't show that she's genuinely thrilled. I wish she really saw it, then maybe it'd be a sign that taking care of me is nothing to regret. It'd prove that the front desk clerk was wrong.

Her success is my success.

I don't even know what decision she *would* be making. I was always told that my parents left me on her doorstep. My dad's sister was the most responsible adult out there. Maybe even the *only* adult out there.

But Aunt Katelyn never told me why I was left on that doorstep. If she was in a circus, perhaps my dad was too. All she ever told me was that they needed to go—and they needed someone to let me have a childhood. To go to school, to stay at home, and to grow up.

Yet I wasn't playing to pretend, the constellation was right there. It *is* right there. It wasn't a game, if only she could know that. If only she could see it.

I looked at Aunt Katelyn's phone from across the hallway, I could possibly take a picture of it. I grabbed her phone and headed outside.

The illumination of the constellation only got brighter. Some of the stars twinkled more than the others, in a way that it seemed as if the bird was flying. And some of the stars were larger than the others.

The stars spread out over the streets, making the street lamps almost seem unlit. So much so that the other stars seemed unlit. It was like all of the roofs were shaded purple, and there was nothing else that contrasted it.

I raised her phone above my head to capture a good angle. I took a couple more to make sure that Aunt Katelyn couldn't miss it. When I lowered the phone to take a look at them, the constellations in the pictures were *gone*. It was like someone cut them out and left the dark sky to take its place. I couldn't see a single trace of it in the photo.

Maybe that's what Aunt Katelyn was seeing from the caravan. But when I looked back at the sky, the constellation was still there. It was still ruling space.

I couldn't figure out what bird it was. It couldn't be something predatorial, like a hawk or an eagle. It wasn't a bluejay or a parrot. It had to be something simple. Perhaps a finch… or a sparrow.

I raised the phone even higher to snap a picture again. I brought my arms down as quickly as I could to see it, and the constellation was in the picture this time…but then it faded away.

I gave up, maybe I was hallucinating or maybe I was going crazy. I guess it's possible that you can be *too* passionate about something.

I climbed on top of the caravan roof and simply stared at the purple stars. I couldn't guarantee if it was going to be here tomorrow, so I better enjoy it while I'm still in this insane phase.

November's gusts rolled in, and the clouds took over. The breeze swayed the redwoods around our house from left to right. And the backyard became a dance floor for the grass.

The street lamps caught my attention, there was something taped to all of them. I climbed down from the top of the caravan and headed to the nearest pole. The colors were striking orange and red and all of the posters were in the shape of a tent. As I approached one of the posters, it started to look like a photocopy of that email my aunt received.

I tried to block out the radiance from the sky to read what it said:

Calling All Children!

The Harrison Circus Welcomes You To Our First ever Circus Camp!

My jaw dropped as my eyes read over those lines again and again.

It could not have been a Trojan Horse.

Chapter Two

We're On A Losing Streak

I grabbed my backpack and skipped through the pale everglades that ran from the trail of our front porch to the driveway. I hopped into the car in the breezy morning for school as my aunt had gathered her bag, had her gymnastic suit ready and jingled the building keys in her open hand.

I sat in the back seat of the car while she drove me to school, with redwoods racing ahead of us.

"Hey Aunt Katelyn?"

"Yes?" she answered.

I said, "You know that Circus Camp thing happening, it's a real thing."

Aunt Katelyn knitted her eyebrows, "Are you sure? Because I'm pretty sure it's a Trojan Horse."

"No it's not, there's flyers everywhere. And…I think I kind of want to join."

My aunt nodded, "Well…we'll see about it. You still have your gymnastic practices."

I sighed, I knew she was going to say that, "But that is with *you*, Aunt Katelyn. You know you can teach me gymnastics at home. This could be a once and a lifetime camp. A circus, bright colors, animals, fire and acrobatics. You've experienced that Aunt Katelyn and I want to, too."

I widened my eyes and tilted my head, trying to make the best begging face, "Please?"

Aunt Katelyn shrugged, "We will see after school, Sienna."

I nodded in response. It wasn't a no, so I'll take it. I glanced towards her, her hands grasping the wheel tightly. Her shoulders were scrunched and she was biting her lip. Something was on her mind today. Her shoulders are usually relaxed, and she's driving like it's her first time, stressed and confused.

"Are you a little stressed, Aunt Katelyn?" I asked.

Aunt Katelyn jolted, "Me? No. Why?"

"You seem that way." I said, calmly.

Aunt Katelyn shook her head slightly, "No, Sienna. There are many things to be concerned about when you're a gymnastic instructor."

"Like injuries?" I've sprained my ankle before while cartwheeling off of the balance beam, but almost everyone gets hurt at some point. It's just part of it, and it's part of

Aunt Katelyn's job too, she's been doing this for a long time. So why is she getting scared now? Of injuries?

Aunt Katelyn took a deep swallow and spoke softly, "Yes. Something like that. But Sienna, as the head of the Idallis gymnastics league, there are many more things to be concerned about."

"Oh…." I began, "That must be nerve-wracking."

For the rest of the ride, we rode in silence. Leaving us to our thoughts. And me to that first period math test I have today.

I peeked out the window, and observed the business buildings with every office decorated in autumn colors dance by. My mind drifted back to the constellation. If I could find a way to show her the purple constellation, something that her *own niece* discovered, then maybe it would make her feel less stressed. More than relaxed, *proud*. Maybe she somehow was looking in the wrong direction yesterday. Maybe what's stressing her took over her mind yesterday. I just need to show it to her upfront, no telescope or anything in the way. Outside, in the open.

She was a whole acrobat in an international circus, even my best back tucks could never live up to that. But maybe this discovery can.

As the buildings ran away and let loose my campus, Aunt Katelyn steered our car into the drop-off curb of Idallis Middle School.

"Have fun, Sienna!" Aunt Katelyn said, with her warming smile, a completely different disposition than the ride here.

I hugged her, "Wait for a second, I have something to show you."

"I'd love to see it, but do it quickly. You don't want to keep the other cars waiting" Aunt Katelyn said, and many cars backed up into a line behind them.

I nodded, asking her to pull out her phone to the latest pictures. She raised her eyebrow, and gave me a cheeky smile, "Who's on my phone past their bedtime?"

I know the pictures faded away last night, but it was worth a shot again. When she opened them up, I could barely see an outline of the bird. It was like someone cut its outline out from black paper and replaced it with another layer of black paper.

Aunt Katelyn blinked twice like she was trying to clear her vision.

It wasn't just her this time. There was nothing. No constellation. Just the sky. The plain, night, indigo sky.

Aunt Katelyn narrowed her eyes, "Wow! Er…it's very um…" She's a terrible liar.

I gave a frustrated sigh, "There was supposed to be this purple constellation of a bird. I guess it's not there anymore."

"Purple? From last night?"

I nodded. "I guess it's gone now." I grabbed my backpack, ready to head out the car door.

She sighed, and plotted a kiss on my forehead, "Bye! Love you Beanie!"

I shut the car door and made my way onto campus, letting the noisy school take over my thoughts.

"Hi Sienna!" A voice called from behind me.

I turned and behind me was a girl with dark curly and puffy hair. My best friend.

"Oh hey, Lindsey!"

Lindsey grinned, her cheeks brighter than ever, "I got an A+ on all of my tests."

"That's amazing!"

"And…….I can't wait until my singing competition tomorrow! I bet I'll ace that one too."

I smiled, "Don't jinx it."

Us two began walking along the cement of the school, passing students playing football, teachers chatting as well as friends.

"How's your art business going?" I asked as they strolled throughout the front of the campus. She always had a running list of extracurriculars, businesses, hobbies, you name it. Even her mother couldn't keep track of it all.

Lindsey shrugged, "Not much but….." She grinned, "My cute animal bookmarks are the best sellers!"

"Nice!" I responded. We began making our way from across the pathway where teachers loved to share their daily dose of student gossip, and over to the benches.

Lindsey turned her face towards me, "What about your astronomy thing?'

A smile spread on my face, I announced, "I don't know for sure" I lowered her voice into a whisper, "*I think I discovered a constellation.*"

Lindsey's eyes widened, "You *think?*"

I nodded, "The best part is that they are purple."

Lindsey's jaw dropped and raised her eyebrows, giving a breathless, "No."

"Yes."

Lindsey opened her mouth to speak. A brown football came flying toward me, hitting against my knee joint. I tried to wobble unsteadily and shifted my balance to my other foot.

"Ouch." I groaned.

"Are you okay?" Lindsey asked.

"Never better." I said sarcastically, shaking my leg out as it still felt sore.

A faint deep voice shouted from behind. "Sorry! I didn't mean that!"

Lindsey rolled her eyes at the boy behind them, "Hey be careful next time!" Although the boy was already on a head start to his friends before he could hear her.

I gave a deep breath, "It's alright, I'm okay."

Lindsey knitted her eyebrows, "But don't you have a roller hockey game today? After school?"

"Yep...but don't worry, I'll be fine by then."

The loud school bell rang, catching the best friends' attention. Lindsey held the straps of her back pack, "Well, see you in the fourth period."

I nodded and waved, "Sure, see you!" and we started to walk their separate ways to our different homeroom classes.

My knee still felt sore. I was standing at the curb pick up at my school, waiting for Aunt Katelyn to come into the lane. I elevated the straps of my back pack further over my shoulders, all I could think about was the constellation that Aunt Katelyn *needed* to see.

A silver car pulled up by the side, driven by my aunt. I stashed my backpack into the trunk and headed into the front seat of the car.

"Hey, Aunt-"

My aunt shook her head, her face was extremely pale, sweaty, and tense, "Don't worry, I am not going to ask how school was."

I shrugged, "Oh that's okay. I was just going to ask about how your day went. I think your morning class coaching is far more interesting than the evening ones."

Aunt Katelyn trembled, her hair hanging loose from her pony-tail. "It was alright," she paused from talking, as she stopped at a red-light signal. She shook her head slightly, "Oh, who am I kidding? I can't lie to someone I live with." She glanced at me, "Sienna, I've -" she paused again, accelerating after the light turned green, - "Sienna, I was let go from my job."

"W-what?" I said, with my eyes completely widened and my jaw dropping to my lap.

Aunt Katelyn gulped, "Yes, it's true."

A million stones filled my heart, her eyes were sunken and she'd never looked this frantic before, "What are we going to do?" I asked her.

Aunt Katelyn bit her lip and shrugged, "At this point I-I don't know yet."

Silence filled the car and everywhere around us. I hardly realized we were already home.

As I grabbed my backpack from the trunk, I hugged her assuring, "Hey, don't worry, I'll bring back the prize money from our hockey competitions."

My aunt blinked and smiled, "Thanks, beanie, you're such a sweet girl."

I grinned back. I glanced at the ground, I guess my priorities have to be shifted around now. "And about the Circus Camp, I actually don't want to join. You know, for the best."

She nodded, although she didn't give any other reaction back, but simply squeezed me in her arms, "What did I ever do to deserve such an understanding little girl?"

We both shuffled quickly inside the cozy house. I tossed my backpack into the corner of the living room and rushed across the hallway into my room, limping on one leg.

"Don't forget! You have a game today in an hour!"

I peeked my head out of the hallway, "Yeah, I know. Just gonna do some homework!"

I ran into my room and unzipped my back pack, setting my homework onto the desk.

I ignored all of the assignments and gazed around the room. I scanned every cupboard and shelf, mumbling to myself, "Now, what can I sell?"

I swung my ginger hair behind my back and knelt toward the low cupboards. I opened the cupboard and took out a cardboard box, dumping almost everything from the cupboard into the cardboard box.

I jingled the box from her room across the hallway into the living room.

"What's that?" Aunt Katelyn asked curiously. She had many flyers in her hands and dove through them, searching for a hiring job from the newspaper.

"It's all my old things. Stuff I don't need. I figured that I could sell these for a good amount of money. It would also save my reputation at school and help you out.

"Oh Sienna, you don't need to do this. All we need is for me to get a decent job and all we need is each other."

"Yeah but..."

"It's fine. C'mon, pack your gear, it's time for your game."

"Okay." I said with a sigh and I set down the box, rushing into the closet for my roller hockey gear.

I gathered my hockey gear: helmet, roller skates, knee pads, shin pads, chest pads, arm pads, vest, and my yellow mouthpiece. As per the coach's instruction, being overprotected was protected enough. And being protected enough, was always being under protected.

I carried my bag of gear outside into the car. I had opened the trunk of the car and paused, "Never mind, I don't want to go to the game. It's not worth it, it's wasting time. We should be thinking about your job."

My aunt gave an affectionate smile, "It's so sweet that you are thinking of all this but really, no need for a young child like you to stress over it." She stroked my ginger hair.

I bit her lip, hesitantly, "Okay, if you say so." I never really argued with my aunt so far, I just wanted the best for Aunt Katelyn and what she wanted was good enough for us.

I sat in the front seat quietly as her aunt drove. I glanced at the static, maybe music would cheer them up. I reached for the dial and switched it on.

Buzz!

I jolted and jumped in her seat and Aunt Katelyn gasped.

"What happened?" she asked.

My face turned red, "I was just trying to cheer us up."

My aunt smiled, "Thanks." She slowed the motion of the car and headed into the parking lot of the roller hockey arena.

I opened the car door, heading out toward the trunk. I walked in very small slow steps, procrastinating on the way to the gear.

My aunt chuckled, "Okay, c'mon. This isn't your first game."

I forced a smile, pressing my top teeth over the bottom as I grabbed my back and headed over inside.

Inside, was a huge skating rink with high barriers. Around it were hard steel bleachers that had enormous spaces in between to let people pass by when going back and forth from the rink to the food court.

I quickly put on my gear by the bleachers and tied on my skates. I was anxious and I just kept thinking of my aunt. And looking back, I should've been less anxious so that I would've properly put on my gear. It came on much looser than it should've been. But regardless, I grabbed my hockey stick and skated over to the rink.

"Good luck!" My aunt waved.

I smiled, "Thanks!" I mumbled through my mouth piece. I looked around to the bleachers, Lindsey wasn't there, and she usually comes. I shrugged and headed over to the rink and began warming up, skating a few laps. There were more important things to worry about right now.

The coach blew his whistle. "Alright kids, the Red Vipers from the east side are coming for this game as I told you last week." He looked at his piece of paper he was holding, "Now we as the Blue Sparrows must play as practiced. I want a clean, nice game. Cheating means no beating. Got it?"

The rest of the team and I nodded. The Viper team from the east side of the town had started rolling into the stadium and into the rink, shooting us intimidating sneers.

"You got the timer up, Joe?" The coach turned over to a man sitting in a plastic chair with a remote. Joe nodded, signaling us a thumbs up.

"Okay, in position." the coach ordered. Two people, with hard gear all over them went to each net, holding their hockey sticks.

The Vipers arranged themselves on the right of the rink as the Blue Sparrows arranged themselves on the left. I was standing in the middle, between two other team players.

The coach had his whistle ready and the puck was right in the middle between the two teams.

"Best of luck to both teams. In three, two….one!" He blew his whistle at the instant and the game began.

A Viper caught a hold of the puck with her hockey stick, racing toward the left net. I chased her although I was going slower than expected. I limped a bit on one leg. The football that had hit my knee joint in the morning didn't heal all the way, obviously. So, I decided to forget all about it instead, I was distracted by the news just dropped on me after school. My leg was still sore, but the game was on. My aunt was watching from the bleachers and counting on me, for this one good news of the day. So, I couldn't let Aunt Katelyn down. I had to try my best in the game, no matter what, not even my knee could stop me.

I gripped my hockey stick hard, I would have to put most of the strength on my left leg and only balance with the sore leg. I paddled my left leg up toward the Viper, kneeling toward and having my hockey open to reach the puck. But the Viper was too fast and easily hit it into the net, scoring a point. Groaning, I dove my hockey stick toward the puck that was thrown back at the rink. *Focus, Sienna. Just for a couple minutes, focus.* I mustered up enough strength, kneeling down...... my hockey stick finally touched the puck!

My eyes gleamed with pride and I carried the puck toward her target: the right net. I raced and raced toward it. Many Vipers circled in front of me, closing me off the net. I backed away further, trying to evaluate a path between them all. I narrowed her eyes and zoomed through them, almost knocking one of them down.

I gave an unbelievable gasp. *Yes!* The pain from my leg was almost gone.

Another Viper closed in on me.

"Over here! Pass!" A Blue Sparrow yelled.

I response, I skidded the puck to her. As the Blue Sparrow was just about to get a hold of the puck, a Viper caught it. The Viper zoomed through them as they tried to race behind. The Viper then passed the puck to another of their team and scored it toward the left net.

"Ugh! They're too good for us!" a team player groaned.

My hope was beginning to go down. I slightly backed away.

A voice came from the bleachers, "The Sienna I know never gives up!"

It was coming from Aunt Katelyn. Too good or not, I have to win. For Aunt Katelyn. I gripped my hockey stick tightly again, my forearm tensed, heading toward the Viper. The Viper was much bigger than me. Even as I reached to steal the puck, the Viper kept hold of it. I raced back, joining alongside another team player.

They passed the puck until they reached their net, and slid it across to the net.

Our guard stopped it, sending it back.

Yes, we have another chance.

I passed the puck next, back and forth with another team player until we reached our net. I took one big breath, stabilized on my good net, and aimed for the left edge–it went in!

"That's my girl!" My aunt exclaimed.

I leaned over the Viper's stick and a team player caught it and began racing toward the right net.

I rolled in from the side, just in case. The other team players closed the other Vipers off from coming in.

Some Vipers came in, heading toward the puck and were closing in on the team player, preparing their next move.

"Here, pass!" I yelled.

The team player passed. I caught a hold of the puck. As I rolled, I caught a glimpse of Aunt Katelyn frowning anxiously at her phone. Her eyes met with mine, instantly setting her phone back down and smiling, "You got this!" She mouthed. But even yards away, her pretending couldn't fool anyone.

Aunt Katelyn's situation flooded back in my mind, and I staggered from side to side. So, I passed the puck to our next player Adeya for my own sake and she raced ahead, passing the puck to another person. Then, another team player threw it into the opposite net, although the Viper's guard caught the puck and threw it back into the rink.

"C'mon, you got this!" I assured the team. My voice was wobbling, but it was better than nothing. The team nodded and raced, sliding the puck into the net.

Three Vipers came in and the others closed off the other teammates when the puck was passed back. The three raced to the puck toward the left net, and hit the side of the net, bouncing off the metal into the middle of the rink.

One team player caught the puck, trying to head for the right net. A Viper closed off her and threw the puck to the middle of the rink

Both teams headed toward the rink and Vipers caught it. One Viper hit it into the left net. Just touching the guard's foot.

When the puck was thrown back out into the rink, I headed straight for it. The bottom of my shin pad was gliding back and forth over my laces, unbalancing me a bit. Many Vipers closed me off in a circle, their hockey sticks angled in every way. I was locked.

The pressure overwhelmed me and the other hockey sticks came closer to me. I tried heading back to pass to someone else. But my shin pad suddenly unstrapped and was loosely hanging on top of my skates. I had a small gasp but I skated back, skating toward another team player if I could.

The other Blue Sparrows came through as the Vipers chased. The puck was right at the tip of my stick. Another stick, one belonging to a Viper, caught the puck. Two other team players came toward it as well as me. I leaned over to the puck. My shin pad fell off, and tripped me, right over the other knee.

"W-Whoa!" I screamed.

I thought everyone circled around me to check on me, but then I realized I was lying right over the puck.

"Pause the time! Player down!" The coach ordered. Joe pressed a button on the remote, pausing the time.

The coach came to me, "Are you alright?" he asked.

I nodded, "I'm fine." I grabbed my shin pad and strapped it on as quickly as I could.

The coach crouched, "I see that you've been limping a lot this game. You better sit out for the rest of forty seconds. It's best not to risk it."

I shook my head, "I don't have the word risk in my dictionary."

Stop Sienna, he is not Aunt Katelyn. The coach raised his eyebrows, perplexed. This was so embarrassing.

"Just please, let me play for the rest of the game. I promise, I can help our team win."

The coach sighed, "No, rest comes before being the best." One of his favorite rhymes, except now he actually had an excuse to use it.

Aunt Katelyn called from the bleachers, "He's right, Sienna. You should take a break and be kind to your knee."

I gave a quiet nod. I should probably sit out the game, it was better than to have someone not limping in the game than to have.

I silently skated over to the bench. I slumped onto the bench, there was nothing I could do now.

For the rest of the game, the Vipers were still in the lead.

There were only ten seconds left of the game and the Viper's scored one more goal. They scored 4 goals to 2 goals by the Blue Sparrows in total.

Buzz!

"And times out!" The coach said, "Well done Vipers! Blue Sparrows, nice work. At least you all made a team effort. Remember your sportsmanship."

Everyone on each team shook hands, saying, "Good game" to one another.

I was sitting on the bench, sitting in guilt and frustration. I just had to do *one* thing right today. Just *one* thing.

My aunt climbed down from the bleachers to the bench, carrying the bag used for holding gear and a water bottle.

She handed the water bottle to me, "Don't be disappointed, my little beanie. You scored a goal and encouraged others. That's the whole point of sports not winning or losing."

I grinned, putting the water bottle on my lap, "Thanks Aunt Katelyn. But I really wanted to win. Especially after what happened."

Her face dulled, "Sienna...you don't have to make up for anything. You hear me?"

I nodded. I stared at the rink, wincing at what I was about to say next. "I actually am going to quit roller hockey."

"What? Why?"

"I don't want you to be worrying about paying the fees of roller hockey just for me. Plus, we have to worry about your job findings and all."

"I told you; you don't have to worry about it."

"It's alright, Aunt Katelyn. Plus, I am not really enjoying roller hockey much." I lied.

My aunt gave a deep sigh.

Other players from the Viper's team came waving to us all on the bleachers, "Good game!"

"Good game guys." I replied.

Aunt Katelyn crouched down closer to me, "Now, if you're sure you want to quit--'"

"Positive." I said with a nod.

My aunt gave a sigh and we both walked out of the stadium.

"Be sure of your decision, please. Don't give up because of my situation."

I nodded, "I'm sure of my decision." We went into the parking lot and drove home. There was no point paying money towards a non-need.

In the car, I asked, "So, does this mean that my gymnastic classes are over too? You know because...."

My aunt nodded softly, "Yes, it does mean that. But don't worry, I can still teach you at home."

"No, you don't have to take the stress to do that."

My aunt gave a deep sigh, "Okay, but you are still going to school. No excuses for that. You must be educated and earn a good degree for a good job."

"I will, I will. But that's years away, I'm only eleven."

"You're still on the path toward it. Are you really sure you don't want those gymnastic lessons at home?"

"I am sure. You don't have to even worry about me. Just please, be focused on the money for our family. Did anyone in our family leave a will of money? Can anyone help us out? What about Dad, you know, your older brother."

Her aunt pressed the wheel a little harder, her hands were silently shaking, she spoke softly, "No, I don't think so."

"Okay." I said dryly, "I am going to start a business for this then. Not as official as Lindsey. You know, maybe a lemonade stand."

Aunt Katelyn was pulling into the driveway of the house. When she parked, she shook her head, "Not so fast, Sienna. You are going to do your homework. And I have to check out your knee."

I reached into the hallway when we opened the door. I sat down at her desk and picked up my pencil, drawing it toward her worksheets. Long division word problems was the topic.

As I began to do my math, only two things lingered in my mind. My aunt had lost her job and I had lost the game.

"Sienna!" Aunt Katelyn called from outside the house.

"Yes?" I called.

"You might want to see this." I dropped my pencil and stormed outside, disregarding my knee that got used to the movement.

My jaw dropped.

Our landlord was tapping on a sign in big red letters that wrote *For Rent*.

Chapter Three

We Sell Almost Everything

"You can't take our house without giving a notice in advance." Aunt Katelyn said. The man just dusted the board and straightened it–having the *audacity* to shrug. "As a landlord, I have many reasons to take this house back, and your un-paid rent for this month is one of them."

"My boss refused to pay me before I…. You see, I was going to get my check last–"

"I'm sorry" He interrupted, his feet tilting on the edge of the sidewalk.

The blood boiled in my veins, "There must be some exceptions. It's only been two weeks." But the man's crossed arms and polished posture stayed as stiff and still as the sign he tacked on. He glanced back and forth between Aunt

Katelyn and me, as if waiting for one of us to say something. He stopped. When he unlocked his car, his hoarse voice struggled a whisper, "I will be showing the house to some new tenants. If you can pay it in before then, perhaps I will reconsider." He left.

Everything was falling apart. Everything.

Warm tears stinged through the corners of my eyes and I bit and held the inside of my lips to stop them from speaking.

Aunt Katelyn's arms wrapped around me and her tears cascaded down my cheeks. "W-what are we going to do now?" I asked.

She straightened herself and grabbed me by the shoulders, "Our life is made of glass, stay intact, Sienna. Stay intact."

I strolled on the trail behind us to clear my head. Leaves crunched under my feet and the cacophony of biker's ringing their bells muddled with my anger. The trail was somewhat therapeutic, with the fiery trees arching over the track and the orange sun trying to peek through the branches—turning the trail into a light show. I used to skate through the trail— everything zipping by in a blur. The smell of crisp apples leaning over fences of backyards that we held back from stealing. It all used to be pleasant. Knowing that I could come to those apples whenever I wanted, I lived *right* here.

I must have made it harder than before, having Aunt Katelyn do everything for me, and now she had to lift the burden off of *both* of our backs. Where are we going to find another home in Idallis City? Another job?

The trail mounted into a small wooden bridge over the creek that flowed into the honeysuckle meadow behind me. I squinted my eyes from the orange sunset waning into the grass and glistening off of the creek. The creek where I dumped our pet goldfish into when I was seven, thinking they deserved a better home. I strolled over the bridge into darker parts of the trail, where the bushes interfered into the path and the sun was fully hidden. Most of the time I walked sideways.

As I walked through the bushy trail. A sparrow flew to its nest, only to find a small toddler disturbed its home, and the baby bird didn't say a single word, but its eyes showed how perturbed it was. The sparrow didn't even touch the nest, and it flew away–leaving the nest to the toddler. It wasn't the baby's fault. I never knew why birds did that.

I cut through the last bit of bushes to get back into the neighborhood. The walk barely cleared my head, only strengthened the memories even more. Every blade of grass, the current of the creek, every obnoxious biker, every tree, *everything*. I've seen it all. I've skated through it all.

The sparrow simply left its problems and flew away. If only we could do that.

The sparrow.

The bird constellation.

I strolled through another neighborhood, trying to dissect the mysterious constellation again. This was the area with copy and paste of the modern suburban houses enveloped in autumn leaves that no family seemed to be taking advantage of jumping into. Every home started to look the same in Idallis City.

I walked through the neighborhood that me and Aunt Katelyn rarely ever skated in because of the steep slopes.

If only she could see what I saw that night. I'm sure I wasn't hallucinating…hopefully not. But if she couldn't see it, then why could I?

Perhaps the greatest discoveries were the most frustrating.

I seriously can't let her down, not with everyone else letting her down.

As I turned to walk back home, a flimsy paper waved in the breeze, with big letters bouncing off the page, *Yard Sale.*

That's it.

I steered through the crisp leaves and rushed home as quickly as I could. There were probably drawers and cupboards filled with things I didn't need.

And I was right.

Aunt Katelyn was flinging her stretch bands across the living room. Aiming the bright ones toward the window. And the dull ones toward the back door.

"To everyone at The Idallis Gymnastics Center, it's all your fault. You were all mad that my light dimmed yours." She flung a bright band towards the couch.

She probably noticed me standing in the corner by the front door because her face instantly went marron. She jogged towards the living room and picked up the stretch bands, looking around the furniture to make sure she didn't leave a scratch.

"My *beanie*, you know…violence is never the answer to anything." Then, she glanced up at me with another one of her cheeky smiles, "But when the world is ending, there's nothing else more satisfying than a fight." I couldn't help smiling at another one of her overly-exaggerated but needed analogies.

She placed all of them next to her other contortion equipment of handstand canes and yoga mats. She shook the bar of the cane, and it loosened off of the wooden rod. "Something's on your mind. Spill."

I gathered the rest of the bands that landed near the front window pane, "How do you know?"

"Well…why wouldn't something be? If my mind is jumping everywhere, then yours must surely be too…it's genetics."

I giggled, "Could we host a yard sale? I have some things I don't need, and we could use all of the money we could get."

Aunt Katelyn placed her hands on her hips and sighed at the broken handstand cane next to her, "That would be *one* way to get rid of this scathing past." Her eyes widened and she gasped, "Sienna, this is *our* dystopian story." Her lips curved from ear to ear as she leaned in to hug me, "I knew this would've been your first step into the apocalypse."

"It would?"

"It's genetics, my little beanie, it's genetics."

I smiled as she patted my head, "Lucky genetics."

Aunt Katelyn said, "Alright, bring everything down here…and try not to break anything in the house, you know how picky our landlord is."

"I won't" I said, my hand tracing the small dents caused by my failed stunts over the years.

When I was eight, I told Aunt Katelyn I was an adult, just like her. I piled all of my toys into a cardboard box and told her to take them away…because now I was an adult. It was only ten minutes after that I cried for them back. So I guess, now it's *actually* time to be an adult. And not just for 10 minutes.

I opened every single one of my drawers in my room and took out almost everything. I don't really use anything except for my telescope nowadays. There was a whole crate of the equipment Aunt Katelyn bought for my size so I could practice my routines like her. But if she wants to get rid of her own equipment, I guess I will too.

I started disabling my miniature beam bar and ring hoops and placed them in the corner of the room. It hit me.

Was Aunt Katelyn not going to search for another job dealing with gymnastics? It was the easiest thing for her to do. She was an acrobat for the Harrison Circus–so teaching children how to do the splits was a piece of cake for her. And she enjoyed it too. I think.

I tried to block the questions running into my mind about her job by dismantling most of the bars set up in the room.

The walls were covered with space posters, galaxy paintings, a map of the famous constellations.

There was one wooden cupboard in the corner of the room. I didn't really use any of the things I put in there. I opened both doors of the cupboard and inside were four green cloth bins. I took out the cardboard box from the garage and poured the first bin in there. All that came out were slinkies, fake makeup, plastic dolls, puzzles, and stuffed animals.

I kept the stuffed animals.

The next bin probably had the same toys so I dumped them all into the large box and took it downstairs. The rattling of the bin almost muted whatever Aunt Katelyn was humming to herself.

She opened the kitchen drawer and grabbed a bundle of markers and threw them across the counter.

"We'll need a to make a sign."

As I put the box onto the table next to her markers and paper, a picture framed on the wall of the gymnastics' staff caught my eye. I walked a little closer toward it to see Aunt Katelyn smiling the way she used to. "If you don't mind me asking, how did um…you know…it happened?"

Aunt Katelyn shrugged, "It just did. I saw it coming."

"But how?"

"Things were unexpected, Sienna. People gave me bad reviews as a coach and they already had another coach set. So this week, I just saw it coming."

"Well, you, Aunt Katelyn, were an acrobat. Who could possibly replace someone like you?"

Aunt Katelyn set down a pen and whispered, "The circus was an entirely different story." She tilted her chin up and forced a smile, "We are on a new chapter of our lives…now, should the border be purple or blue?"

"Purple."

I marched into the drawers and took out more paper I could use to make our posters bigger.

As Aunt Katelyn drew highlights over the large letters on the poster, she said, "The key to advertisement is exaggeration, what are you thinking?"

She glanced over her shoulder as I began to write the next sentence using her advice.

Yard Sale this Saturday, November 20

1907 Bliss Circle. Idallis

Bargain Yard Sale: Purchasing anything will mean more than the world.

It will truly help out a young girl and her independent guardian in need.

The writing started to seep into the borders Aunt Katelyn drew, "Does it look muddy?"

Her aunt shook her head. She narrowed her eyes, "*Independent guardian in need?*"

"You know, it's bold, and captivating. Kind of like clickbait on the internet."

"Well…it's…bold alright." Aunt Katelyn murmured. She placed her hand on my shoulder, "But not all desperate times call for desperate measures."

The next morning, Aunt Katelyn helped me drag the other end of the dining table to the front yard.

In just thirty minutes we shifted the weight of the house to the front—everything was laid open to belong in someone else's home. But it's not like I had any special attachment to it.

"Did you look through everything you wanted to sell?" she said, pushing back her brown hair and raising her hair up to catch the small breeze.

I glanced at the cardboard box, "Pretty much…you?"

She stretched her arms out at all of the balance beams, rings, the printer, the wooden chair from the backyard that none of us used. We were practically selling everything, taking into consideration that our equipment replaced the lawn.

Adults on phones passed our home, their eyes barely turning to look at our yard. Mothers were too occupied by crying infants throwing their bottles outside of the stroller and the only thing the little kids wanted to do was to race to the park nearby.

It was like we were invisible.

"They'll come, Sienna, don't worry." Aunt Katelyn said, but I don't think she was too sure herself.

She walked around the lawn to make sure everything was set at the perfect angle from the front view. She always said execution is more important than the real thing itself.

"I wonder what someone's going to do with all this equipment," she laughed to herself. She scanned the area like she was looking to improve my contortions. "We don't have enough variety, maybe that's why."

She headed over to my cardboard box and started taking out some of the things, "Lay these out for the customers."

She dug her hand to the bottom of the box to get out some of the larger objects, "What's this?" All of the toys rattled to the side as she scooped out a brass clock.

There were brass vines embedded into the rim and the glass was completely broken. The black paint of the hands was coming off and the clock sat perfectly in Aunt Katelyn's hands. The clock became more and more familiar as I looked at the patterns of flowers and birds on the rim. It took me a while to read it, with the small hand pointing to the eleven and the big hand just below the two.

"The 11:11 clock, Aunt Katelyn."

"I know." ...

... "One more story, Auntie." I begged, shaking her hands as she was closing a book and setting it on the couch next to her.

"Beanie, it's bedtime. You'll have plenty of stories coming in your dreams tonight." She lifted me up and placed me on the top of the kitchen counter. I was five.

"What are you doing?" I asked.

"Just making a list of the things I have to buy for our gymnasium." She said, ripping off pieces of paper from her notepad. She placed her pen behind her ear as she bent down into the cupboards to grab a glass.

"Why?"

"Because…the other balance beams broke." She answered as she grabbed a jug of milk from the fridge and poured it into the glass.

"Are the other teachers buying things too?"

"Well…no."

"Then why are you?"

Aunt Katelyn stopped midway in her pour, "Helping never hurt anyone, Sienna."

I remember gulping down that glass of milk and Aunt Katelyn staring at her check. I can't tell if Aunt Katelyn thinks my curiosity was a gift, or a straight-up annoyance.

She stretched out her hands to lift me off of the counter and then she gasped. "Sienna look!"

"Where?"

"The clock, it's 11:11." Aunt Katelyn exclaimed, pointing at her clock she had since the circus that hung next to the oven. "Make a wish."

I closed my eyes and whispered out loud, *"I wish Aunt Katelyn will wear a magical tiara for me."*

Aunt Katelyn giggled, "Now don't tell me, or else it won't come true." She picked me off of the counter and carried me to bed...

..."I didn't know we still had that." I said, astonished that the clock made its way into my box. It stopped working that night, so it froze that minute forever.

I took the clock and examined it closer, "Maybe it's better we don't sell a broken clock."

She nodded, "At least there's people here."

I glanced around, there were a couple of people picking up items, looking at them, and putting them back down. The others were trying to test if the gymnastics equipment were efficient.

"Hello!" I said, trying to put on a cheery expression to the first man holding his wallet. He had a snow globe in his other hand.

"How did that get in there?" I asked. The snow globe had very intricate snowflakes. It had four discrete sections, each representing the four seasons. The spring one would have falling fake flower petals. The fall one would have autumn leaves, and the summer would have small yellow suns. Aunt Katelyn only shook it on the first day of a new season—one of her strange traditions. But it was a pretty one.

The man spoke, his words crisp, "I found it in the box next to you."

"Oh, oh yeah." I gave a deep breath. I really should've looked through everything.

Aunt Katelyn could see the hesitation in my eyes, she bit her lip, thinking of what to say. But she didn't need to. I put myself in that position.

"I'll give you sixty dollars–"

"Sixty-five dollars." I concluded, if I said anything more or anything less, I might start to regret the decision.

The man nodded and handed me a few loose bills from his wallet, smiling, "It's for my grand-daughter's 10th birthday, thanks." He walked off of the lawn and out of sight.

The others weighed Aunt Katelyn's gymnastic rings on each hand moving up and down like a scale, like one was heavier than the other.

To her surprise, they waved their hands at us and left one by one, leaving the yard empty again. I groaned as they left the other items untouched. I mean I couldn't blame them for not buying anything if they don't do gymnastics. But still. "Why's our lives changing so fast?" I asked, slumped down on our yellow and saw-toothed lawn.

"Life's a bookshelf, Sienna. Everything has its own book on your shelf. And its value depends on its size. When you take out a small book, your other books shift only a little. But when you take out a large book, it shifts tremendously. The other books may even fall over." She said, sitting down next to me and serving me another piece of her eccentric wisdom.

I turned to her, "So what book did we take out?"

Aunt Katelyn chewed her lip, "Well, maybe *we* didn't take it out, but as long as we return the book ourselves, the other books will stand up straight again."

"And what if a reader never returns the book?"

"Hm…then either the books stay like that forever or you buy another book and put it on the shelf."

"So I guess you would buy as many books as you would need until it fills the space."

Aunt Katelyn laughs, "Yes, you would. But unlike filling a bookshelf, life's problems take a lot more to heal. It's like … the bigger the book, the longer it takes to read and so longer to heal before it's back on the shelf … if it ever goes back on the shelf."

"Then that doesn't make any sense."

"Why not?"

"Because when you read a book, you don't always read it in one sitting. Sometimes you put it back in and then take it out again. How would you explain that?"

"Oh Sienna, the fire of your brain will always be an enigma to me. Let's see…well that could be because you cover up the problem with something temporary. So the books are standing up for a while, until you take it out again."

"So you're technically suggesting that people shouldn't read then. So their stays life normal."

Aunt Katelyn giggles, "It's just a metaphor dear."

"What if the book you buy is too big to fit the space? What does that mean? Like even if you put the book on another shelf, the first shelf is still incomplete. Does it mean that the problem is still not healed? Because you can't cut a book to fit the space—Like is it even a good thing to take too much space, it depends on the quality of the books—"

"My little beanie, I honestly think it's illegal to be that astute."

Her words let my lips widen, "Really? You think I'm smart?"

"Well of course, I never knew that metaphor had such a big meaning till you dissected it"

My expression was glowing. That comment filled up a space in my bookshelf. A large spot.

I rummaged through the box, making sure there weren't any more items mistakenly put for sale. As I anticipated, there were only my toys and trinkets left—no ancient clock or snow globe this time. I emptied the box and laid out the different dolls with different colored hair and the puzzles of a polar bear or kangaroo that I used to solve every day.

It felt like I was watching the sun travel across the sky like Aunt Katelyn used to joke about using it to tell time when she was my age. The sun was right above me and the shadows of the balance beams were right under them. Noon, I guessed.

"People will come." She promised.

We both decided to take shifts, and to our luck, there were at least more customers around the afternoon.

I was inside, washing the dishes when I heard Aunt Katelyn calling from the front window. I shut off the running water to hear her more clearly.

"Sienna, I just got called for a job interview for a restaurant nearby. Could you watch here for a little while?"

"Sure!" I called and dried my hands off, rushing out of the door. I didn't even question how quick that restaurant was to get back to her application, the only thing that filled my soul was pure hope now.

"I'll be back!" She grabbed her purse and raced to the restaurant that was just a few blocks away.

I closed the door behind me, the yard did look a little less crowded. The beam was gone and so were the rings—leaving just a few more of her equipment left.

And all of the items from the box were sold. All of them.

Chapter Four

My Aunt Has A Plan

For several weeks now, Aunt Katelyn had been working at that fast food restaurant nearby that always had smoke coming out of its roof, carrying its stench of grilled chicken and onions with it.

She usually worked pretty late, and sometimes past midnight. You would think that's too much, but Idallis City is the base of three taxi companies—most *barely* sleep.

I leaned back on the fire hydrant, waiting for the signal to let me cross…

One…

Two…

Three…

Four–

The cars parallel to me started their motors and I began to speed walk across the paused cars.

We made around $452.44 from the yard sale, thanks to some last-minute decisions of those first people over-examining Aunt Katelyn's equipment. At least they made a decision and the snow globe that fetched $65.

Maybe if luck plays fairly into Aunt Katelyn's job, we could keep our home. Maybe if…

I hadn't seen the constellation in a while, now that I think about it. Maybe it was just an illusion, maybe my mind was playing tricks on me. Maybe it isn't real.

But if it is, and I can get my name on it, Aunt Katelyn surely won't be disappointed.

I balanced myself along the edge of the sidewalk, gripping my backpack and playing that little game where I try not to step on the cracks.

I looked for those satisfying, dried leaves to crunch beneath my feet as I trudged up the hill to our home. Like a tetherball, I swung on the streetlamp with one hand to veer into the narrow road ahead.

I darted home—

I paused.

Aunt Katelyn was standing in the driveway, her arms were crossed as she leaned side to side.

Aunt Katelyn? She was home early.

She turned to me and her face faded. Her eyes lowered and she let out a deep breath. The closer I got home, I could see a man stand in the corner of our lot, with a clipboard.

The same landlord with the same hoarse voice and same dry, uncombed hair.

"Expenses in Idallis City are out of control, I'm very sorry." The landlord said. He tried to smooth out his voice to sound comforting.

"Sir, if you could reconsider, it's difficult to find a job with my set of skills with decent pay now. My wages can't pay rent right away."

"I can't reconsider the other factors coming into play here." He scanned his eyes over his clipboard, "You have left several dents on the walls and furniture."

Blood rushed into Aunt Katelyn's cheeks, "One of the flaws of gymnastics--"

"I'm being considerate enough as it is to not have you pay for those damages." He reached out his palm.

Aunt Katelyn bit her lip and she began to take out the keys--her face swerved toward me, "Sienna." she stalled.

I pulled out the sympathy card, "This was our home, Aunt Katelyn. It's where we lived for eleven years…since I was born."

The man broadened his stance and raised his eyebrows sternly, tightening his crossed arms. He had no ounce of empathy.

Aunt Katelyn's eyes watered, "Well, it's probably best for us. It's hard finding a good job here."

"*Here?* You're not thinking of–"

Her aunt was speechless. Words couldn't come out of her mouth, but she quietly nodded at the smiling landlord taking out papers and a pen for her to sign.

"Thank you." he replied, watching her ink her signature over the long lines.

Aunt Katelyn blinked several times to keep the sting from turning into a stream. She ran towards me and gripped me in her arms.

The man drove away, leaving a stream of smoke behind him.

"Farewell house." Aunt Katelyn said.

"Farewell house." I repeated.

My eyes became even mistier and fogged out my vision. I couldn't keep it in anymore, I buried my face and let the tears gush down my cheeks.

Aunt Katelyn stroked my ginger hair and we stood there on the driveway for a while. A long while.

"We're homeless." My voice broke out.

"No, not really. We still have the caravan. We just no longer have a space to park it." She said, straightening up and grabbing my shoulders. "But if there's anyone who survives when the world's ending, it's us."

I opened my mouth to speak, but no words came out. I cleared my throat and tried to blink away the tears so the house didn't look as blurry.

"Do we have a plan?"

She reassured, "My little beanie, your auntie always has solutions."

"We either start new, or we can't start at all." Aunt Katelyn's voice echoed from underneath the caravan. She was loosening the stand grip so we could get this old caravan on it's wheels again after several years.

I handed her a wrench as she slid into the sunlight, reaching out her hand. I put down the toolbox and headed over to the back of the caravan.

There was a small deck that stretched beyond the caravan, with orange decorated pillars and the railing. The orange pillars all connected up top to the ornate arch made of iron. The whole balcony just screamed orange.

"I'm pulling up the stairs now" I said, holding the bottom of a small green and orange wooden staircase. It could almost be a ladder.

I gripped the top of the railing and folded the staircase into the bottom compartment. I hopped onto the deck and pushed it into the gap between the deck and the wheels– using my fingertips to avoid any splinters.

I stood on the deck, my fingers tracing over the peeled paint on the pillars. I let my legs dangle between the two balustrades for a little before using the pillars to lift myself up. I creaked open the brown wooden door and stepped inside.

My telescope still stood at the nook, with the windows open. At least the maroon cushions clothed in dust could breathe.

"Sienna, I'm hooking the caravan to the car now." Aunt Katelyn called from outside. I jumped out the front door as she grabbed the black hook and veered it through the two iron gaps.

Behind me on the side, large curved white letters shouted, *"Harrison Circus!"*

The camp.

Is it still active—

"All set?" Aunt Katelyn stood by the car and zipped up her jacket, chiming the keys in her pockets

I turned away from the caravan. Maybe I'll ask her during the road trip. A road trip with no returning.

"Yep."

Aunt Katelyn set up the navigation system, "about 10-11 hours to Honeyville with our tow. Get comfortable." She buckled her belt and veered out of the neighborhood, making a sharp turn to diverge into the highway.

The olive bushes beside the highway danced in front of my eyes as she drove along the road that stretched for infinity miles. Bisons ate the yellow grass and large power towers were shy of the deep valleys ahead, hiding away in the trees.

"Why Honeyville?" I asked.

"It's the only town *within 500 miles* that we can afford." Aunt Katelyn explained, keeping her hands steady on the wheel, "This is how we solve our problems." She gestured her head behind her.

"We're staying in the caravan?"

"Not exactly–but maybe a trailer…van life doesn't seem too bad."

A trailer.

A trailer?

She changed the subject, "Now, distract me, how are you?"

"Good."

"No, I meant: how are you really?"

I turned toward her, her brown hair glistened from the sunlight peeking through the window. The truth is, I'm scared. I'm terrified, what if "Honeyville" isn't all that great? What's Aunt Katelyn going to do, keep selling over grilled chicken? What am I going to do, become nothing? I don't want to doubt Aunt Katelyn, she's the only parent I've ever had. But it's not her I doubt–it's *everything* else.

I'm Fine, really. I prepared to say by swallowing down the lump in my throat and forcing a quick smile, "I'm stressed." The smile faded and the lump grew its own heart–beating at a million miles per second.

She slowed the pace of the car and reached out her hand, squeezing mine tight.

"I know 'stress' isn't supposed to be in our dictionary." I said, peering down at the gray carpet of the car.

She shook her head back and forth, "Look, without stress, you can't have the word relief in your dictionary. And that's an important word to have."

"You see, I want to help, I really do, but I just–don't know what to do."

"I'm stressed too, Sienna." She looked over at me for a split second and she gleamed, "Hey, what do you know? It's genetics."

We burst out laughing.

The evening was approaching as the sun brazed the ends of the mountains with its red strokes. Aunt Katelyn stared down at the yellow streaks on the road and said, "I think I have a plan."

I fished out a paper and pencil from the compartment in front of me. "Ready." I replied.

"What should the first step be?" She asked,

"Buy a trailer?" I finished.

1. buy a trailer

   "Step 2: Auction the caravan."

2. auction the ca--

"What?" I asked.

She pursed her lips, "Sienna…"

I stayed in the Caravan every night before our late dinners, gazing in the sky. Wishing on every star to discover something. To make me and Aunt Katelyn famous. Call me uncooperative but–

I sighed.

2. auction the caravan

I'd rather let it go than be stubborn.

"Step 3:" I said,

3. help auntie find a job

"Are you still going to teach gymnastics?" I asked.

Aunt Katelyn shrugged, "My reputation is pretty beat up in Idallis City." A smirk gleamed on her face, "No one will know us in Honeyville…it's the countryside, we can start *over*."

She jumped in excitement, "I'll be Amelia Barlowe."

"And I'll be Rylee Barlowe."

"I'm your older sister, and we're–"

"Dancers."

"Yes!" She giggled.

Maybe we *could* be dancers. I tried not to bring up anything else about gymnastics…Aunt Katelyn selling her equipment is a big hint she wants to steer away from that path. So what's the next best thing? Dancing.

"Or," Aunt Katelyn said, "We could be treasure-hunters. We can fool people in Honeyville to join us–how fun will that be?"

"Or we could start a game show!" I proposed.

Aunt Katelyn laughed, "Well, Rylee, get to work, our business isn't going to sell itself!" She said, the lines on her forehead loosened and *life* temporarily rushed back into her face. The paleness left.

Temporarily?

Us joking over our fake identities sustained her flourishing expression. I looked outside and traced my fingers over the racing horses, I'll find a way to make it permanent. I will.

The sun finally resided into the valleys and it was pitch black. The only light illuminating the road were the two beams of ray from our car. Aunt Katelyn decided to rest for the night so we picked up the next exit and veered into the parking lot near a gas station.

Aunt Katelyn reclined her chair back into the middle seats and I followed. We covered the front window with the sun protector we always kept in the back.

"Need anything?" She whispered.

"I'm good." I whispered back.

She unzipped her jacket and gently placed it on top of me. I gazed my eyes up at her and lifted the jacket.

She shook her head, "I'm not cold." She smiled as she tucked her hands underneath her head, "I'll be dreaming about you."

"And so will I."

She gazed off to sleep.

The silver moon shone through the crevices of the window and bounced off of Aunt Katelyn's glowing skin. People came in and out of the gas station, most of them squinted at our caravan. You have to admit, you can't ignore the paintings of the lions, the rings of fire, and the red colors popping off of the caravan in the moonlight. My eyelids became heavier and heavier, weighing down like a boulder. I closed my eyes and pictured someone, some antique zealot will spend loads on this…and maybe get our home back…and…and…

… "Sienna, wake up." She shook me side to side. I forced my eyes open, "Huh–" The yellow sun darted into my pupils, almost blinding them. I shut my eyes again.

"Are we here?" I finally stretched my arms out, only for a gray band to grip my shoulder and stop my arms. My seatbelt was on. And my chair was ascended back up. We weren't at the parking lot anymore. Cars rushed by in a zip and buildings side by side on the streets. Downtown.

Outside my window, a large store with glass walls stood before me. Crowded displays of golden watches and jewel boxes with bulky prices tagged on each wall. Silverware, wooden ships and tea sets all crammed into the display shelves. All of them trying to buy a second of a spotlight for the customers.

"This is it." Aunt Katelyn, "C'mon!"

We went into the antique store. The ceiling was struggling to hold onto each and every chandelier. Wooden cabinets stood in the corners collecting dust in the crevices of their design imprints. Dolls were fighting for a spot on the aisle, it seemed as if they were pushing each other off.

You had to walk on an invisible string through the store, or else you would have to pay more than you'd want to.

"Hello," a man said at the register table. "How can I help you?"

"Can we sell our caravan here?" Aunt Katelyn asked, squeezed her arms together between the aisles.

He stroked his beard, typing rigorously on his computer, "We can certainly auction it. Where did you station it?"

Aunt Katelyn pointed behind her, "It's in the parking lot."

He nodded and opened a drawer below to grab his set of spectacles. "Let me see."

We both stood in silence as he circled and inspected the caravan. He squinted at the designs of the deck, his fingers running through the line of peeling paint. He narrowed his eyes every time he found a new design. He definitely was the guy to take his job seriously.

"It's a bit run down…" He said, peering through the window, "May I take a look inside?" Aunt Katelyn nodded, handing him her keys.

She leaned to the side and whispered in my ear, "Can't tell if he approves of it or not."

"Me neither."

"So," The man began, stepping out from the back of the deck, "I can guarantee this will be auctioned successfully."

A grin lit up on Aunt Katelyn's face.

"Was this passed down in your family? I've never seen anything as authentic as this." He asked.

Her smile faded. She gulped a big swallow and looked at me for reassurance. "Yes, it was my great-grandfather's."

Great-Grandfathers? What?

"Can I have a name?" He asked, taking out a slip of paper and pen.

"Katelyn Cogsworth."

"Katelyn Cogsworth? If you were related to and named after *the* acrobat Katelyn Cogsworth from the Harrison Circus, then wouldn't this be your great-grand*mother's*? Or a female relative?"

What in the world is going on? Is there some relative I don't know about? This man was confusing me more than Aunt Katelyn's "grandfather".

"With all due respect, you are completely wrong." Aunt Katelyn said assertively.

"Maybe I am. Say, what do you do for work?"

"I used to be a gymnastics teacher."

"And where did you get your credentials?"

Silence.

"You don't need to know my entire work experience. You have no right to ask these kinds of questions."

He gestured his hands outward, "If I don't know the full origin of the caravan, then I can't auction it."

Silence.

"Well she was actually part of the circus." I said, "She was an acrobat. This was always her caravan."

The man raised his eyebrows and walked toward Aunt Katelyn, "These types of caravans haven't been made since around the 1910's. And surely for Harrison Circus, they went out of business in 1907. This had to be one of your ancestors. You couldn't have been the first owner."

Aunt Katelyn nodded and she grabbed my shoulder, squeezing it a little. She opened her mouth.

Silence.

She bit her lip and laughed uneasily, "Yes, you see, we need to get going–"

"Hmm." He narrowed his eyes. "If you say so, then how come the Harrison Circus hasn't had a single performance since then?"

"I guess they stopped documenting them."

"Why *wouldn't* there be a video online if it's still in business?"

"Maybe folks got bored of the same acts." She concluded, stepping back a little. I could barely comprehend what point the man was trying to make. Aunt Katelyn always said that when I was born, she had to drop out of the circus and take care of me while my parents…my parents… left? Yeah, some important job or something. Why is she lying?

I looked down and saw Aunt Katelyn's hands trembling and her fingers fidgeting. I feel so stupid blurting out. Maybe it's a good thing she lied, 'cause now this guy seems to think that Aunt Katelyn doesn't age just because he doesn't have his history straight.

"I'm not sure why." She said, she crossed her arms, "Do you still want the caravan?"

I crossed my fingers behind my back, wishing on one hand he would say no. And on the other two crossed fingers, he would promise a stack of cash. But I can't have both. Funny how that works.

The man jolted from his curious conscience, "Yes! Yes. Yes, I'd love to host an auction here."

Aunt Katelyn nodded, shaking his hand, "Then it's a deal."

I sat in my seat and she unhooked the car from the caravan while I fastened my belt. I looked in the rear view, her face was tight and her arms were trembling. She sprinted into the car, letting out a deep sigh.

A sigh of relief? A tired sigh? I couldn't really tell.

"Weird man, right?" Aunt Katelyn joked.

She turned the keys in the engine and started the car, "Alright, back to step 1." She reared away from the curb and drove out of downtown.

"Sienna," She said, merging back onto the highway, "You don't have to prove to everyone the truth. The reason I don't tell people about my circus work is because everyone only believes in rumors. That the Harrison Circus only functioned over a hundred years ago. It's just not true."

I turned to her, "I'm sorry. I shouldn't have said anything."

"Well, you know, there's no point countering their rumors. We have better things to do."

We drove for another hour on the dull road outlined by grassy plains and blue mountains while blasting the local radio station. Songs with banjos, violins used to fiddle, and enunciated vocals. Country music.

Aunt Katelyn's plan unfolded to be laid back now that I think about it. You could auction a vehicle online, or rent a condominium. Were there even trailer neighborhoods in Honeyville? I had to find out.

As far as I could predict, the tall buildings shrunk into flatter houses. The suburban Levi homes vanished into wooden barns and pointy roofed homes. Our theme parks, waterworks, and technology hubs spread into green acres of meadows with sprinkles of flowers here and there.

I gripped on the overhead handle as Aunt Katelyn zoomed into town, the barns multiplied and less cars occupied the streets, because all of those people were walking on the streets.

An old woman with light gray hair slicked back in a pink clip slammed the hood of our car, "Hey! I'm walking here!" She kept walking but her face was still glaring at us across the street.

"Sorry!" We yelled and Aunt Katelyn drove the car as slow as she could, stopping even more frequently because there were no signals. Not even a single stop sign.

The roads are now sanded pathways and every building is a different color. In fact, every wall is a different color. All of the homes have too many windows and I could almost smell the garlic bread from the bakeries. They had more bakeries than restaurants in this town. Not to mention that every house had flat roofs here. And I thought clock towers were long gone, but here, it's the only building with a pointed end.

"It should be nice here…" Aunt Katelyn assured me. She drove in between the bakeries and newspaper presses into the open canyon that merged behind the brick red town hall.

Between the canyon and the rolling hills was a green grassy meadow with sprinkles of either blue sprouting flowers or…just dust.

It's not spring though, I thought to myself. And just a mile beyond these meadows were a full heap of RVs and trailers.

Aunt Katelyn parked the car on the sandy curve. A blue umbrella tent was set up in the corner of the RV park with a woman standing by a table.

She led us through several trailers. One's roof could emerge into another bed, others had multiple bedrooms. Hardwood floors, carpeted floors, brown wood, big bathrooms, decorated rooms.

But we only had two things in mind: One bedroom and a decent kitchen.

She took us through the trailer alleys, opening doors to give us a peek inside and then shutting them again.

She would tell us which ones had a laundry machine, and which ones had a bed that would come out of the walls…somehow.

Only one of them caught our eye.

A light turquoise trailer stood at the very end, with its window shutters open. It was small, but it had one bedroom. One bathroom. One living room. And one kitchen. The wood inside was painted light yellow. The very end of the trailer had two nooks facing each other with alternating patterns of brown and white. The window between the nooks could open, just like our old caravan.

"It's perfect." said Aunt Katelyn.

Aunt Katelyn told me to wait under the tent while she made the purchase. We wouldn't be driving the trailer anywhere, so fuel wouldn't be something we would worry about. And she promised that there were no campground fees for a year either, which is excellent. So, after we make up the money we spent on the trailer from the auction, we just have to make sure we have, and can make enough money for food and water.

Shouldn't be so hard.

I grabbed a newspaper from the plastic table. I opened one corner, only to open the whole thing.

The front caught my attention because there was a girl on the page. A girl my age.

The Daily Dose of Honey

Hold the Press!

An Eleven-Year-Old Girl's Advice

We all thought Honeyville's news always swelled with gloominess. Here and there, nothing would get better. County leaders told us that we need to be aware of these facts. If we covered it up as if nothing ever happened, the problem would not be solved.

But a young girl, Disha Raj, brought up a better point. Of course no one was expecting it, but we were happy she stepped into the printing house with a fist in the air and valuable words to say.

"I felt like the news these days would just pile up with negativity. I know it's important to know the truth. But something was missing. It was the positiveness that was missing. We needed something for Honeyville residents to look forward to and feel happy to read the paper every day. Something to add." Miss Raj says.

Mayor Michelle McDawson asked, "How do you suggest we incorporate positivity and solutions into the Daily Dose of Honey?" The mayor herself had even chuckled at the irony of the press name.

"I have a theory on something called the 'reciprocal'. Whatever you give, you get it back. It's like a force. If we give out positive affirmations and motivation, residents can reciprocate it back. If we suggest solutions to these problems. If we open a new section highlighting the townspeople's opinions, it would be a stronger connection between the council and residents."

Disha Raj decided to start this new section of the newspaper, as a way to merit the true issues throughout town.

"What's lost can be repossessed." She says, "With just a shifted mindset."

There you have it, Honeyville, we are truly serving you a dose of honey.

I can't tell if she's *actually* trying to help out the residents, or doing it to collect her own charisma. Either way, she's kind of milking it, because the word "reciprocal" is just another word for *karma.*

At least she's right. I would be tired of hearing sulky news every morning, and if she can provide solutions, then I'll be fine. If she can find a solution to our situation, if she can help us move back to Idallis, if she can fix Aunt Katelyn's reputation, then I'll be happy. If not, then I honestly don't care.

A shadow casted over the newspaper and blocked the sunlight. I looked back, it was Aunt Katelyn jangling a new set of keys to the trailer. She glanced at the sun from the corner of her eyes and smiled, "Sienna, are you ready to step into the new chapter of our escapade?"

Chapter Five

The Annoying Guy Hosts An Auction

A couple of days later we drove over to the next town,

back where we met that guy who kept pestering Aunt Katelyn with questions. I have no idea what textbooks he reads, but the Harrison Circus closed the year I was born. Not 1907.

On the drive there, Aunt Katelyn was extremely silent, mumbling to herself loud enough I could hear *that* she was muttering something.

"Okay, Sienna, how much do you bet our caravan is going to sell for?"

I shrugged, "At least over 10,000, I hope."

She glanced over at me, crossing her arms over the wheel to make a turn, "Well, the antique store owner said he would send flyers around his town."

A smile peered on my face. *Finally, something good is happening.*

Aunt Katleyn drove to a park near downtown. One gazebo among several green rolling hills and our caravan erected upon one of them. There was a crowd. A small one, only seven people who all stood on one of the hills.

The man stood in the center of the gazebo, holding a large megaphone.

"WELCOME TO A HISTORIC AUCTION!"

The buzz of the crowd silenced. Dog-walkers, children, and runners coming from the park's trail all paused to watch.

I thought it would be a bigger crowd, but who knows, maybe one of them will be promising.

I held onto Aunt Katelyn's arm and stood on the tip of my toes as the man was getting started calling out numbers.

The host looked at his list and turned to the auctioneers. "Alright," -he turned his head toward their red and orange caravan, "Early 1900's circus caravan from the legendary Harrison Circus, authentic, brought in by–." He then glared at us from the corner of his eyes, "Someone *close* to the owner of this caravan." Aunt Katelyn rolled her eyes.

"Let's begin. 9,000, anyone, 9,000?" A man yelled.

"9,100!" another person yelled,

"Alright, 9,500 anyone, 9,500?"

"9,300!" Someone else yelled,

"10,000!" A woman shouted from the back.

The jump of prices startled the man, and the people glanced at each other, their hands on the verge of raising.

"Okay, okay, 10,500, anyone?"

"11,000!" The woman screamed

"11,001!" someone offered.

"11,040!"

They began bidding around the same price, not escaping the 11,000s.

"12,000, anyone got 12,000?"

A man raised his hand.

"I got 12,075, anyone got 12,075?"

The numbers kept climbing as the sun glided across the sky. Whenever silence filled the small crowd, Aunt Katelyn gripped my hand harder. "How high are they going to get?"

Soon, we were almost reaching 100,000s.

"75,000 dollars, anyone got 75–" A man raised his hand

"80,000!"

"I got 80,000, anyone got 80,500?"

"80,705!" The woman yelled.

"Alright, 80,075, anyone got 90,000?"

No one raised their hands.

"90,000? Going once?"

No one stood on the verge of shouting out a number. My heart was beating in my head, it felt so surreal. 80,075? Really?

"GOING TWICE AND SOLD FOR 90,000 DOLLARS…TO ME!"

Aunt Katelyn scoffed, "Is that even legit?"

The woman narrowed her eyes at the man, "The host can't bid!"

The man set down his megaphone on the floor of the gazebo and crossed the hills to the caravan.

"No rules were written against it."

The rest of the crowd backed away to avoid the anger of the woman and scampered away. Honestly, they are probably relieved they didn't win the auction, their wallets are at least intact now.

The man and the woman started arguing back and forth.

"This is preposterous!" She protested.

A smile appeared on his face as Aunt Katelyn and I approached them.

He reached out his hand, "Well, it's up to the owner."

Aunt Katelyn said sharply, "Whoever is willing to give the $90,000 can have the caravan."

"Not a penny lower?" The woman begged.

Aunt Katelyn turned to the man, "Can you pay 90 grand on the spot?"

He nodded.

She sighed, "Well, whoever is willing to pay the highest."

The woman shook her head in disbelief and said, "Well then, it's yours." She crossed her arms, glaring at the man once more, and rushed away.

When the man opened his wallet, it exploded with bills and bills.

"Where do you even—"

"When you own an antique store, many things get brought in without clear owners."

"So you just keep the money? Is that even legal?"

"Do you want the 90 grand, or not?"

He was copying her words from last time, that's a new level of annoyance for me.

He handed her the money and she snatched it without making any contact. He let out a heavy breath, "Alright, then, enjoy your stash." He fiddled a silver brooch shaped like an owl between his fingertips. Aunt Katelyn looked befuddled as he still paused at the car window, not moving an inch. She opened her mouth to ask a question, but she closed it again.

"Enjoy your caravan."

She gave a firm nod to the man and grabbed my hands, racing to the car on the other side of the park.

Aunt Katelyn turned the keys in the vehicle and initiated the engine.

"Is that him?" Aunt Katelyn narrowed her eyes, the man was walking toward our car.

As the man's figure grew closer and closer to our rearview mirror, Aunt Katelyn lowered the glass, raising her eyebrows.

"Yes?"

"I want answers about this caravan, Cogsworth. Soon. Or I will bring in some investigators."

I saw his eyes flash green and back to brown. Now he was only an inch away from our window. As his eyes flashed back to brown again, a red feather appeared in the crevice of the window.

There wasn't a single bird in sight, and it was so chilly outside in the autumn cold, I don't think birds with feathers as bright as this would be active right now. Would they?

Strange. I just put it in my pocket to look at it later.

Aunt Katelyn turned her head back to the road, "It's in your possession now, you may do whatever you want with it, but do not involve me or my niece." She quickly closed the window.

Aunt Katelyn's forehead tensed and she gripped the wheel even tighter. She said nothing and rolled up the glass again, driving off as fast as she was allowed to.

Chapter Six

Our Youngest Neighbor Just Retired

So, I've been living in a trailer for several days now and here's what I've learned so far.

You can't take long hot showers. Why? Because hot water only lasts for a few minutes. And I don't think anyone wants to take a freezing cold bath in the middle of November.

And you also must be cautious with cooking. Heating up the oven can heat up the entire trailer, and it takes a while for it to cool down. That being said, we have to keep track of time with the stove. But since our mobile home park is on a vast, vast meadow, opening the doors and windows usually helps out.

The property lines around our trailer are basically non-existent, and so is privacy. We don't have much of a "backyard" since fences aren't allowed.

I've always been told that you get really close with your neighbors here—not with us. You see, Honeyville feels kind of like a retirement town to me. Every time we take a stroll on the streets, I haven't seen a single person who could be in grade school. I can't find anyone close to Aunt Katelyn's age either, as she's only in her late twenties.

Maybe because we're the youngest in our neighborhood is probably why others won't mingle with us? It's not like I want to anyways, all they do is play cards behind their trailers, sip tea, gossip, and that's…pretty much it. Even that time we found a lost dog in return for prize money, the owner said nothing, gave nothing, and closed his trailer door on us.

Here in Honeyville, they give a week off from school for fall break—which Aunt Katelyn decided to enroll me in.

The first question I have is, are there even kids here who can go to school?

And the second question I have is, does that make living here official? We can't move back to Idallis?

She promised it was just until she could get financially stable, and then when she heals up her reputation, we could move back. But when you think about it, *buying* an RV, *auctioning* the caravan, *living* in a new neighborhood. That's so much stronger than just renting, *leasing*, and *staying*. Isn't it?

And the thing is, I'm only eleven. I can't work anywhere for a job, and a lemonade stand doesn't sound like the best idea during November.

What does sound like a good idea is, having that constellation appear again, get famous for spotting it. Or discovering it. Then carve myself a big pathway into astronomy, make Aunt Katelyn proud, and move back home.

But if no one can see it, then how is this supposed to work? I already got Aunt Katelyn to fake her appreciation.

"Hey beanie?" Aunt Katelyn called from the kitchen, wiping the counter clean. That's another thing, you have to keep the trailer clean at all times. It's a small area, and one mess can lead to another really fast. And one smell can stench up the whole trailer.

"Yeah?" I called from the bedroom, separating our laundry into several piles.

"The woman next door…Norma Huxley, I think that was what her name was, invited us over this afternoon." She said, drying her hands on the white rag that hung over the oven handle.

Our first friend here, this should be nice.

"Is the laundry ready?" She asked, peering into the other room.

I skimmed the folded shirts and pants on the bed. "Yep." We had ten of each clothing, and now we're down to five. I first thought that our ninety grand was for household expenses. But no, it's for college. For the future.

She nodded and took out a lint roller, setting it on the table. It rolled sideways into the sink. Aunt Katelyn sighed, "Looks like the level block…isn't leveled."

That's another thing about living in a trailer, if you don't have one or place it in the right spot, you shouldn't be surprised when everything rolls off the bed. Even yourself.

That being said, I think it's also time we need a water filter.

🚐

Aunt Katelyn curled her hand and knocked on Norma's RV door and it swung right open.

Norma chuckled, sitting right in front of us on an old couch, "Come in you two." She wore her gray hair slicked back in a bun with a pink clip. The same pink clip, the same bun. The same woman who we almost ran over. As we stepped in, she squinted her eyes and looked back down on a folding table in front of her. She was sewing some coasters or something with a thin needle.

"You enjoy sewing?" Aunt Katelyn asked.

Norma nodded her head back and forth, "Yes, yes, I do. Knitting and crocheting is a bit—well it isn't as exciting, is it?" She lifted up her fingers, "My fingers never tremble."

Aunt Katelyn was always good at starting small talk, I would sometimes copy her words whenever trying to make new friends. But if you ask me to start a conversation, I would simply ask what your favorite color is. I tried to give it a shot,

"So…what's new?"

Norma looked around herself at her vases painted with watercolor, wraps of thread laying over the kitchen counter. An old vintage camera set on a wooden plank.

"Well…nothing here is."

Whoops.

She squinted her eyes and looked at me, "Where'd you two come from?"

"A city down south." Aunt Katelyn replied, "Have you ever visited Idallis?"

Norma set down her project beside her and shook her head, laughing a little. "Oh, I've never left this area."

I couldn't help but widen my eyes.

She continued, "My dear, everyone who's born here, never really leaves the town. And no one ever moves here either."

I gave a big nod, "Must be nice with family always living close."

"Oh well, I'm the youngest…"

My jaw dropped. So everyone living in all these other trailers, are older than her?

Norma gestured her hand towards the couch and we took a seat. She stood up and headed over to the kitchen counter and brought over a small china tea set. The tea pot's lid rumbled as the tea sloshed around.

Aunt Katelyn arose quickly to grab the teapot.

She took one hand off the tray and paused Aunt Katelyn. "I told you, my fingers never tremble."

"Say," Norma began, handing us each a tea cup, "Why did you move here?"

Aunt Katelyn shrugged, "Well, we thought we'd start a new life here."

"What was wrong with your old one?"

"Nothing really, just, it was hard finding a good job."

Norma began to chortle, "Good luck finding one here."

I narrowed my eyebrows, "What do you mean?"

She took a sip of tea and set the plate on her lap, "Well, everyone around here retired years ago. I just retired yesterday and…we've learned to adapt and live on our own. There's no doctors here, barely anyone to teach, no courthouse, no jail, we have all the chefs we need, and no actors, no athletes…the list goes on."

Aunt Katelyn gulped. Her eyes began to quiver. Maybe moving here wasn't the best choice.

"Is there anyone here to take care of you?"

"I used to have a grandson," She pointed to a picture of a teenager framed on her wall. "But he left."

"Out of town?"

"Disappeared."

Oh.

He just left her?

She gazed at us for a full moment, we didn't know what to say and she threw one hand in the air. "Not to worry, like I said, we can all handle ourselves on our own."

"Is there not a retirement home?" I leaned closer.

She knitted her eyes, perplexed, "A what?"

I shook my head, "Never mind."

Wow, this town…it needs help. Like a lot of help. Why couldn't *this* be a headline on the news?

Norma looked at the cold tea wavering around in my cup, it was still full. "Kayleigh," She said, turning to my aunt, "Why didn't you move here earlier if Idallis was so hard to live in?"

"It wasn't always hard, I just…got laid off."

"Why?" She asked.

Was everyone here always invested in things other than their own business?

"It was out of my control…nothing too drastic." Aunt Katelyn concluded.

"I see. I see, why didn't they like the way you did your job?"

This Norma was a *savage.*

I looked over at my aunt, she sat there with no expression. Numb to this idea. Numb to this conversation. She didn't say anything.

Norma opened her mouth and turned to me, "I've never met a ginger before." She slipped her hand through a couple strands of my hair.

"I've heard it's a rare trait." I added on.

"It certainly must be. How can your mother have brown hair and you have red?"

Aunt Katelyn giggled, "She's my niece."

"Oh, well you two keep surprising me every second." She said, chuckling again. Aunt Katelyn laughed uneasily along with her, and so did I.

"Life here is slow, we don't get too many surprises, Kayla."

"*Katelyn.*"

Well, our life has zipped by in a brisk. One minute, I was just contemplating about a constellation, and now, I don't even live in the same house, the same town.

I turned back to look at the aqua colored drapes that she most likely knotted because you could still see the sunlight peer through the stitch lines. The picture of her grandson was baking in that sunlight, he was smiling, his uncombed hair spilling over his shoulders and his arm wrapped around Norma. I could only think of a few reasons why he would leave, an invasive grandmother, bored of this town, possibly found a job that's obviously not here.

There has to be *something* for *someone* to do in this functioning town. Surely it can't just be bakers and cleaners who run this place.

"Well since Aunt Katelyn is really flexible," I mentioned, "She could help you all out with contortion, yoga, and all that sort."

Norma took a small sip of her tea and scrunched her eyebrows, "I don't think anyone here would be interested."

"A gym?"

The cringing still didn't leave her eyebrows. She shook her head.

Aunt Katelyn gave an uncomfortable laugh, "We'll find something."

She finished another sip, "I'm sure you won't." Norma dropped that sentence like a bomb on my aunt. At least we don't have to worry about payments for now, I said to relieve myself. The job search will come later.

Aunt Katelyn shook her head, smiling. Her eyes were jolting, if Norma wasn't old and retired, I would give her a piece of my mind.

I looked down at my china cup, the gusts of wind swirled the little bit of tea left in there. Aunt Katelyn was finishing, too.

"Do you miss your grandson?" I asked, Aunt Katelyn shot me a *why-would-you-ask-that* look.

Norma looked out the window, the gusts of wind turning her huge earrings into chimes, "Yes, I do. You know my heart isn't made of stone. I'm just bold." She narrowed her eyes at me, like I was suspecting her of being a coldhearted woman. I am not suspecting, I know.

Aunt Katelyn got up to her feet and patted my shoulder, "We should really get going now. It was nice meeting you, Norma."

Norma gave a slow nod and resumed her sewing project.

"Bye Karolyn."

We unlatched her door and trudged through the wind swaying the grass from side to side. As Aunt Katelyn unlocked our trailer, something caught my eye.

My jaw dropped, "Aunt Katelyn, look." I pointed.

Over the colossal plains of the green meadow, sheets of red and orange laid flat over the grass, each tip connected to thick wires. The other ends of the wires were hammered down beneath the meadow. The sheets soon stretched into smooth pyramids and small red flags propped up into the air.

"Well I'll be." She whispered breathlessly.

Chapter Seven

The Circus Camp Is Practically Everywhere

The bright sunlight from the window stinged my eyes open.

I gazed at the bare ceiling for a while. It was the first day of fall break. Not that it made a difference, except for the fact I would be starting school in a week. Whatever that looked like.

I finally forced myself out of the sleeping bag and neatened it. I decided not to comb my hair, but just threw a couple of splashes on my face. That's better.

When we wake up, we always have to brace ourselves for any blemishes the trailer surprises us with. Leaks from the bathroom, the compressor of the fridge breaking, any bats finding their way inside, you name it.

Aunt Katelyn was already in the kitchen, pouring herself a glass of milk—our usual breakfast. "A mouse and his family came in this morning, and now they're living over there—" She pointed toward the nook where if I focused enough, I could hear their chitter and chatter.

I still don't think that moving here is the best way to go about it. Sure, it's more affordable, but is it worth it? Is it worth adding the word *stress* back into our dictionary?

Every morning, we would go into town, looking to see if any store or bakery could give Aunt Katelyn a job. And most of the time, they said no—everyone here had pride in their family business, and kept it within their family.

We were giving up hope, until we saw a bakery that we missed.

A cupcake shop.

The second we walked into the red-bricked bakery, the sweet aroma of cakes and cinnamon filled the air. Aunt Katelyn would always start by handing the manager a copy of her resumé and it would always end in a denial.

I was standing behind her, gazing around the bakery, it was strange, just like the others. I'd always assume that they enjoyed puzzles because a table-sized Rubik's cube would always be seen in every kitchen.

The manager gently smiled and shook his head no.

But that's why we went every morning, to see if we missed anything—or to show our eagerness to the owners. Yet today, I had something else on my mind.

I gulped down a glass of milk, "I have to go." I wiped the milk off my face and ran outside. I sprinted across the field, fighting the force of the wind.

The circus tents were fully set up and the flags rippled in the wind. Every circus had the same warm colored theme. But these exact hues twanged a sense of familiarity beneath the surface.

I trudged a little closer, reading the front curtains with the title:

THE HARRISON CIRCUS

It can't be.

There's absolutely no way.

A man with a tall dark hat and a maroon suit covering a golden vest spun his baton, "Come all! Come all! Experience the magic!"

I paused in front of him, and he kneeled, handing me a flier, "Join our camp!" He exclaimed, stretching his smile from ear to ear.

A rip-off camp trying to reboot itself in a big city—and now that same "business" is coming to Honeyville. This town gets uncanny every day.

I grabbed the flier and looked up at the tall ringmaster, and said as candidly as possible, "I'm your new employee." I reached out my right hand for him to shake.

He raised his eyebrows out of sight into his hat, his eyes staring in thunderbolt, "I'm sorry—"

"I'm here to work. I have all the skills you need to walk on a tightrope, ride a unicycle."

"We have all the employees we need–"

"There's been a mistake in the system." I said, putting my hands on my hips to fake a splinter of confidence, "You see, I signed up for this job, and…and I think there's been a glitch."

He rolled his eyes and turned his back to me, "Have a nice day, young lady."

"Wait!" I called, running after him. Don't call me desperate, unless you know any other job in Honeyville. "My aunt worked in the actual circus! She was an acrobat!"

He wavered, swinging his baton at his side and let out a long sigh, "You can volunteer."

I sliced a block of cheese on the wooden board while Aunt Katelyn heated bread on the stove. That's what we've been eating for the past week. Fresh bread from the nearby bakery, and a block of cheese from the old man who lived in the trailer behind us, Jerry.

I mean, we change it up sometimes, like last night. We covered the bread with apple slices. It works out.

I nibbled the edge of the crust, as Aunt Katelyn set the pan in the sink and sat down at the counter with me.

"So," She began, "Where'd you run off today?"

I shrugged, "Nowhere." *Volunteering* at the Circus Camp would be useless. Futile. Vain.

She nudged my shoulder, "Where is this *nowhere?*"

I slumped my elbows further down the counter, and said softly, "The Circus Camp."

"And how was that?"

"Pointless. The…ringmaster told me I could *volunteer.*"

Her eyes lit up, "Well, that's perfect! You get the full experience for free."

I shook my head, No. no. I would never attend a camp for the fall when our situation is like this. "No, Aunt Katelyn, it's not perfect. He wouldn't pay me to help there."

"Isn't that what volunteering is about?"

"You could just stand in some charity event, and call it volunteering. No one really cares, you're not getting paid."

"Well that's the thing, it's about helping out of free *will.*"

I completely lost it, "Aunt Katelyn, why would I help others out of free will if we have no one to help us? Why would I waste time there for a week, for nothing?"

She set down her sandwich and moved a strand of hair out of my face, "Don't worry about wasting time, Sienna." Her expression grew concerned, she closed her eyes for a moment longer than a blink, and forced a smile when she opened them.

"You should go, it'll clear your head." She whispered softly.

I shook my head, "I don't know…"

She tried lightening up the mood a little bit, "Don't worry, they won't make you do the Thomas Salto."

The Thomas Salto.

It was crowned one of the most dangerous gymnastic moves in history, and Aunt Katelyn got in a lot of trouble for trying to teach it to her students back at the gymnastics center in Idallis.

"Auntie?" I called, as she left to rinse her plate in the sink.

"Hmm?"

"Could you show the ringmaster your stunts? Maybe he'll let us both work this week."

Aunt Katelyn shook her head, "I'm trying to leave behind my gymnastic days, Sienna." She turned off the faucet and glanced at me for a second, "Maybe starting everything over isn't such a bad idea."

"But…if you just let everyone see how talented you are, then maybe we'll have a better chance of success in Honeyville. Don't you think it's unfair how they all overlooked your talent? We'll get the whole town talking about your skills if you just show them."

"We all lose too loud and win too quietly sometimes." Aunt Katelyn said, "My reputation may have been destroyed back in Idallis and people always seemed to ignore the stunts I taught. And that's okay." She leaned in to hug me.

And that night, I decided to volunteer. Maybe not out of *free will*, but maybe because Aunt Katelyn would get that I found a place in this town, and maybe that will put one book back on her shelf. A small book, or a big book. I'll have to find out.

The next day, I grabbed all of my clothes and stuffed them in our bag. I ran water through my hair, and–

"Sienna, let me braid your hair." She separated my hair into three parts.

"You sure you don't want to come?"

"If I came, it wouldn't feel like a camp, would it?" She joked.

And with her persistence, I trudged out of the trailer, plowing across the meadow for several miles and strapping the bag over my back. I'd only be so far away from our trailer.

When I got there, there was already a line of kids waiting by the entrance. And if you're wondering how many kids, only three. I'm serious. Only three.

I thought this camp would prove my perception of the demographics wrong, but no. It didn't.

I stood behind in the line, swung the bag to my other shoulder. The nylon fabric of the tent that hung off of the edges swayed in the air.

"Alright, what's your name?" The Ringmaster called, skimming over his clipboard as I got to the front.

"Sienna Cogsworth, I'm a volunteer."

"I don't see a Sienna–" He straightened his hat and glanced at me, "Oh, it's *you.*"

I smirked and nodded, "Yes, it's *me.*"

He looked vexed, rolling his eyes while copying my name down on the page. "Since you're volunteering, why don't you go see if the unicycles have their training wheels on." He pointed inside the net.

"Yes sir."

It was muggy inside the tent, as humid as a summer in Idallis City. Just think of how sultry it'll be when there is an audience. Thin lights lined up to the rim of the tent, and a large open ring occupied the middle—circumference by curved blocks painted with stars. The floor was flat and grainy, almost like the circus was in a desert. Poles on each side of the ring, holding up the tent—and possibly the poles we'd use for tightrope walking. Or something like that.

I walked over to the bleachers, and found a hallway, leading to another tent.

"Hey." I called. A woman was screwing on the bolts of the gears. Gears to a unicycle.

"Hello." She said, lifting up the unicycle and spinning the wheel.

And that's how I spent the two hours before the camp started. Greeting the circus performers, retelling that I was in fact, a volunteer. They wouldn't believe me until I showed them the things Aunt Katelyn spent her life teaching me.

"Watch—" I flipped back and caught myself landing on my hands, crunching my core to walk a few steps backward before I tried to jump up again and do another handspring. They're expressions were blank, crossing their arms and raising their eyebrows. I guess I'll have to wait until the tightrope, it's just like a balance beam—that'll show them.

Here me out, if I do in fact, impress the performers, they could invite me to join them—or even invite Aunt Katelyn.

We'll be living her old life–and we'd finally get out of this town. Aunt Katelyn may not see the vision now, but I do.

Honestly, it feels harder to do a stunt here, on the grainy surface with more pressure on me. It makes me mess up even more, but if I don't prove it to them, then we'll never change our lives. But if I fail, then the same thing happens.

And an hour later, we started teaching the other three kids who came in early. We started with basic juggling from a devoted clown. He didn't have a red nose or frizzy hair, or anything, just white face paint, pink circles over his eyes, and dark red lips. Overalls too.

We started with one pin, then two, then added a third. I can't juggle, but I can sure collect them, and pick them up, and put them away. That's volunteering. The jugglers signaled to me that it won't be the only time I'm picking up equipment.

The sun was almost an inch away from the mountains, and we hadn't learned a single stunt other than a somersault. The trapeze and the tightrope won't ever be taken out, I'm guessing. And neither will the training wheels.

When the sun almost set, the Ringmaster placed logs in front of the camp, surrounding a plinth grasping onto the cackling fire.

A girl sat next to me on the log, and rolled it back and forth with the force of her knees. "How'd you like the camp so far?" She asked. She looked very familiar. Like someone I haven't met, but have seen her face before.

I shrugged, "It's fun."

She nodded, clasping her hands together. Probably thinking of another question. "How long have you been working for the circus?"

I giggled, "Oh, I don't perform with this group." She looked at me and narrowed her eyes. It almost seemed like her eyes shook their heads, expressing doubt.

"My aunt used to." It wasn't *technically* a lie.

"Oh…that's actually really cool." Her voice crescendoed. She rocketed the log back and forth again.

I opened my mouth to say–

The sun fully dove into the ground and sprouted the purple constellation.

The constellation?

The constellation!

It radiated off of the sheets of the tent, illuminating the sky once again. The purple haze dominated over the other blurs of planets seen in the distance. It was here. It was here. I wasn't crazy. It really exists.

"It's back!" I thought out loud.

"What's back?" The girl asked. I turned to her, her eyes and mouth widened as she looked at the sky. Wait. She could see it too?

"The–purple stars." I whispered softly.

The girl jolted, "Huh? What stars? I don't see any."

She clearly did. The way her pupils grew smaller as the purple constellation reflected off of her eyes, captivating her vision. She clearly saw it.

"Yes you do." I nudged.

She shook her head and looked at me, glancing up for a second again in the sky to give her eyes the illuminating glow that consumed anyone's thoughts. I looked around, the other kids chattered among themselves, not even taking a second to glimpse at the purple sky.

"I don't know what you're talking about."

I sighed, giving up. Maybe this constellation has a spell that keeps itself a secret by closing off itself from being communicated by others. But not me, I joked to myself, I broke the spell. Maybe *that's* another thing I could talk about in this town. This theory of my *spell.*

I looked at the girl, she could be my first test subject of this theory.

The Ringmaster stood up and splashed water over the firepit. He stretched out his arms to gesture to all of us to get ready for our tents.

I got off of the log and turned to the girl, "I'm Sienna by the way."

She smiled, stretching out her hand, "I'm Disha. Disha Raj.

Chapter Eight

Disha Won't Give Me Answers

We all spent the night in one big tent next to the circus, each one of us taking a corner. I didn't pack anything to sleep on, but they did lay out a blanket on the floor of the tent. It was the most they could do from keeping the spikes of the dried grass underneath from poking us.

However, I couldn't sleep. And I'm pretty sure everyone else here is pretending to sleep.

I gazed into the roof of the tent, contemplating the stars again. This plan of trying to impress the performers was—well, it's in progress. But now this constellation has come back…

It's impossible. But I'm so glad it's possible.

If Disha wants to keep it to herself, then fine. I honestly don't know why she would lie, it's not like *she* wants to be the discoverer of the stars, does she?

How would I learn more about this weird, purple constellation if no one could see them? But if someone else could see them, it would spoil my plan. There was no clear way. It'll only work if Disha can see it when I want her to see it. And that goes for anyone else too.

I got sick of tossing and turning from that feeling I had in my stomach. It's the fact that I only have a week to figure things out, before I lose sight of the performers or even the constellation. If it'll ever come back.

So I opened the flap in the front and tried to find those stars. Up over the large circus tent, stars stretched over the flags. The six hazy stars that formed a bird that looked like it was flying away from camp.

I just stared at them for a while, the stars were much dimmer than they were when I was by the fire pit. Maybe they're like radioactive rocks. Once they appear in the sky, they get dimmer as time goes on.

I gripped my knees and gazed up until my eyes became heavy as boulders…

…"What was the Harrison Circus like?" I remember asking just a year back.

Aunt Katelyn was frying up a batch of her breakfast donuts, her specialty.

She paused, midway when dipping the first donut into jam and peanut butter.

"Oh Sienna, it was pretty much nothing."

I shook my head, "C'mon, lions, elephants, fire, acrobats? How is that nothing?"

She placed the donut onto a plate with the others and responded, "Because this lifestyle is definitely an upgrade." She wiped bits of chocolate sauce off my cheek.

I crossed my arms, frustrated with no answer, "Did you have any friends?"

She nodded, "Tons, there were so many animals, the other acrobats, my brother…" she trailed off.

Ten-year-old me just knew that she never liked talking about him, or the circus in general. But I still couldn't quell the curiosity inside me.

"Sienna, the past is in the past, and you are my present and future." She said with a smile, which made me gleam.

"I know, I'm the perfect present." Aunt Katelyn giggled, "Yes, you are." She took the plate of breakfast donuts and set it on the table, "Now come on, we've got donuts to eat."

I remember cheering, and sitting down to decorate my donut with sprinkles shaped like fruits, fried eggs, pancakes, bowls of cereal to truly make it the epitome of *breakfast* in the Cogsworth household.

She bit into her donut, a look a satisfaction on her face, "I think this is the best batch of donuts so far,"

"So far…" I repeated, then getting distracted by another bite of the donut.

She nodded, "Exactly, the future will always improve if you try, beanie. That's why the past is gone and away. And the future is approaching."

"Future…" I contemplated.

She set the donut down and grabbed me at the sides, lifting me up higher than her head, I screamed in cheering, "Yes, our future will only get better!"

…. I caught my eyes drooping while watching the stars. I guess it's time to go to sleep. I lifting myself off of the grass and headed back to the tent. Oh, how the times have changed.

The next day at the camp was just like yesterday. Only this time, I was holding a plastic hoop for the three others to run and jump through. You could say it's a bit of a modification from the "ring of fire".

The meadow was quiet today, the grass didn't dance, staying still for anyone who decides to count the petals of the small flowers. I'd stretch out both of my hands to hold out the ring and watch the other step back and run through the ring.

The rest of the day, I only got a chance to hold the equipment and props for the others to use. Obviously, no Thomas Salto stunts, or even *cartwheels*. To be honest, it's a waste of time. It's almost like a daycare. But a *week-care*, masked in the name of a circus.

I'd also be organizing some planner in the back of the tent. Apparently, they would all showcase their talents on the last day of camp to their families–and I was supposed to jot down all of their specialties throughout the week.

Disha took more than a few steps back and darted at the ring. As she saw the ring just an inch before her face, she stopped.

My fingers were getting tired holding the ring, "What's wrong?"

She shook her head, taking a deep breath, "The ring, that's the problem, it's *unjumpable*."

I shook my head, "No, you just need to trust yourself, girl."

She backed away again, mentally preparing herself, breathing. She closed her eyes and rocked back and forth a little, "Okay, Disha, you got this…"

As soon as she started her run, the lunch bell rang.

A wave of relief hit her face.

During lunch, everyone swarmed toward the benches outside the large tent for the usual, make-it-your-own sandwich buffet. It was pretty conventional.

"So," I began, talking to Disha, "I read your interview in the newspaper."

Her face brightened, "You did? What'd you think?"

I grabbed a piece of lettuce to place on top of my bread, "Well if it gets the moods of the residents up, then I'd say yeah, it's pretty good."

She smiled, grabbing a slice of turkey onto her plate, "I mean I've lived here forever, and let me tell you how negative the news always is. And the thing is, there is nothing happening in Honeyville at all."

She's lived here *forever?* That must be rough.

It was like she read my mind, "My parents like staying in a small, safe, and almost isolated town. You know, for safety and such."

"You could get safety in the suburbs, too. Say, Idallis City."

"Never heard of it."

Wow, Norma was right. No one really leaves this town…or barely enters it.

The circus master stood erect at the front of the tables, "Alright, children, as you know, you will have to perform for your parents at the end of this week. And to do that, we will have some group acts, but also individual acts as well. So after recess, please choose and practice your specialty. Thank you." And he walked away.

"What trick do you think you are going to do?" I asked her, there was an entire list set out on the tables for us to choose from:

1. Unicycling.

2. Multi-hula hooping

3. Clowning

4. Illusion

5. Human Pyramid (Group Stunt)

6. Trapeze Art

7. Contortion

8. Aerial aerobics

9. Tightrope

Disha shrugged, "No idea. I'm not very flexible to begin with, or a master at flying in the air. But one thing is for sure, I'm phenomenal at balancing. How about you?

I replied, "I'll go with contortion. You know my aunt was a gymnast."

I guess I could've thrown myself out there and have chosen aerial aerobics or trapeze art. But I'll get there, first showing my flexibility before attempting those moves. You know, if I perform by the end of the week with a jaw-dropping stunt, maybe Aunt Katelyn will consider a chance for us to work with them. It's a far stretch, since she wants to leave those days behind, but there's not a lot of opportunities to work with here.

Yet at the same time, I didn't want to waste time at a camp, helping people with hula hoops and carrying clown makeup from one room to another. I wanted answers for the stars. I *needed* answers for the stars.

I tried not to think much about the cards I was working with and simply threw my trash away, getting ready for the next set of tasks thrown at me.

Disha was also one of the older kids around, since most of them weren't really older than nine. And so, we both just strolled around the tents, having her tell me about the life here and me responding with how the outside cities are.

"You know its crazy." I said.

"What is?" She narrowed her eyes.

"I thought no one here was close to Aunt Katelyn's age, let alone my age. I was seriously considering why they have a school."

"Well, they *don't*. That's why living is extremely affordable. Less tax toll."

"But I thought–"

"There's a school *program*. For tutoring and homeschooling, but not an actual school district here."

"Oh, I see."

"Cogsworth!" A voice outside the tent shouted, it was the ringmaster. "We need you to untangle all of the nets before stunt practice begins!"

I sighed, "Coming!" I turned to Disha, "See you around…" A shiny object caught the corner of my eye. It was in the shape of a little owl and it was a brooch, or something, falling out of Disha's pocket. It looked familiar. Like what that Auction man was fiddling with.

"What's that?" I asked. Disha's cheeks reddened, "Oh, it's nothing, Sienna." She quickly walked away, "The ring master is calling you, by the way."

First the lying about seeing the constellation, and now this. As smart as she may be, she's a horrible liar. Just like my aunt. There's something she isn't telling me. And if it has anything to do with that constellation or its origin, I *need* to know. Now.

I shook my head subtly as I walked inside, with a couple of stuntwomen tossing nets to each other for them to untangle.

While the other children were on the rest of their recess break.

"So are you volunteering here for fun?" One of the stuntwomen asked me, straining their arms at a ridiculous tight knot in the rope.

I nodded, I couldn't really think of a better reason, "Yes, I thought it would be a good use of my free time."

"Well bless your heart, little girl." She replied with a wink, "Planning to join a circus?"

That'd be amazing.

"I'm still letting my future run its course." I replied, trying to play "hard to get".

"If your heart is here, and you find yourself to be talented contortionist, then why not? I'd ask."

I nodded, I wouldn't say I'm a *talented* contortionist, but an above average one. My heart is anywhere me and Aunt Katelyn can live comfortably. Maybe it's here. Or maybe it's in Idallis.

The ringmaster was clicking his pen repeatedly, taking an inventory of the hula hoops, the juggling clubs, balls, rings, etc.

After my blistered fingers untangled the last net, the ringmaster asked, "And as for the individual stunts—"

"I'd like to perform in the contortion category." I replied, smiling.

He shook his head, "You won't be performing, you will be helping."

His words hit me cold and deep. Then what's the point of being here?

"Please sir."

He took a huge sigh, "If you can stay on your toes, and keep the schedule running on time, every day, then, I will consider."

I nodded, "Yes sir, I won't let you down." It was good news and bad news. I guess I have to help even more intensely now.

The rest of the evening went on, I was on a quick break. I was sitting in the bleachers with my clipboard and pen resting next to me, and Disha talking beside me.

"Must be hectic running a circus, even if it's just for kids."

"It sure is," I replied, making sure the ringmaster wasn't in sight, "The crew is nice, though. I mean I've only spoken to the acrobats, but I'm sure the jugglers and clowns are pretty chill too."

"They probably are."

I was swinging my feet out and under the bleachers, my mind racing back to the owl brooch,

"You sure you don't know what that brooch is for?" I asked.

Her face paled, feeling personally attacked, "It's just a decorative piece, what's so wrong with having an ordinary object in my pocket?"

"Your expressions don't make it seem ordinary, Disha."

Disha's eyes widened and then lowered, looking at the owl brooch in her hands, caught red handed. "I'm telling you, its nothing."

I let her go on that. If there was something I needed to hide, I'd find it pretty annoying if someone kept asking me about it.

"That purple constellation last night," I began, "It's really pretty and splendid."

Disha nodded, "It sure was pretty but I don't know about splendid–"

"So you did see it?" I asked, she almost jumped at her own words.

"Well, yes…I did. But where'd you hear about it? From whom?"

"I didn't, I just saw it."

Her expression lightened, her muscles relaxing. "Well then, you're a Philoxenian, too?"

I've never heard that word in my entire life before. What was it? A country?

I shook my head, "No, I've only lived in Idallis my whole life before coming here."

She smiled, leaning towards me, "You can tell me."

I shook my head again, seriously, "I've never heard that word before."

Disha looked at my expression, "You're serious? You've only lived in Idallis? You haven't even heard of Philoxenia?"

I nodded sincerely. She could read the confusion and honesty off of my face and replied quietly, "Well then, never mind."

I regretted my answers. Because now, she won't give me any.

"Alright, those in for juggling, come to the arena." The ringmaster announced.

That was what Disha signed up for, giving me a chance to volunteer with something I'd rather do.

A couple of other kids joined the arena and the ring master told me to grab them hula hoops.

Apparently, their warm up was to hula hoop while jumping on one leg and tapping your head.

"What even is the point of this exercise?" Disha thought out loud.

"I honestly don't know." I replied, I was only doing my job, barely thinking about the reasons for the ring master's exercises.

"Multi-tasking is the point. Young jugglers. If you do not learn the art of multitasking, then you won't be able to accomplish your stunt." The ring master answered.

After that tedious warm up, the jugglers brought out a dozen different clubs. Everyone started with one club, tossing it from one hand to the other.

"Go at your own pace." One of the jugglers advised. And once someone was ready, I would toss them a second club.

They spent that hour getting comfortable with juggling and increasing the number of clubs little by little.

Meanwhile, I'd be helping the stunt woman tie the safety nets together to prepare for the tight rope and the acrobatic categories which spoiler alert, no one signed up for.

The performances we had were clowning, juggling, and only a couple people for the unicycling stunt.

The ringmaster was growing impatient, "Folks, we need at least *someone* to do one of the other stunts for the performance."

"I can!" I raised my hand from behind the arena. All the other kids were all sitting in the bleachers while he was standing in the spotlight, hosting the meeting.

The ringmaster continued, "Anyone *else?*"

Everyone looked at each other, and shifted uncomfortably.

No response.

The ring master put his hands over his nose and mouth, "We can modify stunts, but we need diversity in our performances. I have an incredible crew on deck here to teach you all these stunts. We can even modify them as you like."

No response.

A low voice raised her hand, "I'll do the trapeze one." Disha said.

Disha?

The ringmaster smiled, "Perfect."

She nodded and went back to writing down in her notebook.

"Dismissed." The ring master said and turned away to walk backstage, with his long coat wavering in the wind.

He approached me holding one finger up, "Remember Cogsworth, our condition. Keep everything running on schedule and you've secured yourself a spot."

My mind wasn't even *thinking* about if I could perform or not, but Disha's choice to.

All the kids left off to their tent or to freshen up before their training, but Disha was still sitting down at the bleachers. Writing.

When I approached her, large words like *Philoxenia* and *Orb* were written down in her notebook.

As soon as I walked over, she shut the notebook close and put on a smile, "Hi, Sienna."

"Hello," I replied, "I heard you're going to be a trapeze artist." I sat down next to her.

She shrugged, putting her pen behind her ear, "Just said it so he wouldn't bug us. While you're working, he's been keeping these meetings like every thirty minutes."

I stood up, concerned, she's still going have to perform the trapeze stunt, whether she means it or not, "I'll help train you." I suggested.

She shook her head, "No need, but thank you."

I narrowed my eyes, "H-how are you going to get out of this?"

She looked up at me, giving a cheery grin, "Don't worry about it."

My jaw half-dropped, flabbergasted. This ring master was by far the strictest person in all of Honeyville this week. It'd be *pure magic* just to convince him of something he was remotely against.

"What's your magic plan?" I asked her.

She looked a little startled. Okay, something was definitely going on here.

She brushed off her jolted-ness with another smile and soft tone, "Don't worry about it, Sienna."

I randomly asked her, "Do you like to write?"

"W-what?" She asked, confused.

"Do you like to write. I mean, Philoxenia, is that a creation of your own–"

"Y-yes, it is. Um, there's this story I'm writing, where these fairies live there. And they go on quests and such."

So, if that was a fake, magical world, why would she be asking me if *I'm* from there? Something wasn't adding up. Is that a forbidden city around here?

"You know, Sienna." Disha said with a huff, "You've been working really hard at this camp and your efforts haven't been so unnoticed here–" She took out that owl brooch from her pocket and pinned it onto my olive-green shirt, "You should have it."

"Wow, thank you, Disha." I said, feeling the intricate pattern of the feathers and the eyes on my fingertips.

"Anytime," she said.

Another group of children marched in, holding loud horns. Some wearing red noses and others shouting about throwing pie at each other's' faces.

I said, "That's probably the clowning group, I don't think you'd want to get cream pie stuck in your hair."

Disha nodded intensively, "I'd rather not, see you at dinner." And she scurried away outside.

I spent that mid-afternoon testing different wigs, different red nose sizes on these children for their costumes. Not without the annoyance of those horns, however.

The two professional clowns, who were brothers were explaining to them the art of comedy like they were lecturing physics.

"You have to fool the audience into thinking they know what you're doing, and then you flip up and do the unexpected."

They demonstrated with simple actions, like walking in a straight line toward the exit door, and then jumping up and running to the other one.

I regret saying that teaching comedy was like hearing a physics lecture because what came next was worse.

Pie.

Before the clown brothers even *got* to talking about the next activity. The children were already throwing them at each other's faces.

This'll be fun to clean up.

"No, no, son." One of the clowns said, "Please don't"

Too late, the kid already hit him with a cream pie.

The two clowns looked at each other in regret at this horrible idea.

In the evening, I helped clean up with the clowns all the cream pie frosting and the props that got left behind. Then, finally, the dinner bell rang. Finally.

We got to eat in the tent today, where there was some lighting because the children weren't in favor of eating outside in the dark. And the ringmaster wasn't in favor of having dinner early. The dinner menu today had some chicken and noodles. Delicious.

"You know, this Circus Camp would make a really good article in the newspaper." Disha said.

"It would, wouldn't it?" I said after a slurp of my noodle, it's been so long since I had them, "I'm sure the town would love to know about these hectic kids throwing pie everywhere or breaking the only training wheels we have."

Disha nodded, giggling, "Those kids really do put you through trouble, don't they?"

"It's all part of the experience, I guess. I think the ringmaster thinks I'm scamming him by "volunteering" to get the Circus Camp experience. So, he's making sure to use all of my volunteering potential."

"I will say though, he's definitely a difficult guy."

"Oh, did you try to talk out of the trapeze stunt?"

She shook her head, "No but when I told him I have to go home early, he said I can't."

"You're going home early?"

"Yeah, my dad's going to pick me up."

I decided not to ask why, because even if I did, she wouldn't give me an answer.

"He probably doesn't want the one and only trapeze artist going home." I suggested.

She twirled the noodles on her fork, "Probably because it wouldn't help his circus promotion, I assume."

That was a good point. Always keeping everything running on time, no changes, strict day by day plans, everything had to be perfect. I can start to see why Aunt Katelyn hated it here. Maybe she had a horrible director too.

For dessert, the acrobat woman was serving fortune cookies on a large sheet tray.

All the children swarmed up to the table with the cookies, their hands reaching over each other's heads to steal more than just one.

I managed to get one unharmed, and so did Disha. I cracked my cookie which wrote:

You will NOT get what you desire the most.

It was mysterious and frankly frightened me. What did I desire? I knew many things I did want in life yet they all flew away from my head as I read this note. I couldn't point out anything. Fortune cookies aren't supposed to be negative, let alone eerie.

"What does your fortune say?" I asked Disha.

She cracked her cookie and opened the note which she read aloud, *"You will always remember who gave the most important gift."* She shrugged, "It's one of those general ones; I don't really pay attention to these things any way. What about you?"

I sighed, "Um, well, it just says, you will not get what you desire."

"Well what do you desire?"

"Honestly, to go back to home in Idallis."

Disha patted my back, "I'm sorry, I guess you'll have to live in Honeyville then."

"Disha."

"What?"

"Don't tell me you believe this."

She shrugged, "Sometimes, you just have to."

"Okay, then who gave you the most important gift?"

"Probably my tutor, she helped me get a scholarship."

"You got a scholarship at age eleven?"

Disha nodded with a smile, "I sure did."

Disha definitely left me in awe with a lot of things. One including this.

Everyone wrapped up dinner together, and the ring master had us go to bed pretty early, so we could train even better for tomorrow.

I pretended to yawn, "Alright Disha, see you tomorrow."

She paused while walking to our tent and gave a small nod, "Sure, see you."

▲

I closed my eyes and forced myself to sleep that night. But as always, my curiosity got the best of me.

In the other corner, Disha was uncomfortably shifting from side to side. Her eyes were open and she was scanning around the tent. She turned to me—

I shut my eyes.

She started breathing heavily and carefully got up, grabbing her satchel. She tip-toed to the front of the tent and then hurried away.

I moved my bag to the side and sprinted after her.

She paused, digging her hand in her pocket and took out another pin. Just like the owl brooch. All I could make out was that it was round and gold.

"Disha!" I yelled.

She jolted and ran into the Circus tent. I followed her underneath the bleachers inside and she kept turning her head back, picking up her speed each time.

"Disha, wait!" I yelled. I was running out of breath, but she seemed to be slowing down. I was still far behind her.

She sprinted behind a fold of drooping curtains near the ring. She stopped and yanked down the handle of the small

119

door the Ringmaster built to a small closet backstage. She pulled out that brooch and kicked it under the gap between the door and the ground. "C'mon, C'mon!" She muttered impatiently.

I was so close to catching her, she gasped as she looked behind to see me. The door grasped onto Disha's momentum and swung open. Blue wisps of glitter seeped out of the door, connecting and separating. She grabbed the handle and slid inside, trying to keep the door as barely open as possible. She jerked the thin door close.

I tried to grab the handle and follow her, but this time it was too heavy. Like pulling pure metal. I knocked on the door and tried to tug on the handle. "Disha?" I called, knocking intensively. I can't think of a single reason why she would be hiding in that small closet of all places.

I let go of the handle and grasped it again. I forced all of my strength into my own two arms and put one of my feet against the wall to yank the door open. It collected its momentum again and swung out–dropping me to the floor. I picked myself off of the ground and went into the closet.

"Hello?" I called, looked around. It was only a very small room with house supplies, no other doors or corners or sections. And…she was nowhere to be found.

She was just here. I saw her, I'm not crazy. Maybe I was just seeing things. Seeing things because I was so stressed about Aunt Katelyn. Or seeing things because I want to convince myself that everything will turn out fine in Honeyville, but it won't.

Still, I'm not crazy. She opened the door and went in. How could she not be here? She opened the door, went inside, and closed the door. That's all she did.

Wait.

She slid something underneath. Some random pin, round and gold. Too bad I didn't have any–

Wait.

The brooch. The owl brooch. I rushed back into the tent and scavenged through my bag. The one Disha gave me.

I pulled it off of the shirt too hard, leaving a rip. Never mind that, I crumpled the shirt at where the hole was and ran back off to the tent.

I took a deep breath and kneeled. I have no clue where Disha is, but if she can see the weird constellation, then I'll ignore my doubts. So following what she did, I placed the brooch at the front of the door, then sidled it into the gap with my fingertips.

I took a step back, underneath, the blue wisps were flowing out again. They were soft and cold, juxtaposing the humid tent. I glided my hands through them to feel the mist. This isn't real. This isn't real. This isn't real.

I embraced myself and opened the door. It was like your house was floating and you opened the door when you were soaring through the sky. Shadows were flying through the air, the houses were flat rectangles, mountains reached so high, they touched the glimpse of the sun, illuminating everything. It was like you were standing on the edge of a skyscraper.

My feet are set in place perpendicular to this strange portal. It was like you were sticking a magnet to the fridge. You could take off the magnet, but you'd still feel the force.

I blew out all the air from my lungs, trying to process what I'm seeing. This is real. This is real. This is real.

I turned my head back; it was either this risk or Honeyville. Either find Disha, or stay in this depressed town. Either discover something new, or struggle with Aunt Katelyn forever.

1, 2, 3…. Jump.

Chapter Nine

Philoxenia Is A Real Place

My heart was racing faster than ever. I was falling, and falling and falling. But I wasn't falling *down*. More like diagonally, through precarious winds swaying me left and right. I was getting closer to the ground, but the townspeople never got closer. And I never saw anything but the tops of the roofs. It was as if water rolled into a hollow passage, its winds gushing up and down and erupting from the sides. The hollow passage opened below me, its current promising a rollercoaster of a ride.

It's now or never. I told myself, and stepped in.

I slipped and the current of the passage skidded me through the tunnel–pushing me onto a cold crystal platform and then disappearing. The whole platform was covered by a dome and it was like the floors were doing everything they could to keep them from floating off into the universe. Ironically, the stars from above bounced off the dark nothing into the crystal complex. And…the stars from below.

There was an old man standing in the middle of a room, twisting his scepter slowly side to side. I tried to approach him, walking on the small design imprints on the glass and trying not to walk on the risky crystal.

I stood behind him, "Excuse me sir, but…where am I?"

The man turned and lifted his scepter, painting a stiff expression on his face, "Where are you from?"

"That depends." I said, shifting on my feet. I couldn't just give my address to anyone. And then again, I wouldn't know if I would say Idallis City or Honeyville. You already know which one I *would* say.

"Don't play games here. Tell me where you're from." His muscles tightened and his voice became stern.

I sighed, "I'm not from here…hey, how'd you get that space illusion going from underneath the building?"

He set down his scepter and massaged his temples, "Oh, you're one of those people. From the Tech World."

The Tech World, I thought. In that case, that's Idallis—there's no way he's referring to Honeyville. "The city, you mean?" I murmured under my breath.

"Stop mumbling!" He growled. He shook his finger at me, "I hate mumbling."

I winced, not letting my eye go off the scepter. Technically, that's technology.

The man walked away from me, and sat down on the edge of a short cylinder. Everything in here was either gold or glass. Glass floors with gold design. Or gold cylinders with gold corners. But more than that, a large *silver* table stood in the middle of the entire dome.

"Where do you want to go?" he grunted.

"Wherever I should go." I said softly, if he works in a taxi system I've never seen before, then he should have strong expertise in getting me home without asking anymore questions.

He narrowed his eyes at me and yelled, "Stop mumbling!" He looked at my hair up and down, "I hate children like you....you *vibrant mumbler*."

I patted my braid up and down, sure it's vibrant alright. And so is his impatience. He gripped that scepter so tight spines crawled up my back just thinking what he uses that for. To get out his anger? Probably.

"Answer to me now, or I'll make sure no one will answer you ever again." The gold knob of the scepter was pointed at me. I gulped and blurted out loud without thinking, "Home."

He shook his head, "I can't send you home."

"What?"

"How'd you get here?"

"I don't know…I just slipped a brooch under a door and–" He shot a dubious look at me, raising both of his eyebrows. One minute he's going to break something, and the next minute he refuses to fulfill his job. Wow.

"No *Techie* can just come here from the Tech World accidentally. I can't trust you. Who knows what you have planned back there. "

I took a step back, was an old man seriously suspicious of an eleven-year-old girl for trying to go back home? Well maybe I'll stay in this implausible neighborhood.

A moment of silence passed within the dome.

The Platform Manager crossed his body with his scepter and stood behind the table, leaning on his elbows. "You're not the… are you?" He said with a loud whisper.

I raised my eyebrows in confusion, "I'm not who?"

"Don't play like this at me!" he yelled again.

"Just send me *somewhere!*" I yelled back, "If you're that desperate."

"Board the Philoxenia Express. It couldn't hurt." he then shook his head and rubbed his hands on his long neck. "But no! I can't risk it." He looked up and turned his head to a very thin table. "But she can't stay here." He said out loud.

I'm starting to understand how much this man hates conversing softly.

The Platform Manager stepped toward the very thin table. "Put your hand just above the table."

I cautiously approached the silver table and reached out my trembling hand. My fingertips where shaking and–

"Don't touch it!"

I jumped. "My bad!"

My hand, just hovering over the silver table, attracted some electric light flowing from the table to the top of the dome. As the blue light zapped from the table and up, it shimmered white, outlining my hand with a thin line.

The platform portal manager instructed, "Board the Universal Express with a ticket to Philoxenia. And just stay *there*. It's safer for everyone."

I nodded but then stopped, "I don't have any money."

He growled and slapped his hand on his forehead, "If you can come to the Platform 'coincidentally', then I'm sure you can sneak on a train." I thought taxi systems were supposed to be loyal to the law—or at least follow it. And I've never met anyone who was so desperate to do their job. How am I supposed to know how this country works? Or this world? This universe?

"Here. Now," he said "Stand on the table." A minute ago he just said—never mind.

I climbed on the table and a circle just an inch smaller than the table emerged. Then another circle an inch smaller than that circle emerged. As the table layered up and I grew taller and taller, a big metal stand appeared on the top circle. I stood on it.

The Manager pressed his scepter on a gem beside the table.

"Don't come back, vibrant mumbler."

The blue electricity bordered around me…and I felt myself fade away. A million questions rushed into my head. How could he do that? How is this happening?

And then none.

I'll just accept it.

It's better than a Circus Camp.

I was racing down that void with the gushing wind that almost had the current and polarity of water. Sucking me and and–

Dropping me on a stone hard ground with a thud. I'm still recovering from the first one.

I stretched my arms out to carry myself off of the station. And when I got up, I was standing in a pool of people, all holding tickets that said: *The Universal Express.*

There was a ticketing office behind me, I moved away from the window, covering my hair as much as possible. It was like one of those train stations in Europe that I had seen pictures of. Light stone concrete but green grass everywhere else, everyone eagerly waiting on the edge of the station while you could just sit behind them all and solve a crime, the average steam whistle–

Whoot! Whoot!

And the black iron train.

I crouched behind a family's set of luggage. The mother held the set of tickets, I squinted my eyes to read across the words, **PHILOXENIA**.

Philoxenia.

I tried to walk within the condensed spots of the crowd, keeping my eye on the family. I could hear yelling from the front of the train, but I don't know if there's anyone to inspect tickets here.

The family in front of me started to board and lifted their bags. I let go but still stayed near. I crouched near the edge of the door and slipped in, walking close to the family to seem like a part of them—but it still felt like I was just a stranger in the crowd. I guess a criminal's first crime is the most vulnerable of all.

The family sat in the front of the train, greeting the ticketmaster and kneeling down to point out the lower windows so their children could spot their favorite colors in nature. I hid behind a wall, away from their luggage to avoid eye contact with any adult.

I pushed through the crowd of passengers in the narrow hallways to the back of the train and hid there. I had no ticket. I have no money. I can't get caught.

If anything happens, I'll blame it on the Platform Manager—he's the one who told me to do this.

I stretched my shirt over my knees and sat in the corner of an alcove. My shoes were full of dirt from the meadow, ruining the soft maroon carpet. It definitely stood out from the rest of this clean train.

I could hide in the compartment above me and stay there until the train stops at Philoxenia. Perfect.

I stood on the seat and opened the compartment, crawling in there as fast as I could. Through a small crevice I peeked out just in case anyone came into the booth. So far so good.

I sat there for what it seemed like hours, listening to the whistle hoot as the train made small pauses in its trip. I don't know how far 'Philoxenia' is, but I'll leave if it sounds anything close to the muffled yell of the engineman through the window covered in steam.

To hear it better, I opened the cabinet just an inch to let the cool air in. I could see green grass soften into snowy mountains through the crevices letting in a speck periwinkle light. But it wasn't before the train rolled away from the mountains and the snow faded into misty oceans roaring onto the shore.

Season to season. Like Aunt Katelyn going person to person in Honeyville. Person to person in finding someone who needs another hand. Person to person to find someone willing to pay her. I told her she should've made the best of her skills. If only she listened. Then who knows, maybe we would've been the sensations on our way around the world.

I opened the cabinet a little more to widen the gap. The ocean mist snuck its way through the window corners and softened the air a little. I laid flat in the wooden compartment, scanning my eyes below me to calculate the distance between the seats and me.

I don't even have a plan. I already angered someone and I doubt I'll find Disha. The purple constellation or returning back home; I don't know what matters now.

"Tickets! Tickets!" A voice echoed and he stamped the tickets that reached out into the halls.

Shoot.

I closed the cabinet door again and breathed as softly as I could. He poked his head into the booth and poked it out again. *Phew.*

I'll have to find that Platform Manager again, he knows what he's doing. Suspecting me of some crime while telling me to commit one. If he can send me anywhere, why can't he send me directly to Philoxenia? What's the point of this? I could be anything here. An experiment on his futuristic transportation method. Or just some random girl. A lost girl. A lost girl trying to find a solution back home by leaving the world. Or better yet, I could bring Aunt Katelyn here. Then we can win loud and lose quiet.

My chest tightened and my stomach dropped. She doesn't know I'm not at the camp.

Oh no.

I'm already a burden to her, and now I'm a bigger one. She's going to be so mad, or worse, disappointed. But if I get home before she finds out, If I make something out of the constellation before–

Footsteps patterned down the cabins, "Mom! An open booth!" A girl shouted and slid the glass open. The same family.

"Dad, what's Philoxenia like?"

I heard a heavy sigh from the father, barely whispering, "Only the safest dimension right now–and the serene."

Safest?

The mother replied concerningly, "Edmonia is a beautiful kingdom there, sweetie. You'll love it."

"How long are we going to stay there?" A small voice whined.

"I don't know," The mom said, "We'll see. But don't worry, it'll be fun."

So I just followed Disha into an unchancy world. Well, this is so great.

Their voices continued chattering about living in Edmonia telling promising stories about the kingdom and the squeaky little voices becoming engrossed in little creatures flying across the window.

I could feel myself getting sore from staying crunched in the compartment, but it was worth it, worth waiting for a new world; Philoxenia. Waiting to see Edmonia.

I'd look out the crevice to keep track of the family. Observing how eager the father seemed at moments, how he sat on the edge of his seat where the rest of his family didn't. Anytime he stood I would grip onto the wooden corners. Anytime the children looked up at the compartment, I would hold on as if it would make me invisible.

The journey of the train seemed endless and my fingers grew tired of balancing the wooden compartment an inch open at their tips. I scrunched my fingers into a fist and slowly opened the compartment a little more. Gushes of salty mist from the sea swarmed in around me, saturating the air.

"Almost here, children, almost at Edmonia. Just a few minutes more." The mother grabbed the youngest son into her lap and cradled him. She kept humming to the children to soothe their restless impatience. The most it did was slow them from bouncing on the cushion that vibrated up here. I could almost feel the wooden planks jolt.

Through the gap, I saw a glimpse of the children wheeling the luggage back and forth and back and forth and back and forth—

"Here." The father paused, he grabbed the bottom of the suitcase, "I forgot to put them away…"

Oh no.

Oh no.

I backed away far into the corner, as if that was going to do anything. My heart jumped into my throat and roared in my ears. This was a bad idea. A terrible idea. The train would stop any minute—how could he remember? *Now?*

It was completely dark inside here now. The two doors swung open and forced wind through my hair. I couldn't help but grab the bottom edges as if that would help. But he just pulled the door open with all of his momentum and I crashed to the ground with my hair fully wrapping my face.

The three kids thrusted the wooden planks up and down and screamed to the top of their lungs. "A monster! A monster!"

I swung my hair back over my head to show them that I did have a face, "Wait! No! I'm…playing hide and seek!" I shouted.

The father said nothing and the mother held her children close. But they both were backing away.

I stood up and took a deep breath so the world wasn't spinning again, "I'm Sienna." Aunt Katelyn always says to make your name known. "I was just thinking that this was a good place to hide—"

It was too late.

The ticketmaster came rushing in from the cacophony the children created. "What's the emergency?" He promulgated and looked down at me.

"Where are your parents?"

I gulped, "I was playing with my cousin and I decided to hide here. I'm Sienna."

The Ticketmaster crossed his arms. The train was coming to a stop and the planks stopped rattling below me.

"I'm actually supposed to get off here—" I said.

"If I can just see your ticket and any adult here with you, then that's fine."

The mother whispered to her husband and they started leaving the booth. The entrance was just to the side of the train. I could run.

I underestimated how much it could hurt to fall three times. I forced all of my weight onto the cushion as I struggled to balance myself standing.

He only gave me a stern look, a look saying: *Show me your ticket.*

I can only try so hard at stalling, "You see, I was lost but my family is right over there…" He looked over his shoulder at a large family pushing out a single file through the entrance. He pointed at my head, "Is this child yours?"

They shook their heads. Can't someone just at least try to help out a kid here? Sheesh.

The Ticketmaster kneeled, "You don't have a ticket, do you?"

I stammered leaning back on the cushion, "I-I-I do, you see, I'm from…Edmonia…it's true, I was lost. Just me, a small, lost girl trying to find her way back home."

I looked around, everyone was getting off at this train. It almost felt like the train was a little *lighter*. Weird.

He raised an eyebrow. "Oh really? Who's the king and queen?"

Oh no.

"I suffer from memory loss. These details slip my mind so quickly. That's why it's hard to find my family–"

He laughed, "I've met people like you before and you all seem to never understand how terrible train hopping is for your reputation."

No. No. No.

This can't be happening, I can't just ruin my reputation before I even *step* into Edmonia.

I thrusted my arms over the cushions again before trying to shift my weight to my legs. Just a couple of sore muscles and bruises, I can still run.

"Thank you, sir." I saluted to throw him off a little and I darted off—well limped off.

I gripped every piece of corner to throw me into a faster momentum as I bolted onto the station. And the ticketmaster wasn't too far behind me.

This really isn't such a big deal, though. One kid is train hopping, really? That's an issue?

I pushed aside my thoughts and ran straight into the village market. There were dusts and wisps of cinnamon from the mountains blocking my eyes. And eventually, the dust got caught in my lungs and I couldn't taste anything but cinnamon flavor.

As I tried to hold my breath, my hands were snatched behind my back and I was shoved forward. Every joint of mine throbbed, I didn't fight the force.

The wisps cleared and a large gray castle emerged in front of the market. There were patches of grass circling it like a moat and discrete from the grainy sand underneath me. The maroon flags laid low and flat against their poles on the palace. Interesting.

"You're taking me to the castle?" I asked.

A deep voice growled, "No." She gripped my hands tighter. I looked behind me, a rough woman dragged me through the sand with her firm hands.

She grabbed my wrists and dragged me across the sand, letting the cinnamon wisps blind me. The castle on the hill didn't look so small anymore.

Was train hopping such a serious penalty?

We approached the moat, but the bridge didn't arch over the water. There wasn't any water. The red bridge crossed over blue powder that gushed around the castle.

I glanced behind my shoulder, the woman gruffed and glared down on me, squeezing my hands tighter. As we crossed the bridge, I placed my shoe into the crevice and repulsed myself from her. It did nothing.

I blinked the dust away from my eyes as I waited for the main doors to open. But they didn't. Instead, she dragged me to the side of the castle and pushed a tall window open.

"Get in."

I hate this dream. Why did I follow Disha? Was Disha even here? What's Aunt Katelyn doing right now? Does the circus camp even care that we're gone? I want to go back home, I want to go back home, I want to go back--

"You can't go home."

The halls were dark and cold. The windows stood out against the walls. They were perfectly clear, but couldn't even carry the sunlight inside, weird.

There was a small hallway that she tugged me through and led me down a flight of stairs. A dungeon?

I shouldn't have listened to the Platform Manager, even if he did "magically" send me here.

A man stood inside and stomped his fist on the throne, "Another one?" He shouted.

"Indeed, sir."

It was just like the books. A long red cape stretched from his neck to several feet below his throne. Silver and gold rings shone on each of his fingers–just barely reflecting a hint of light. The gray bricks arched over his throne and I could feel my hands loosen from the woman's grip.

"Just send her to the inspection."

This is a dream

This is a dream

A dream…

"I'm just dreaming about them, beanie," Aunt Katelyn said, stroking my hair. I was probably nine, sitting in her lap on a summer evening. The sun was just setting.

"But I dream about stars at night, Auntie, and there's stars in real life."...

"I'm only a child." I said, glancing for a second behind me. The walls were closing in as the King contemplated his decision.

My hands tightened again.

The woman's voice darted in my ear, "Sir, we mustn't underestimate children ever again."

The King stood up, "That much is true."

I stood there as the two shared expressions of doubt and faces of worry. Between frowns and shrugs. Between, eye raises and sighs.

The windows began to reflect light. The invisible curtains began to pull away and the windows brought in light and the doors brought in townspeople.

Their walkways formed hallways and their curtsey's dominoed across the palace. Suddenly it wasn't so bad.

I turned my head back to the King, "I swear I'm innocent–"

No reply.

From across the castle, a teenager juggling three potions threw each bottle one by one across a side of the wall. She reached out her arm and the potions disappeared, leaving only dust.

I turned my head and for a moment she glanced straight at me. Her hand lingered behind her.

The dust swirled into the wall and back, the gold dust fell to the ground. Slowly, it rose and each particle stuck to each other–forming rods. My eyes swayed left to right as the rods bent into a harp-like instrument across the teenager's hand.

My attention was drawn back to my wrists that were gripped snug by this woman. It almost seems that *she* didn't belong here. Among the townspeople.

The King concluded in a deep voice, "Send her–"

"She's my sister!" A voice echoed from behind. The teenager's hand waved in the King's sight. She swayed the harp and her brunette hair to one arm and hastied toward me. Not only was she tall, but I could see her arm barely quivering to hold the seemingly heavy instrument. It almost looked like a harp.

"I lost her for days, Your Majesty," She bowed, "I told her to take the Geoport here but it may have malfunctioned."

The woman leaned towards her with a raised eyebrow, "She didn't come from the Geoport–"

"Ah well, this girl never listens to me. Whatever I say goes through one of her ears and comes out the other."

I gazed at her subtle expressions. She was sure I was her sister. The way she leaned in and out. The way she nodded at everything she was saying. Her brown eyes were convincing enough. I gulped when she made eye-contact with me, she winked.

"Mazie Polaris, simply take your immature sister and don't let her scare the authorities like that. You know we can't divert our attention to these trivial matters."

Mazie bowed her head and grabbed my hand from the woman's. Her palms were soft and eased the tension that the woman caused, "Yes, Your majesty."

She placed her hand on my shoulder and lead me out. As she plucked a string from her instrument, the window stretched and enlarged into an opening door. She gestured my head down to draw attention to the water. We crossed the narrow bridge–

"And Mazie." The King called.

She turned back, "Yes?"

"The children want to hear your song again, play it for them, will you?"

"Of course, your Majesty."

The doors closed as she led me out. She rubbed my shoulder and grinned, "Welcome to Philoxenia, little girl."

Chapter Ten

I Impersonate A Stranger

"Thank you…" I trailed behind her, watching her braid swing from side to side.

She paused and waited for me to catch up to her. The swirling dust came to a rest as they slid off the sides of the tents.

"How old are you?"

"Eleven."

She paused again and looked at her harp and looked back at me and looked back at her harp. "Hold this." She shoved the instrument in my arms. I braced my arms however, the harp felt as light as a feather when I held it.

We continued strolling down the aisles of the bazaars. She stretched out her fitted suit and took out a watch. The breeze pulled back my hair and the low strings almost vibrated. Children were running around with iridescent pendants and every time they saw Mazie, they swung their arms in the air. There wasn't a single kid that didn't notice her.

"Do you think you're dreaming?" She asked me. I raised my head from the harp, "Sorry?"

"I said, does it feel like a dream?"

I looked at the women next to me swirling powder in the air and their family pulling yellow string into thin rods behind counters.

"Well, honestly, it does."

She looked at her watch again, "Maybe when the clock strikes three, you'll wake up back in your bed."

She held out three fingers and counted down each second. "In three, two…"

Wait. I can't leave now. Not without Disha. Not without proof of the constellation. Not *bare*handed. Can't just leave this cornucopia.

She closed her last finger, "One."

"Hold on!"

Nothing happened.

Mazie giggled, "So, you *are* from the Tech World."

I stammered, "How did you—"

"Your world is completely dry of magic. No sane person would want to wake up from this dream."

My jaw dropped; I can't be so predictable anymore. A smile spread over her face as she watched my eyes widening.

My eyes traced her, pointing her watch towards the side of the street, a large yellow tent laid with its flaps fluttering in the wind. It was nothing out of the ordinary, just a tent. But as she led me inside, there was a raised wooden stage with other harp-like instruments. I set hers next to them.

"This is my home."

It was spacious and the deep wooden scent of the instruments reminded me of the fireplace back home. And the yellow walls were like the everglades of pale grass near our home in Idallis.

She placed her hands on her hips, "I still have a lot of work to do, but as long as the little musicians are happy." She turned to me, "You Techie's are so unexplainably curious—any questions?"

I inhaled a deep breath, "So first of all: What's Philoxenia? Why am I here? How am I here? How is this working? Is magic actually real? Is this whole thing real or is it just fake? Does this place have anything to do with that constellation? Does it have anything to do with that purple bird constellation? Can stars even be purple?"

Mazie slowed me down, lowering her hands, "Whoa-whoa-whoa. One thing at a time. We want to steer into the garage properly."

I cocked her head with perplexion.

Mazie shrugged, "Isn't that a phrase you use?"

I shook my head.

Mazie took out a large book with a golden design from underneath the wooden stage. She thudded it in front of me, letting that sparkly dust rise from the ground.

"There is so much to learn about this universe, but let's just cut to the basics." Mazie said. She opened the book, "The people of Philoxenia are the ancestors of magic. This is the first dimension ever created."

"I thought Philoxenia is a kingdom."

"No, this is Edmonia, a kingdom *in* Philoxenia."

She turned the next page and all of the illustrations were instruments—but not just harps. There were long tubes, and drums, and boxes, and stars shapes.

As Mazie pointed toward the illustrations she explained, "Magic was formed from music and logic. As musical vibrations passed through the force of nature, logic enveloped into it. The force that emerged is now called the reciprocal. The practice of the reciprocal is called *natounding*."

"But we have logic and magic back on Earth. We don't call magic as reciprocal. That doesn't make any sense."

"Yes, it is a mystery, but the reciprologists claim you in the tech world are missing a special factor to invoke this magic" Her voice faded to a whisper, "But we don't know what."

On the next page stood a large group of people, all in suits and ties stood proudly.

"These people," Mazie pointed, "are responsible for the reciprocal running in other dimensions. They founded the

Whislow Agency. And the people who showed magic in the Tech World had the reciprocal to begin with."

My eyes grew wide. The world's first fantasy authors has magical powers? Even the basics were hard for me to wrap my head around. I narrowed my eyebrows, "I thought the reciprocal just means the opposite."

"In some cases, yes. But it really means the *energy* that's common among two things here. It's the *energy* that's returned to you. The force you give is the force that comes back to you."

She could still see my confusion and stretched out her hands, "Watch." She pushed her hand an inch and the flap of the tent miles away pushed out too. "That's one way." She concentrated and pushed her hand again, the flap inverted. "It returned the energy I gave."

I see. *Reciprocating. Natounding.*

Mazie went over to a wooden table and there were two types of mini jars. She picked one that had some chalk-like consistency. "This is Logic Chalk. It is extremely fragile and never ever use this without a proper experience. There could be disastrous consequences. And I will be using it on this instrument which is called a Hayur." She then spread the chalk very gently over a bow and strummed the strings with the bow—bursts of color shot and erupted into the air. Mazie put her hand in the burst of colors. She waved her hand at the book and concentrated, it turned into a shelf.

"You see," Mazie explained, "This is how the breakthrough of magic began. Most people in Philoxenia have a simple magic force within themselves. But only those with the *reciprocal* can activate the magic like I just did with the instrument. After time, magic began to evolve into things like witches, wizards, fairies, trolls, elves, you name it."

I nodded and pointed to the second jar beside the logic chalk. "What's that one for?"

Mazie's face became serious, "That's a more concentrated Logic Chalk." She walked over to an instrument that looked like it had springs on each side of the box. "That's the Manipulating Mertila. It sounds beautiful on its own." She twisted a couple springs within her fingers and let it resonate a long tone. "But if it ever comes in physical touch with the concentrated Logic chalk, anyone playing it can manipulate someone who hears it." She then held up the two jars, "You can tell which one is which." The regular logic chalk was silvery white but the concentrated one was a deep sage.

I nodded, shifting my eyes from each jar from left to right and right to left. "How come I never read anything like this?"

Mazie sighed, "Most origins of things are unknown, sometimes it just isn't credited. And I'm not sure how you got here."

I mean, it's not like I wanted to go back to Honeyville. Not yet anyways. I'm not going to leave this *dimension* just now. That would be like leaving a galaxy undiscovered…

"Do you know anything about the purple constellation? I think it's a bird–"

"You mean the Sparrow Constellation?" She interrupted and her voice fainted to a whisper again. "It's just a constellation."

My heart crumbled.

Mazie bent to reach my eye level.

"Little girl, what is it exactly that you're looking for?"

I gazed straight into her eyes. The words *looking for* always ebbs me.

You will NOT get what you currently desire.

"I don't know…just something to…"

Mazie grinned, "Did you know I worked for the Whislow Agency once?"

I wasn't surprised her smart mind worked for a prestigious sounding corporation. And the blank expression on my face made her smile even more, she probably wasn't used to high expectations.

She closed the book and placed it to the side. She paced around the wooden stage back and forth and back and forth.

"The Whislow Agency has all the answers you need. So much more than what I can explain."

Oh, simple. I just go there, drop all of my questions at the officers hoping one of the answers will help. Use that to get something from here, show Aunt Katelyn, go back home–

"But they don't allow visitors."

Uh oh.

"But if you become an agent…"

"That's so much work," I groaned, I peered at her instruments, "I could *learn* the Manipulating Mertilda in that much time."

The smile on Mazie's face widened, "Who said you had to go to training?"

She took my hand and sat down on the edge of the stage, "I still have my badge from when I was fourteen. You could use that.."

"And go in as…*you?*"

"Precisely."

"Isn't that dangerous?"

Mazie scoffed, "I wasn't even that important in the agency, they won't even notice a thing. They never notice anything."

If this works. If this truly works. It won't be hard coming back to Idallis. It won't be hard at all.

"Under one condition."

Uh-oh.

She stood drumming her fingers on the wood and peeked underneath. She took out an envelope and handed it to me.

"If you could give that to Chief Faryyan, that would be appreciated." There were black edges on each corner of the envelope, like each side was burned. Ironically, the paper was colder than my hands.

"How come you don't work there anymore?" I blurted.

Mazie's hands shook and her lips quivered. "Well, I wanted to achieve so much and, in that process, I guess I had to lose something."

A moment of silence lapsed between us.

What could it mean? Lose something? Her position at Whislow?

Mazie lifted her head, "Are you planning to find a way back home?"

I shrugged. I never think that far ahead in life. Mazie left the tent and scavenged for something in a drawer nearby. It was weird. When I first went into the tent, I only saw the stage and the instruments. But now there was a drawer, a vanity, and maybe even a bed will pop up in a few minutes.

She threw a flier at me like it was a disk and gestured at me to open it.

THE WHISLOW AGENCY
All Training Details Are Listed Below

I raised my eyebrows, reading the manual "Mazie, I can't get into the Whislow Agency without taking the test."

Mazie smiled, "Sure you can, give me your thumb." Before I could respond, she pressed her thumb onto mine, "Hold on for a second." My hand felt numb like it woke up from a decade of sleep. Mazie's lips curled as she removed her thumb, "Now you're me."

The ridges on my thumb were discrete, new mountains that emerged and replaced the old ones. "You didn't–"

"Swap our fingerprints, I sure did."

A rope knotted in my throat, "Mazie…"

She squeezed my hand, "You'll get into the building, and have access to anything you want with just the touch of a fingerprint. You'll find out everything you want about everything there."

From the same drawer she pulled out a magnifying glass and muttered joyfully, "I forgot about this thing." She glanced at me from across the tent, "It's funny how I was looking for this thing for ages when I was younger..."

I scanned my finger, doubtfully as she played with her detective tool. "Why are you helping me?" It still felt wrong to doubt her, even though I am impersonating a stranger.

"Because you seem really dedicated. Plus," she admitted, "I have nothing better to do."

She pinned the badge onto my black leather jacket, I was wearing a white shirt inside, a pair of blue jeans, and sneakers. Apparently, the inspiration for the uniform came from the tech world too—not to mention the pair of peach colored Canvas shoes.

I tucked the envelope into my inner pocket and Mazie gave me a hug. "Thank you for doing this." She gave a huge sigh.

I slowly wrapped my arms around her, partly strange, but I'm not going to say anything.

She straightened out my collar and waved, "Remember, the location of the Whislow Agency looks like a big glass door, and nothing else. You'll see what I mean later."

She handed me a blue key and a blue pouch and in it, she poured in green powder.

I backed away from it, "What is that?"

"It's *Grandom*. Sprinkle a little in your mouth whenever you're hungry, but only a little." Mazie tied the pouch with a string and handed it to me. I rubbed it between my fingers, it felt like grains of sugar.

I nodded my head and waved as I started to leave the tent.

"Enjoy your escapade–" She paused, her mouth half-open.

"Sienna" I answered, "My name's Sienna."

"Enjoy your escapade, Sienna."

Chapter Eleven

The Whislow Agency

I went into the meadows just like Mazie said. The grass here wasn't dry like it was back at Honeyville. It was vibrant and green and if I looked closely, I swear there were little fairies in them.

There was a small pad on the ground, it was made of marble and it vibrated every time I touched it with my foot. There was a small hole on the edge of the marble—

The blue key.

I turned the key and waited for the marble pad to do something.

It started to vibrate.

The dots of fairies jerked and bolted behind the blades of grass.

I decided to stand on the marble pad–because apparently, Philoxenia works that way. Just like standing on the table back at the Platform, a light began to illuminate around the pad. The sound of a trolley came ringing from up above, signaling that my ride was here. The Geoport was nothing like what I thought: a golden cage that was the same size as a telephone booth.

It hovered a couple inches off of the ground and its gate opened. I held onto both sides as I wobbled on. The cage abruptly shut behind me and I jolted–so much for a smooth transportation.

It slowly started to take off so I sat down in the corner. Did it even know where I was going? I swiped my fingers over the rails to make them ring. The ringing stopped until I reached a small tablet that had a map. There was a castle and acres of forests and ponds and meadows and everything. What did she say? A big glass door?

I kept scrolling and scrolling until I found an area with a ring of bushes and in it stood a transparent trapezoid. Close enough.

I let out a heavy sigh. Finally, a break. The wind swirled in and out of the cage and ocean mist turned into smells of pine trees. The Geoport never flew straight, it only glided through the clouds carelessly.

There were so many other castles and buildings but each village looked different. Instead of tents or houses, there were huts, ships, and even miniature forts.

But Philoxenia was rich in meadows because between every kingdom was acres of these vibrant blades of grass. In some parts of the trip, I mainly saw people in their villages but as I reached closer to the destination, there were scooters zipping over the meadows and more Geoports glided past me: each holding at least a trio of kids wearing the same uniform as me.

The scent of the powder grew stronger and stronger and I was starving. I poured a little in my hands, and sprinkled it in my mouth, it tasted like candy. Just by one taste, I was already full.

The envelope laid flat next to the bag of powder…

I reached my hand out for it–No. No.

It can't hurt just to look. Right?

I picked up the envelope but the Geoport had something else in mind. The black edges of the paper were drawn to the corner of the cage and the harder I pulled, the faster it went toward the crevice. I tried holding onto the edges but another envelope came out of the crevice. Its edges also looked burned and it connected to the side of Mazie's letter.

Magnets?

Mazie's letter flew out of my hands and into the crevice. I was left with this new note laying perfectly still in front of me.

This whole situation was already so confusing that it's not morally wrong to read the note, right? I'm just making sense of Philoxenia's whole "mailing" system.

This note didn't move unlike Mazie's and so I carefully ripped it open:

Mazie,

It's time we give each other a second chance. Meet me at the Realm in 3 days, right before the optimal time of the Sparrow Constellation.

Campbell.

Weird.

The ranges of mountains that covered the land below began to flatten out into forests and a ring of bushes stood prominently in the middle of the woods. The Geoport began descending and I held on as I thrusted to the ground.

I almost tripped off of the cage because the glass door was so tall. It reached higher than the evergreen trees that perched on the hills.

My Fingerprint.

I slowly pushed my finger against the door and the color of the blue glass door lightened into periwinkle.

Well, here goes nothing.

The doors clicked and let out a low hum as they opened.

I was standing on a large main floor amidst hundreds of kids and adults who were pointing at files or aggressively typing on their tablets or rushing to and from offices. The floor was filled with white tiles and the ceiling was glass, its theme taking place of whatever the sky chose to be. Everything else was clear: the bridges, doors, and stairs. Each window had a hazy blue light bordering it and outside were silver skyscrapers connected to the headquarters entailing their own purpose for the Whislow Agency. Strange contraptions floated around the palace followed behind their designated agents. Some walls of the headquarters were holographic, displaying the latest data from a detective's case. Everyone looked so engrossed in their work that I don't think I'll have to worry about identity theft.

This place was so big and the spiral clear escalators seemed endless that I almost forgot to breathe.

Everyone was waiting in crowds to get on the escalator so I joined them—best way to blend in. The second I put my foot on the step it zoomed all the way to the top floor.

The others on the escalator went their separate ways through different halls and into different offices. Some even went into what seemed to be another elevator moving sideways near the back of the halls.

There was one large room: **CHIEF FARYYAN'S OFFICE.**

Oh shoot.

I patted my pants and searched through my pockets. I even looked in my bag of powder hoping that the envelope would magically appear.

I had one job from her. Literally one job.

It's fine. I told myself, if the message was that urgent, Mazie would've just given it herself…so it can't be that important, right? And what if the Geoport was so smart that it mailed it to Chief Faryyan herself? It'll be fine.

"May I help you?" A low voice called from the office.

I turned around to face the office, where an old man with a silvery white beard and hair sat in his rather large desk that stood from one end of the office to the other.

"Hello, Chief." I responded, not knowing whether to salute or curtsey.

He gestured for me to come inside and the doors closed behind me. After reading my badge he squinted his eyes, "Miss Polaris? What a nice surprise!"

I opened my mouth to speak, *what do I say?*

He spoke again with his beard barely indicating anything he was saying, "That time machine has surely affected your age, I'll say."

Time machine?

I just went with it, "Y-yes, I'm still experiencing jet lag from it. It's not easy becoming a child again."

He let out a laugh, "I would surmise the opposite."

A moment of silence lapsed between us.

"What is it that you need from me?" He asked again.

I figured my fingers in stress, "Nothing sir, just dropping by to say hello."

He tilted his head and eyed me through his small glasses in suspicion.

Gulp.

As I walked out the door slowly, he stopped me,

"And Miss. Polaris?"

"Yes?"

"Why was it that you resigned from the agency?"

I turned, glancing at the portraits of all of the chiefs that came before him.

"Time travel has just had such a big toll on me that I really needed a break."

He lifted one eyebrow and in that moment I respectively speed walked out.

"And Miss Polaris?"

"Yes?"

"Welcome back."

I nodded with a sigh of relief, "Thank you Chief. It's good to be back."

I rushed down the hallway as fast as I could, zooming through crowds of agents.

"Hey!"

I bumped into another girl and we toppled on the ground. Her papers and files flew everywhere and small bags of little blue dust scattered over the floor.

"Watch out!" She groaned. I gathered the files closest to me and stood up. She pushed the papers away from her face and tried to neaten her leather jacket. Her black ponytail was still in good shape…wait–

"Disha?" I asked, handing her some of her files.

"Yeah", her eyes widened, "Sienna? Since when do you work here?"

I straightened my badge, "For a w-w-while." I stammered.

She eyed me up and down, "Is that how you saw the constellation–"

"Yes." I interrupted, stepping back a little. She squinted her eyebrows to read my badge, "Your name's Mazie?" She shifted uncomfortably on her knees. She opened her mouth to speak but closed it again, not knowing what to say.

I looked at her leather jacket, it was bare and she didn't have one.

I gulped, "Yes I am." She nodded like she was pretending to believe me so she could end the conversation. So, I handed her some more papers to do the same.

But curiosity seemed to grab the best of her and she said, "There's no way *you're* Mazie Polaris." She seemed disturbed by that circumstance. Narrowing her eyes, her eyes didn't leave the badge, and she seemed strangely uncomfortable.

"Well, uhh, I'm not," I conceded, "I'm her sister and there was a misprint on the badge."

She slowly nodded, "Uh huh, likely story."

So, I decided to shift the conversion and be curious about her situation, "What are these files for?" I asked her.

She gave a sharp response, "The Zecron Orb moved and it's been latent for years. I'm also responsible for plugging the idiosyncratic dust leaks as well."

"So, if you don't mind, I have to go." she snatched the rest of the files off of the ground and headed down the hallway.

"Oh, and Disha?" I called, "Do you know where the library is?"

"Down this hallway and to the right." I watched her take out a key and head into an office with large, glittery tape across the big door: **THE ORB ROOM**.

One thing's for sure, I'm not following her anywhere again.

I headed towards the library, locked by a tablet asking for my thumbprint. When I pressed against it, the words, *Welcome Mazie Polaris* faded in and the doors clicked.

Inside were shelves and shelves of books, just like ordinary libraries back home. In the front were countertops and desks of all different shapes and sizes for agents to work and communicate. There were even different types of lamps and sources of light for each desk. The shelves were silvery white, and books automatically floated off the shelf and into a wagon, which was then wheeled away outside the library. The desks on the other hand stood in their original place, but only one other person was working there today.

This is perfect, there *has* to be at least one book that would help me here.

I rummaged through sections and aisles of the books. There were thousands, maybe even millions of books. It would be impossible to find the right book. Or would it?

As I searched for something remotely related to the constellation, a scratching noise came from behind me. I ignored it and continued searching.

But the scratching noise continued so I turned around in part curiosity and part annoyance.

"Sorry." Someone whispered. I traced where the voice came from--a boy my age wearing the Whislow Uniform was using a stubby quill over a large blue sheet of paper that looks as if it has been crumpled and straightened out over and over again.

I decided to take a break from my tedious task and go see whatever he was up to.

The boy traced small marks with the quill and said, "This part of a project is a little scratchy. So don't mind me."

I nodded as I leaned over to see the drawing, "Don't worry about it." It was filled with notes in the margins all over a backpack looking contraption. A jet pack?

He pointed his quill at small screens in the area of the library. "You know, there is an easier way to search for books. You can just search there. The book you click on will glow."

"Oh, right." I said, "Thanks."

He joked, "You not knowing that and still having a badge makes me feel a little better about my journey for the badge. I'm Robert by the way."

"Mazie."

I went to one small tablet. I opened the search bar and typed:

Constellation of a bird in purple stars.

A result instantly popped up.

I hovered my finger over the option and it was a book titled:

The Legend of the Sparrows--by Macladez Zecron. A complete guide to magic and of constellations.

I clicked on the option. But nothing happened. I looked at the shelf number of the book and went there.

There, I searched for the book yet, it wasn't there.

Then, I found a bin all at the corner of the with the tag: Discarded.

There was a barrier around the bin, so I couldn't get in.

So, I decided to ask the librarian.

I approached her desk, where Robert stood in front of me holding up his blueprint. She responded to him.

"I'm not sure. The blueprint looks good to me. After all, you've been tirelessly working on it for the last 4 years."

Robert nodded, "I know, ma'am. But the thing is, it's not about the time, it's about the quality. It still feels like it needs more work, honestly."

"Maybe you need a break from the project." the librarian said, "Next."

Robert sighed and went out of the library.

I asked, "Have you heard of a book called the Legend of the Sparrows?"

The librarian took out a magical container from her wooden desk. He opened it and whispered, the Legend of the Sparrows. The container resulted with wisps of lavender.

"Hmmm." She said, "I believe it might have been discarded. The last person to check it out was several years ago. The reader had a rather emotional response to the book. We checked it out and it could be mentally dangerous."

"Then why did it appear on the search results for books?"

The librarian shook her head, "It shouldn't be. If it's discarded, it wouldn't appear. I'll take a look."

I nodded, "Thank you. It means a lot because I *really* need it."

Just as I left, I asked the librarian, "And um, do you know who was the one who last checked it out and where I can find them?"

The librarian glanced at the container, "Estrella Rivera--she's always at the Creature Sanctuary."

I nodded, "Thank you."

I followed the map to where it was written: Creature Sanctuary.

I followed the map through the halls and until it led me outside amongst a large place with trees, plants and animals of all sorts.

A little girl, about ten years old, was feeding seeds to large birds. She had brown hair, and a unicorn's horn was sticking up in the middle of her head.

"Hello." The girl said. "Are you here to see the animals, adopt one? Or to receive one of the magical things the animals create?"

I shook my head. "No, I'm sorry." I stepped forward with my right hand, "I'm Mazie, by the way." I had to keep up with my fake story.

"Estrella. Mucho gusto."

"So," I began, "Have you ever read a book, like the Legend of the Sparrows? By Macladez Zecron?"

Estrella's horn lowered, "Oh yes, I've read it before." Her voice softened with each word.

I rocked on my feet, awkwardly gazing into the stream of little fish that flew by, "Well, could I please borrow it?"

She lifted her head, "I would give it to you if I could, but I lent it to my friend Rex. He should have finished it by now."

"Oh," I began, my attention distracted by a flock of pink creatures flying above me and blocking out a fraction of the sunlight with their shadow overcasting the gold sand, "If he ever gives it back to you, do you mind lending it to me."

She gave a slight smile, "Of course, Mazie. In fact, I'll ask him for you."

I smiled back, "Thanks, Estrella, you're incredible." I shifted uncomfortably at my fake identity, but sacrifices had to be made if I wanted this for Aunt Katelyn and me.

Estrella nodded her horn, its tip shimmering in the sunlight. As I began to walk down that sandy path from the meadows and flowerbeds back to the main lobby, a little squirrel stopped my tracks. He held a colorful cube with roses on top of it. With every step I took, it stopped me.

"Looks like he made something for you." Estrella explained from behind. I kneeled down to take the cube, "What is it?"

"You'll never know if you don't taste it."

I took a bite, the cube melted in my mouth, and exploded with a million different flavors. From sweet to sour to savory, it was a blend of all the best types of meals into one, in a good way.

"Tell your little friend that he's an excellent chef." I joked, as I headed on my way out.

I decided to take a stroll around the Agency, every single corner and room was completely unique. But I had to be sneaky about this. You know, since everyone here is supposed to be extremely busy.

I peeked into the Council Room, a large antique room that covered much of the first floor. It had a red velvet carpet and a golden chandelier to illuminate all of the seats. It was completely empty except for an old woman standing up at the front. She pointed to the wall where a big tablet stood: COUNCIL CONVENTION TOMORROW MORNING

Bring your questions and concerns in order to have your voice heard.

This is perfect. I can ask about the constellation. I can figure out how to transfer some of the magic from here to Honeyville. Maybe it'll even help me and Aunt Katelyn.

What could go wrong?

Chapter Twelve

Conventions, Cravings, and Consequences

"**W**onderful suggestions." Councilwoman Cordelia said, looking at a long list of papers that rolled off of the podium. There was barely anyone in the room, however. "Alright, anymore concerns?"

I took a deep breath and stepped forward. The room was filled with so few people, yet so many at the same time. It wasn't like they were listening, but like they were *judging*. So I closed my eyes, and now no one is in the room. "What would happen if we share magic, or stars, rather, with another dimension? We have a taste of the technology from the Tech World, so it's only fair they have a taste of the magic from ours." I let out.

The room was silent.

Silent.

I opened my eyes, Cordelia was thinking hard, her eyes switching from her list back to me and back to her list. "Well," she trailed, "Just like any other decision, it has its positives...and its negatives."

I bit my lip, Great, just a few hours into another world, and I embarrassed myself.

She spoke again, "It's dangerous, really. And sharing magic with other's unknown to it can lead to confusion and chaos."

I nodded, I mumbled under my breath, "I know…" I decided to step back into the crowd of a couple people.

"It is a good idea." A young man with short brown hair that had a streak of red running through it said, "If we share magic or stars with another dimension, it allows the dimension to share their perspective which would be unique and different from ours. Our two perspectives communicating could allow us to be more progressive."

I smiled.

"That's true." Cordelia said.

"And-" I said, "It's not against the law or anything, right? Like if magic just happened to be shared, it's not said otherwise in the rules, right?"

Cordelia replied, "You see, it's not so much about the legal aspect as it is about the consequences if a naive dimension were to be exposed to such a great force."

"I mean, the Tech World isn't dumb. They'll figure out a way." A voice behind me said. I turned, it came from someone whose face was dug into a large blueprint. *Robert.*

Cordelia shook her head.

To be honest, this is just straight up greediness. The innovative scooters here and effortless transportation is just the iceberg of what this dimension has to offer. But I still tried my best with the cards I had:

"So what about that Sparrow Constellation being visible back at the Tech World? There's reports that there were sightings of it there. "

Cordelia clapped her hands to commence silence even though it was already quiet. Her eyes were struck wide and she opened her mouth. It looked like she was trying to say something, but no words came out.

She started coughing as she tried to speak and pointed at a small table near her podium, "Some r-r-etaw please." She struggled to point as she massaged her neck. I was the closest to the table so I grabbed the glass of blue juice and handed it to her. She gulped it.

Suddenly, a large wave of blue dust swarmed in and she screamed at the top of her lungs.

"HELP!"

I rushed towards her and held out my hand. As she tried to dig herself out of the blue dust she grabbed my wrist. She locked eyes with me and I tried pulling her out, but she disappeared in less than a blink. Her grip was so strong that

I still felt a heavy weight on my arm even after she disappeared. My heart was pounding.

The murmur turned into a loud, chaotic swarm.

I gasped. People called on their watches for help. Professional agents scurried into the room holding large kits.

"Evacuate! Evacuate!" They yelled, "Let's go! Let's go!"

Everyone rushed out of the room, several heads eyeing me as they left.

What have I done.

What have I done.

What have I done?

Chapter Thirteen

The Whislow Agency Actually Trusts Us

Sirens were wailing inside the Agency. Officers were closing gates across the Council Room and every few seconds someone would scream.

I leaned my head against a wall and tried to breathe. I didn't do anything wrong. I didn't do anything wrong. This was just a *coincidence*.

Breathe. One. Two. Three. Breathe.

"Hey." A voice called in front of me. I glanced up, Disha was standing there, with her hands crossed and half a smile on her face.

I turned my head back against the wall. Look what just happened. I tried to introduce an idea just to *see* if it isn't against the law. But instead, people disappeared. I caused a calamity. So much for a 'plan'.

Disha took out a yellow folder and ran her fingers through a few pages. She clicked open a pen and checked a few boxes, writing down notes in the margins.

Robert walked down the hall from the Council room holding his obnoxiously large blueprint. "I'm so confused about what just happened." He asked.

Disha's eyes bounced from her folder to Robert, "Weren't you just over there?"

Robert shook his head and gave a laugh, "Sure I was, but that doesn't help me understand anything more than what you know."

"What about your usual 'hunches'?"

"In this big incident? Normally yes. But today, no. I'm guessing you have a detailed analysis and estimations about this whole event even though you never even witnessed it?"

Disha rolled her eyes, "No, I've recently been busy with the Zecron Orb malfunction. You know, since I've been given the job to volunteer in the Orb Preservation room. And I can't seem to find a single clue for it."

Robert cocked his head, "That's tough."

"Wait—Disha" I began, "What happened during the blue dust powder case you were talking about?"

Disha shrugged, "It was nothing major. I just plugged a small leak."

I cocked my head in confusion, that blue dust had to have come from *somewhere*. I shook my head, "No, what I meant was, what happened after that?"

Disha sighed, "Well there's still some small leaks here and there. But I have help from the other agents to stop it."

Robert raised his eyebrows, "Disha, you mean that *big* pour of blue dust in the Council Room was a small *leak*?"

Disha, "We all make mistakes." She glanced at her yellow folder, "That's why I'm still filling this out."

Robert said, "Everything that has to do with this blue dust has to deal with the birds."

I put my finger on my chin, "I mean I found a random feather back home where there were absolutely no birds around."

"The Path of the Birds..." Disha whispered.

"You mean Zecron's scavenger hunt?" Robert questioned.

I narrowed my eyes, "But, I didn't notice anything about birds in the council room."

Robert said, "Hmm....maybe it does. You made the councilwoman speechless because you mentioned a sparrow constellation."

I shook my head, "But I was just *saying* it."

"Well..." Disha began, "Maybe the Sparrow constellation is a significant factor. When I took the case, there were just sprinkles of dust here and there. But that was a whole *swarm*."

He nodded, "If this has to do with Macladez Zecron, then maybe it also has to do with his orb. Maybe that's also the reason why the Zecron Orb's been acting up. There's your first clue, Disha."

"So the blue dust, the constellation, and the orb are all connected?" I asked, my head spinning.

They both nodded.

I gave a solid nod, "Alright then, let's go catch this case." I began walking out of the hallway. Finally, a plan that's working.

Robert and Disha silently stared at me.

"What?" I asked.

"Usually, Sienna," Disha began, "A case is given to us, we don't choose that. And anyway, this is way too dangerous for us."

"Sienna?" Robert brough up, "I thought your name was Mazie."

I frantically nodded, "Well it is Mazie, Robert." I slammed a fist against my palm to change the subject, "Well, you guys, we have to do something." Anxiety raced into my chest with the thought of *being* on the suspects list. Not happening.

I did my best to convince them, "Not only will this help solve a case but you guys could get your badges. Don't you two want that?"

A smirk perked up on Disha's face, "Sienna, your badge isn't real either."

I stammered, "No, I told you, it was a misprint. I'm *Mazie*."

She leaned closer and whispered, "You think I don't know who the real Mazie Polaris is?"

I was speechless. My jaw opened and I slowly backed away from her face. It felt like the agents rushing too and forth starting to slow down and each picture snapped in the Council room took ages to form.

She smiled, whispering, "Tell me how you got in and I won't tell anyone about your identity theft."

"I didn't steal anyone's identity—"

Robert butted in between us and waved his hands, "Guys, we don't have all day."

Disha nodded, "Alright, let's go tell the Chief."

The Chief.

I gulped down the knot in my throat and covered my hand over Mazie's badge. Around me, every single investigator had their badges except for Robert and Disha. But we were only eleven. I felt a tug on my arm.

"C'mon!" Disha tugged.

I dragged behind them as they shuffled through the crowd of agents onto the escalator.

Breathe. One. Two. Three.

The further we went up, the less people there were. Even Chief Faryyan's office *looked* empty compared to the Council Hall.

I held onto Disha's wrist as the glass doors slid open and a transparent blue desk stood prominent in the room.

The walls were almost clear but opaque enough to keep the privacy of the other offices.

"Chief." Disha said, neatening her leather jacket and standing taller. There were interviewers in the rooms speaking over each other and aggressively writing down notes as they discussed.

Chief Faryyan came out from among them wearing a tan trench coat and several tablets in his hands, "Yes Ms. Raj?"

"We think we can figure out how to find Councilwoman Cordelia."

He set down his tablets onto his blue table and stroked his gray break. It felt like the walls were becoming more and more opaque, "The only thing I know about this mystery is that there's been reports of Natounders going missing and any magical object as well."

Robert followed up, "Well none of us have the reciprocal, so..." I quickly unlatched the badge off of my jacket and threw it into my pocket while he spoke... Chief Faryyan shifted his attention to me, and he narrowed his eyes, "I've never seen you before."

"I'm..." I lied, "I'm Mazie Polaris' sister." I gulped down another knot as I watched him stroke his gray beard.

"Ms. Polaris hasn't worked for us in years–"

"–And isn't it nice to have someone just like her on the team?" Disha interrupted.

I was taken aback, first Disha wanted to report me for identity theft, and now she's covering for me. Funny.

Chief Faryyan inhaled a sharp breath, "You want to take on this dangerous case?"

Interviewers stopped writing, cameras stopped clicking, and everyone looked at us. We didn't look so confident anymore.

Robert cleared his throat to compensate for the awkwardness, "Please?"

Chief Faryyan stared at the sky through the window, trying to recalculate everything we were saying. "You want to take the case?" He repeated.

Disha nodded, "You always said our flexible and young minds could do much more than we think. Maybe we shouldn't *take* the case, but join in."

Chief Faryyan nodded, "Yes, we do already have a lot of agents investigating this. And I do understand that you want to help, but it's just not safe."

I pursed my lips and raised my hand, "Yes, sir. But the thing is--we kind of can already connect the dots."

The chief looked at us with a deeper interest, leaning in.

Robert gestured to the audience, "Well---ok, interviewers, take notes." He turned to them. I could see his heels raise as he gained confidence again, "The Zecron Orb was acting up right before this all happened. I mean you said it didn't even budge for years. Isn't that kind of suspicious? And not to mention the dust leaks that's linked with almost everything Macladez Zecron used to be known for." He pointed at Disha, "She's skilled in this dust leaks and I'm skilled in research, alright." "And this girl," he pointed at me, is a key witness too.

I gulped, No Robert, don't phrase it like that.

"So, you'd be lying if you said we weren't one step ahead of you." The interviewers bit their lips. Robert shrugged and his heels went back on the ground. "Just sayin' "

Disha added, "This could be a big chance for us, if you let us, who knows?"

Chief Faryyan sat down at his desk, "All right, I'll let you join the others on this. But I want to warn you--"

Robert interrupted, "That--things could get dangerous?"

Chief Faryyan gave a playful scoff, "Oh Mr. Wilgrinton, I already know that things will get dangerous. But this is something that you must hear--"

We three leaned in.

"You may feel at times to give up, but don't. You are the first to ever ask for a mission. I realize my mistake here--I need to get more of your children out on adventure and less at your desks researching at the Whislow Agency. I need to set you all onto a rhythm for your own future. Your capable minds have it in them. You can do this."

I smiled now that I'm not a suspected anymore, "Thanks Chief."

Robert nodded, "Yeah the pep talks really helped."

Disha saluted, "Alright, we'll find Councilwoman Cordelia as soon as possible. C'mon guys, let's head back to the Council room."

We three young rookies, on our first case, scurried over down the hall and to the left, back where we came from.

Chapter Fourteen

Who Knew Shoes Could Come In So Handy

It wasn't difficult for me to find the Whislow Council room because that was where everyone was congregated. The glitter dust was scattered everywhere and I could've sworn I saw other agents holding onto each other so they wouldn't slip.

Bright, yellow tape was wrapped around the area to warn people to stay out even though no one listened to it.

"Coming through!" Robert waved, trying his best to tunnel a passage through the crowd of agents.

We all peered through the agents who were snapping pictures from in front of the entrance and we ducked under the tape.

Robert inhaled a big breath. He took out his watch and clicked it open. "Anything unusual?"

Disha put her finger on her chin, "Not sure yet. We should check Cordelia's podium?"

I chuckled nervously, "Is that necessary?"

Robert nodded, "It's kind of is."

Two tall investigators were jotting down notes of the corners of the room and dictating through their watches.

"Whoever has the audacity to commit such a crime will face dire consequences. " They both concurred.

I gave a small gulp. *I swear, I'm not the culprit.* I said to myself. It was obviously a coincidence. *Chief trusts you now.* And even if it was me, why would I be solving the case in the first place? So there, I'm not the culprit.

While I was repetitively convincing myself I wasn't the kidnapper. Robert pointed at the large wall of the council room. "Look!"

Disha narrowed her eyebrows, "What?"

"Those picture frames."

"Yeah, they're the pictures of the whole council framed on the wall."

"I know but what I mean is…. *look.*"

I approached the pictures a little closer, "Is there a pattern you notice or something…?"

Disha squinted her eyes carefully at each of the frames. "Well, they're all standing formally, in suits, nice shoes, the same well-preserved council room. All are smiling…. except for that one man in the back---"

Robert clicked his tongue, "That's what I'm talking about! The uniforms."

My eyes widened, "I think I have met him somewhere. His face is very familiar. But there has to be some kind of brand where these clothes came from--or at least they're hand stitched by *someone*."

Disha nodded, "This is a great start for the day." She jumped and clasped her hands, "All right, let's see here....I don't notice...."

Robert pointed to one woman from the council who had her feet angled ever so slightly that a logo was visible. The logo consisted of a pinecone a golden 'S' imprinted in the middle.

"My dad has a collection of all sorts of things," Robert began, "This guy named Samuel Orion makes shoes exactly like that. My dad loved his brand so much that he made me go buy more in this really tiny village."

I smiled, "This is perfect, Robert."

Disha nodded, "Yeah maybe he'll tell us a little more about them." She then snapped a picture of the picture frame from her watch and I could see her zooming in on the man who didn't smile for the photo. The man's frown was quite familiar, if I might add.

We headed outdoors to the entrance of the W.A. There was a small courtyard, with the sunshine bouncing off of the bushes. In the back were charging several heavy bicycles with countless pieces of gear.

"So, are we just gonna walk a few miles there?" I asked.

"Are you kidding?" Robert asked in disbelief, "No! We're gonna try out these new Galactic Bikes." He said, turning his fists up and down as if he were initiating a motorcycle.

"Yeah, but remember how we're supposed to keep everything low profile?" Disha warned.

"What if we use the 'Invisible Mode' " Robert said.

My eyes lit. "There's an 'Invisible Mode'?"

"Sure is."

I set my foot on top of the bike pedal and steadied myself as I sat down. As soon as I gripped the handle, the bike started zooming and my fingers were disappearing in front of me. For the first time in my life, I was invisible.

We headed into the nearby town until they found a shoe shop. The top board had that identical logo of a pinecone and the letter S sitting on top of it.

We parked our bikes and headed into the shoe shop—barely anyone walked past it on these busy streets.

No one seemed to be there--at least of what we knew of.

"Hello?" Robert called, "This is—"

"Shush." Disha whispered. "Robert, if you're going to disclose your entire identity then you might as well give up on the entire case."

"Well," Robert began. "What if he was friends with Councilwoman Codelia? He'd trust us more if he knew we were agents."

Disha chuckled, crossing her arms, "Would *you* be friends with the person who made your sneakers?"

He shrugged at her, admitting defeat.

"That's what I thought."

The noise of crinkled tissue paper followed a middle-aged man with a name tag spelling *Samuel Orion* to the front counter.

"How may I help you all today?" He said, examining his unfinished shoe on the counter, its seams were loose and much of the soles weren't stitched to the rest of the shoe.

"Are you familiar with Cordelia Shears?" Disha prompted.

He nodded, "One of my devout clients, yes I do know her."

I glanced at Disha, confused on what exactly to ask next. So Robert took a try at it, "Was she ever your enemy?" He asked, squinting his eyes in suspicion.

Samuel frowned and shook his head, "No, we had pretty diplomatic conversations, young man."

That made me think, we could just look at the Council's previous problems they solved and rules they made—to see if they had anyone who could potentially be their enemy. It would be so much easier.

Disha cleared her throat, "What he means is—when was the last time you made shoes for her and her council?"

Samuel began polishing another shoe on his counter in thought, "During the last new star, perhaps."

Disha began to count on her fingers, "That was in August then," she muttered to herself.

Samuel turned his head towards Robert, giving a perplexed look, "You look vaguely familiar."

Robert raised his eyebrows, "What a fascinating memory sir. You must've met my father. He's rather an obsessed shoe collector. Jonathan Wilgrinton."

The keeper nodded, "Not good with names but I see, I see."

On the next counter was a strapped shoe and a magnifying glass that hung over the shoe. There were pieces of thread lying side by side next to it.

He was sowing thin thread into the side of a shoe.

"Just fixing up a pair." He said, picking up the threads. He turned and spoke, "Are you here to buy anything?"

Disha set the photo of the council on the counter that she took from her watch. "No, sir. But we were wondering if you knew any of the others from the Council."

The shoe maker smiled, "Yes. Yes. I know each and every one of them. The Whislow Council isn't it? I made shoes for *all* their uniforms."

"Sir, " I began.

"Please." The shoe maker insisted, "Call me Samuel." I squinted my eyes at Samuel's self, a strange book with a familiar title was collecting dust behind him. "What book is that?"

Samuel replied, "Oh nothing. It's simply a book by Macladez Zecron, and his rather cruel ambitions. Do you know anything about him?"

I nodded, "I've heard of his name, yes."

"And have you heard anything of the *Zecron orb*? Anything at all?" Disha asked.

Samuel tensed and shook his head rapidly. "The Zecron orb has many terrible uses. I dare say, you children shall never go near it. Haven't they destroyed it already?"

Robert put his hands in his pockets and shrugged, "We just thought you might have information or news about it. You see we are on a case, to find council woman Cordelia.

"She disappeared."

Samuel narrowed his eyebrows, "Is that what you are here for? Has she gone missing?"

"Yes" I said, "And we don't know who took her away.

Robert nodded and slammed his fist into his palm, "And we need to catch that crook responsible."

I swallowed a huge gulp. *Be quiet Sienna, it wasn't you.* I don't know why my heart started pounding. But being in that room, as one of the few people there, made it very likely I was a suspect. I turned to Robert, I was glad he didn't suspect me. Even though he was standing *right there.*

And I don't even have the reciprocal, but you don't know what could happen in the agency *without* good quality security.

Samuel nodded, "She's not the first one to have disappeared, you know. There's been so many cases of people vanishing and magical objects disappearing. People have been speculating about this for a while."

"So, it's been in the news for a while?" I asked. He nodded. A huge knot of stress untangled in my chest. Well, now I know it's a coincidence. I just have to make sure that *everyone* else knows that too.

Disha asked, "Well, do you know anything about that man in the back of this picture, the only one who's not smiling?"

Samuel chuckled, "Ahh, the Platform Manager, is it? He appeared in this picture because he was constructing a new leverage of Philoxenia's portal. Could never get him to smile."

"Oh." I replied. So that frown *was* familiar.

Robert asked, "So, uh, got anything that could help us?"

Samuel nodded, "Follow me."

He led them into a vintage room. He took out a key and unlocked a large case.

But when he opened the case, a frown appeared on his face, his grin turning upside down.

"What's wrong?" I asked.

Samuel shook his head, "I-I, had a magical map in here that could've helped you guys, but it's…gone."

Disha shook her head, "It's alright, Samuel, don't worry about it."

He let out a sigh, "But I want to help you all." He stood there, pondering, and then clicked his tongue, staring at our worn-out Canvas sneakers given by the Agency. "You all need new shoes." Mazie must have gone on plenty of adventures, because mine were almost torn.

So he took us out back to the front, flipping through wooden shoe boxes he had.

Other customers started coming in and browsing through shoes in the store. Now that I have a chance to look at the shoes, there were unlike anything I've ever seen before.

Some were fairy themed, with wings fluttering in the back of the high heels. Others were the theme of mermaids, with the shoes having fins on their sides.

Others were plain, just like the ones back home in the Tech World. But most of all, there was not a dull colored shoe in sight.

Samuel took out a box of purple sneakers with colored glass embedded in them.

"Here you are." He handed a pair to me, it was incredibly small.

"Don't worry," Disha said, "It resizes to fit you."

I went to sit on a bench, and stretched on the shoe…

… "Alright, Sienna, let's go." Aunt Katelyn would say on a Saturday afternoon when I'm sitting on the ledge of the caravan and swinging my legs.

"Where?" I asked.

She stretched out her hand, "To the mall, of course, we're going to get you some new shoes."

I shuffled on my feet, "But these sandals are still purple and sparkly." I raised my left leg for her to see up close.

Aunt Katelyn nodded, tossing a handbag on her shoulder, "But you can't run in them, Sienna. We need some good running shoes for school next week."

I sighed and got up to my feet, letting Aunt Katelyn help me up to my car seat. It was bluer than usual that day, no clouds, and the sun was warm but not scorching hot. These days flew by quickly.

Aunt Katelyn put on some pop music as she started the car and went off to the mall. Shopping was by far the most boring experience I had endured until then.

"When you're my age," She began, "It becomes your favorite pass-time."

"*Favorite?*" I'd repeat in disbelief, "You've got to be kidding me."

She giggled, "No, I'm not. There's just something magical about stepping into a world with so many new things that you just–get lost in it."

I shook my head, "You have no idea what you're talking about, Aunt Katelyn." I never understood the idea of people looking at items for evermore and then moving on to the next item–contemplating for forever on which color dress, which style of a fridge…it was endless.

When we arrived in the mall, Aunt Katelyn treated us to some soft pretzels, getting both a cheesy and a cinnamon one to balance it out. She always adored balance.

The shoe store was the epitome of sliding measurement scales, the sound of crinkling tissue paper, and the cashier scanning thousands of things at one.

"When picking your shoes," Aunt Katelyn said, "Theres four things you have to consider. Aesthetic, durability, and comfort."

I narrowed my eyes, "Then why are you wearing high heels?" I said, pointing at her white stilettos.

She looked down at them, lifting up the soles like she just realized she put them on, "Sometimes aesthetic is weighted more heavily. And other times, it's the comfort you're looking for. But no matter what, durability must always play a factor." Looking back now, I don't think she was just talking about the shoes.

She gestured to a little bench, "Now, why don't you try on the shoes you like?"

I picked out pretty much the same shoes I was wearing, just in sneaker form. And durable.

She took out the first box, and placed on the purple sneakers on my foot. But she was struggling as she couldn't get my heel to fit.

Aunt Katelyn gasped, grinning up at me, "My little beanie, you've grown!"

"I did?" Shaking my head, now that she's mentioned it, the sandals did feel a little smaller.

So, Aunt Katelyn happily placed the shoes back and returned with the same exact ones, just a size up.

"See what happens when you eat well and sleep and run around with your auntie?"

"I'm going to be a big girl now!" I exclaimed, wrapping my hands around Aunt Katelyn, she hugged me back, "Now don't grow up too fast, okay? You will always be my little beanie" ...

…"Thank you," Robert said, taking the shoe box with large lightning stripes streaked across his shoes. He reached into his pockets, trying to find–

"No, no." Samuel insisted, "It's on me. Consider it as my contribution to Whislow."

My eyes lightened, "Wow, thank you, Samuel."

He gave a small nod, "My pleasure." His eyes started flickering green from its original blue and a feather appeared on the counter right next to my shoebox.

Another feather.

How weird. I shrugged, grabbing it to be alongside the other one I found with that annoying auction guy.

As we were about to leave, the store started rumbling. The faces of the happy customers inside turned into confusion and surprise.

The ground below me was shaking the shoeboxes off of the shelf.

What's happening?

The only reasonable explanation was that it could be an earthquake. But something is telling me it isn't.

And before my eyes could blink, all of the customers disappeared. My heart started pounding, Cordelia isn't the only one. Why is it happening where we are? Here? Right now?

Samuel was breathing heavily, he turned behind himself, upset at all of his shoes hitting the floor, "Not my beloved creations," he said, kneeling down to pick them up.

I looked at the shelf again, "Zecron's book–it's gone."

Disha placed her hands on the counter, stretching herself to see it, "Oh my gosh, you're right."

Disha commented, "Maybe the clues of Macladez Zecron and Councilwoman Cordelia are related."

Robert narrowed his eyes when he saw the shopkeeper standing in the far corner end of the store.

"Wait," Robert said, "Samuel, how did you get from the counter to over there?"

Samuel cocked his head, confused, "What do you mean?" He paused, and then he sighed, shaking his head. But really, we should be shaking our heads.

My fingers were trembling on the countertops, the atmosphere became eerie, and I couldn't wrap my head around anything going on.

He glanced at me. "Little girl, what were you saying about Macladez Zecron?"

I stepped away a little bit and chuckled, "Oh nothing, just that the book on your shelf disappeared to, the one which Zecron wrote."

Samuel laughed, "Oh he's more than just an author. He's the greatest man who's ever lived." He brushed off some lint on his shoulder pad and continued strolling around the store.

"That was so weird." Disha said in our ears, "I thought he hated him."

"Oh my gosh," Robert exclaimed, "That dude's totally an imposter."

"He's gotta be" I agreed.

We turned to him again, he looked up from polishing one of his items, "May I help you? You've all received your shoes, haven't you?"

We nodded, and he responded, still confused, "Well, is there any more favors I can do?"

Disha shook her head, and I craned my neck to see past his shoulders. Yes, the book is still gone.

He followed my eyes to his shelf, concerned, "Was there something you'd like to see?" He asked.

I shook my head, "No, just that the Zecron book is still gone."

Samuel's jaw half dropped, "I would let you borrow it, but it isn't something for your young mind. The inhumanity…the inhumanity."

Weird.

He loved Zecron a minute ago.

Robert placed a hand on the counter, and shrugged one shoulder, "Just a thought man, how do you feel about everyone else in this room vanishing?"

Samuel frowned, looking around, "It certainly has been a slow day today."

Robert nodded his head in conclusion, "Alright, alright, you were definitely possessed."

Samuel squeezed his lips together, "I'm sorry, young man?"

Robert shook his head, sliding his hand off of the counter, "No worries, Sam, you're fine now."

Samuel cocked his head to one side, letting go of his shoe project and contemplating what Robert had just said.

I tried providing Samuel for some context to at least shoo away some of his confusion, "The case we're on–."

"Ah." Samuel interjected, opening a drawer to find another sewing needle, "I recommend you all search through Whislow's records, they have a phenomenal number of files to guide you in the right direction as to who caused Cordelia's disappearance. Afterall, it has to be someone tied to the Agency, if the Agency's Councilwoman, someone who creates law and order, was severely targeted."

Disha nodded with a confident smile, "Thank you, kind sir, that is what we will do." We backed up, and Robert stretched his hands over our shoulders, muttering, "That man was definitely possessed."

I felt my heart still palpitating, it was another occurrence of the vanishing happening right in front of my eyes. And more odd Reciprocities controlling Samuel's mind, or he just has severe moral changes. But either way, this case is muddier than I thought it would be.

Don't worry Aunt Katelyn, we'll solve everything. Soon.

Chapter Fifteen

Estrella's Story

Robert and I waited patiently in Disha's office while she went and allegedly was bringing a box of newspapers, records, and old council files to help solve whatever got into Samuel, or whoever got into Samuel. Someone who adores Zecron, that's all we came up with.

Robert spun his chair in circles, "So…" he began, staring at the ceiling, "Where are you from?"

"Edmonia," I quickly replied.

"Oh I see. I see." He spun faster in his chair, the transparent walls must look like a kaleidoscope to him, "My mom is from the East and my dad is from Italy."

I leaned forward in my chair, "Italy?"

"Yea, it's crazy. My mom's worried that I won't ever get the reciprocal because of my dad's genetics."

"But you're still *half*-magical."

He grabbed the ledge of Disha's desk to stop himself from spinning, I could still see his eyes adjusting to the stillness of the room.

"Would you rather live here or in the Tech World?" I asked him.

"My whole family lives in Italy because my father couldn't cross dimensions even if he tried. It's kind of messed up if you ask me."

Since I'm here, does that mean…? No way. No way am I "magical". But if I was, then Aunt Katelyn must have been too. Or my dad must have been. Or my mother must have been–

"Let's get to work, guys." Disha thudded a whole box onto her desk and the aroma of parchment paper arose into the room. She took out a metal pen and drew two boxes side by side that imprinted into her desk, "Relevant information here and irrelevant information here." She tapped her hands on the boxes to emphasize her directions.

"Got it." I said.

So that entire afternoon we sifted through papers and papers of Wanted signs and newspaper clippings. I wasn't sure what was "irrelevant" because almost every one of these criminals were "evil" with no further description. That was insane.

I took a rather stiff paper from the box and dusted off some of what seemed to be dried cement.

Rupert Cogsworth

Princess Victoria has been missing. If found any trace of Rupert Cogsworth, please contact the Whislow Agency immediately.

Cogsworth? You're kidding, right? Is that just a coincidence…or am I from here? My mind kept sidetracking, thinking of all the possibilities that this man named Rupert *really* is my dad. But this was incredibly vague. And so were most of the news clippings I found in the box.

"Speaking of criminals," Disha leaned in, "How'd you get in? I know you aren't her sister. And our badges never make mistakes. They are not made by technology; they are made by the reciprocal."

My mind stopped thinking about that last name. Robert paused on the three newspaper clippings he was reading and looked up, confused.

"Well…" I gave a nervous laugh. Suddenly, my hands became sweaty and the room felt hotter. "I met this girl—"

"Mazie Polaris. Mhm, continue."

Man, when will this girl stop interrupting?

"So…she a-a-a-sked me to come here—"

"Why?"

"She said it would help answer all of my questions about the universe and I think it just made her feel better to....I don't know, help someone."

Disha leaned back in her chair and laughed, "And she…what? Just handed you her badge just like that? Very funny."

"No, she really did." I said. But when I said that, it sounded a lot stupider than I thought. So I even took off my badge and handed it to Disha just to prove my point.

Her eyes widened as her fingertips reached for the badge.

Robert set down his newspapers and lifted his arms, "I'm completely lost in this conversation right now."

Disha rolled her eyes, "Robert, *basically*, a girl committing identity theft is helping us solve a kidnapping case. Her real name's *Sienna*."

Robert shrugged, "Fine by me." He smirked and turned his head toward me, "Criminals are better at solving cases anyways because they can think like the culprit."

There was no going back.

"Yeah Disha," I said, "We'll solve this case faster."

She crossed her arm and squinted her eyes at me, curious "How did you get in through the doors?"

I showed her my thumb, the ridges weren't prominent anymore and my fingerprint was finally flat against my finger.

She took my finger and analyzed it carefully, "You stole her fingerprint?"

"More like she *gave* me her fingerprint."

Disha's face was hot and I could see the blood rush into her cheeks, "She couldn't have trusted you *that* much. Not after you just met."

I smiled, "Well I guess she did."

"No, there's just *no way*." Disha's voice grew infuriated, "I've known her for years! And we've never been *that* close. Let alone giving me her identity." She started breathing heavily, and Robert looked up, concerned.

"Disha, remember to count…it helps."

"Don't tell me to count!" She shook it off and went back to sifting through the news and Wanted signs.

The piles were growing bigger and bigger but they were just filled with vague descriptions. I guess the agents here finally learned what "copy" and "paste" was.

"I'm guessing you're not from Edmonia then." Robert said.

"No." I admitted, "I'm from the Tech World."

Robert looked stunned, "Next thing you know is that you're secretly an acrobat."

I couldn't help but snicker, "My aunt used to be one, actually."

Robert's jaw dropped and he raised his eyebrows in disbelief. I decided to go back to the papers.

We spent almost another hour doing so but it felt like we weren't getting anywhere. It's weird how back home I had to be as *specific* as possible in my writing but here, top-secret agents could get away with writing anything they absolutely wanted. Crazy.

I looked outside of the transparent walls; it was almost dark and the sunset illuminated Disha's office a dark orange.

"Oh, wait a minute" Disha said, she skidded her chair back and stood up. "I think I found something."

Wanted:
Reeva Harvey-The Vanisher
If found, return for prize money.

She turned the paper around for us:

Reeva Harvey, a twenty-eight-year-old female resident of 275 Shipley Drive but nowhere to be found. She was accused of thievery by Macladez Zecron a few stars ago, yet the Whislow Agency didn't take this seriously into our own hands. This was deeply regretted.

"Disha…" I began, "This is *perfect.*"

Her eyes lightened and she gave me the 'we're-getting-somewhere' look.

"To Shipley Drive!" Robert announced. He gathered his bag and started heading out of the office. He paused and twisted his head back, "That's not where we're going, is it?"

We shook our heads.

Disha took out her metallic pen again and started writing on the desk. "This is going to take forever to find her."

199

"Not if we split up." I said, "And…" I gave a sigh, "research".

Robert hung his head back over the ledge of the chair. And Disha, boy she had the most energy out of all of us left her chair spinning as she darted to the library. Robert saluted saying, "Okay I'm off to the file room."

I watched them both rush out and so I sat in my chair for a little bit longer. A million questions rushed into my head but they all dissolved when I tried to acknowledge them.

What's a retaw?

Where can I get a watch like Disha and Robert?

Who's Reeva Harvey?

Where do I belong?

What even is the quest for the Path of Birds?

Wait, why am I even in this case? Just because I need to "prove" myself innocent? If only Cordelia liked my idea, if only I went home and showed Aunt Katelyn the constellation I was talking about—not to mention showing the world. If I show the world that I discovered it, that would mean interviews and articles and being famous and—

And not having to live in Honeyville anymore.

And freeing Aunt Katelyn of her career stress.

But I didn't really discover it.

I shrugged to myself, I'm not being a bad person for lying, am I? I'm just helping Aunt Katelyn and myself get through this.

Wait…would solving this case get me anywhere?

I spun around in my chair again…man how I wish I could send Aunt Katelyn a letter.

A letter. That's it.

Reeva Harvey has to communicate with people in some way and some form.

I threw myself out of the chair and rushed to the sideways elevator. The mailrooms are always in the back of every building.

I followed all of the arrows in the Whislow Agency until I finally arrived at this big storage room. But it wasn't at all what I had imagined.

Instead of bins and slots and carts filled with overflowing paper, there were just *doors*. That's right. *Doors*.

And nothing was overflowing. The lights were dim and there were only a few people in the room, closing up their envelopes and sliding them through the bottom cracks of the doors.

Estrella was standing in the corner; her hand was at the bottom of a pink door and she was waiting for a letter to slide right out. The door rumbled a little bit and out slid a small note–Estrella's eyes and horn lit up the room.

I looked at the closed green door next to me and tried opening it–

"No lo abras!" she called out.

I jolted my off the door handle like it was piping hot.

"If you open a door at the wrong time, mail can get lost."

"Sorry." I winced.

I watched some people coming and going. Some with letters, some waiting for letters. It reminded me of that time Aunt Katelyn had to isolate herself…

…It was probably only three years ago. Aunt Katelyn had to quarantine herself for two weeks so I wouldn't get sick. She barely left the guest bedroom but sometimes she would call me from there.

She always thought I was watching a movie on the television or sneaking through her vanity in our original room but in reality, I was spending hours making arts and crafts for her.

When I finished drawing notes with flowers and stars and little gymnastic fairies or acrobat princesses, I slid them underneath her door. Nothing made me happier than seeing her hand pick up the cards from the floor.

"Thank you, my little beanie" she would do her best to whisper through the wall.

Sometimes I would make little figurines out of corn straw but they turned out so big that I felt like cutting the door shorter just so I could send them.

Sometimes when I was working on the cards by the door, she would slide little notes from her door, too. They had little telescopes on them because she had gifted me one for my eighth birthday. That was when my obsession with stars began.

"I have Zecron's book for you" she would say.

Wait, what?

Estrella stood in front of me, holding a couple more envelopes in her arms and a book underneath, "I have Zecron's book for you."

I leaned against the door to snap back into reality, "Thanks, Estrella." She handed me the book from underneath.

Her hooves echoed through the room, bouncing off of each door as she pattered through the mailroom.

Why did she have the book anyway? I know that's a terrible reason to be suspicious, but if she knows anything about Zecron, then every bit of information counts.

"Estrella, can I ask you a few questions about it?"

She nodded.

We went back to the animal sanctuary and Estrella sat me next to her at the water fountain. Instead of those water fountains you'd wish on by the mall, it was more like a waterfall trickling into a pond.

I just came to the realization that I didn't have a pen—or anything to write with so I decided to rely on my brain. Even though I did have that note from the Geoport, it wouldn't help if I didn't have a pencil.

"So," I began, "When did you first come to learn about Macladez Zecron?" I tried holding back a laugh, it's funny how I was interrogating someone about him even though I barely knew anything.

She was wavering her fingers through the shallow pond when I asked the question, but her arm abruptly stopped. She didn't make eye contact with anything but the water.

"A few years ago." she said softly.

Another moment of silence lapsed between us. It's probably insensitive to ask another question.

She took a deep breath and exhaled, "My brother went to a camp several years back led by Macladez Zecron."

"Macladez Zecron is still alive?"

"No, he was almost a hundred years old when the camp was open." She continued, "Well, you see…my brother and his friends never returned."

Her eyes became misty and her horn stopped shining.

"Did Zecron do something to them?"

She nodded, "The Sparrow Constellation appeared in the sky when they disappeared." She pointed to the book in my hands, "I read all of the books he published after that— and they all talked about the Leyenda de los Gorriones. The Legend of the Sparrows."

"Did he get in trouble?"

A tear trickled down her cheek as she screamed in rage, "No! No, he didn't! Everyone thought someone else wrote these books!"

She flipped the book open to the first page and gestured me to read it:

Chapter One: The Legend of the Sparrows

Six children were always the culprit of any misdemeanor at the Obsidian Harbor Camp. It wasn't an incongruity as to why they were intelligent yet so clueless—they weren't simply clueless. They were reckless.

The Obsidian Harbor Camp was founded to evoke the reciprocal in young individuals. However, if children were willing to disobey rules and unwilling to discover their inner magic, then there is no further answer than the consequences.

Stepping into the Obsidian Forest and eliciting a howl out of the Wolf was the final straw. Out of the six children, three of them were given plentiful warnings yet Mr. Rivera, Ms. Faryyan, and Mr. Huxley did not obtain their reciprocal simply due to their ignorance.

After the howl was heard, there was only one choice left. These six children were transformed into stars to form the Sparrow Constellation that will forever serve as a reminder that misconduct will always have consequences.

I get it, maybe pranks and dares to go into a risky forest and awaking predators isn't the best-case scenario at a camp. But c'mon, turning them into swirling spheres of heat for the rest of their lives? Is that necessary?

Estrella blinked several times to push all of her tears back. She wasn't sad anymore; she was in rage. Her face was red and if she had the chance to throw Macladez Zecron down the fountain, she would.

Ms. Faryyan—was that Chief Faryyan's granddaughter?

Mr. Huxley. Mr. Huxley. That sounds so familiar…

Norma Huxley. Our elderly neighbor. Her grandson who 'disappeared'? No way. It's gotta be a coincidence.

I flipped through the book until I came across the Path of the Birds.

Chapter 17: The Path of the Birds

Every path leads to a destination. The Enchanted Orb shifts into different birds ever so often. Follow its path, retrieve a handful of dust, and a feather from each distinct bird it transforms into. The mix of the feathers over the Platform Scepter will unlock one wish.

This wish must be cast under the Sparrow Constellation so that every star shines on the feathers in order to be fulfilled. However there is one renunciation, the wish may not regard wealth, health, or love.

That's it, I follow the path, I wish for my astronomy hobby to skyrocket or I could wish for this constellation to be seen by everyone, so Aunt Katelyn would know what I'm talking about.

"I tried following the Path of the Birds, and it didn't work." Estrella said, pointing at the page with her horn.

I had the urge to ask, "What sort of magic does your unicorn horn do?"

"It just moves objects and casts temporary conditions. But I'm still little, so there's still a lot of magic that it can't do yet."

Her face seemed to calm down, maybe it's best we didn't talk about her brother. What else was I here to ask?

"Have you heard anything about Reeva Harvey?"

Estrella gave a huge nod as a small pale-yellow bunny hopped its way to her lap. I almost forgot how many critters lived here. "I met her when I spent last year trying to follow the Path of the Birds."

My eyes lit up brighter than the sun illuminating the wings of the butterflies near the wells. "Where'd you meet her?"

"The Brierwell Mansion."

I hugged Estrella and thanked her almost a billion times.

"Take the book with you." She said, I grasped it in between my fingers as I sprinted across the bridges and jumped over the little streams filled with enormous fish.

Chapter Sixteen

Reeva Harvey Connects the Dots

"The Brierwell Mansion?" Disha asked, "Where's that?"

I told them Estrella's story and watched their eyes widen at each word I said. We met in Disha's office again this time—because Robert's office was filled with parts for his blueprint that he's been sketching out.

Disha used her metallic pen again to input a map into her table. It was like those search engines I had back home, minus the globe…and the table.

The landmass on the table kept swirling around until it slowed down into a completely green patchy area. It wasn't too far away from here. But then again, I'm probably underestimating just how big this world is.

Disha led us outside using her complicated watch, "The battery's almost dead." She said. But outside, it wasn't too bright anymore. Blue moons replaced the sun and the stars were blazing across the sky. They were definitely brighter than what I've seen in any city.

We followed the map on Disha's watch towards the Brierwell Mansion with what we could do with our eyes.

"Don't we have any flashlights?" I asked.

"Opps…" Robert trailed off. He stuffed his hands in his leather jacket. He kicked the stones away from the small windy paths amidst the dark forest that were approaching to shift the conversation to something more important. "Well, here's the forest."

Disha held out her arm with the watch so it could quickly point us in the right direction. No matter how advanced it may be, I don't want to be in this forest for long. The watch started beeping louder and louder. Maybe we were almost through the dark woods. I let my heels touch the ground and my shoulders loosen–

"It just died."

"Disha, are you kidding me?" I groaned. She gave me a sharp look. It was true, I had no right to be mad considering the fact I had none of that glamorous technology with me.

We paused and let the hum of the forest sit with us for a bit. The leaves didn't move and the silence was almost deafening. My hands trembled at the premonition that there was something lurking nearby. But it was so quiet that maybe my mind was trying to fill in the gaps.

"Wait, guys." Robert paused us. His voice was soft. As he concentrated on the movements of the leaves in the forest, Disha and I stayed back. As he walked forward, he picked up a small feather off the ground. It was too dark to see the pattern. Because it wasn't purple. And it wasn't blue or any other vivid color. It was like the birds back home. Oh, it's just a feather, he mumbled. No dust nearby. Feathers. Dust. Question mark? Was he on the path of birds too? My heart slowly jumped into my neck. It's my throat. I didn't want to face another competition again. Knowing that he's far more experienced, far more. But I'm not going to drop this. I'm gonna find the rest of the feathers. I'm going to make the wish.

We three let the movement of the leaves fill the silence again. Nothing else seemed to be lurking nearby. So we started to tiptoe around. The tiptoeing turned into a walking, and the walking turned into a stroll, and the strolls turned into a search. I looked up at the sky. It looked dark this time. No constellation. And the moon was so dim that invisible clouds seemed to be covering it.

We almost gave up and just tried searching around the vicinity, but through the dark and deep woods nothing could be seen for miles.

"We're lost," Disha said.

"You think?" Robert added sarcastically.

It almost felt like we were traveling in circles because with every step I made, I always ended up near where Robert found a feather. But there wasn't a nest, so I wasn't exactly sure what could be nearby.

As every turn we made, it seemed as if the same trees were in the exact order as they were when the friends reached it. Not that I could distinguish the trees well.

Robert chuckled. "Come on guys, we gotta keep going. I mean, if all else fails, we can at least get that prize money. For finding River Harvey."

I rolled my eyes, "They never give the prize money in the end, believe me."

"That's probably because you found the wrong thing, Sienna. You have to actually *win* to get that money." Disha joked.

Sometimes you lose too loud and win to quietly.

A weird feeling stung my fingertips. I never felt so vulnerable before. I struggled to make. Words flew out of me. A cactus filled in my vocal cords.

"Well," I said bravely, lowering my head, "You just don't understand Disha, is that it *helps* some of us."

She scrunched her forehead, "But the Agency helps with that."

"Yeah...maybe. If I was *legally* here."

Disha bit her lip. A little guilty? Perhaps. She turned her head and changed the conversation. "Well, what should we call the person that took? Councilwoman Cordelia."

"The Vanisher." I said.

"More like the kidnapper." Robert said.

Well, the first thing we have to do is find the motive. If River Harvey was the Vanisher or the kidnapper. Or whatever she is. Why would she take her in the first place?

"Guys," I said, "How can we find her, if we don't even know where we are?"

"You got a point." Robert said.

As we walked, Disha stumbled over a bush. Robert and I grabbed her hand but we fell down with her into a ditch.

"Shh!" Disha hushed. There were these weird devices floating in the air. One was green, one was black and one was gray. They had a little dome at the top that was almost clear. They were like UFOs, but only smaller. We ducked through the branches as we approached the opening of the meadows.

Up ahead in the dark night forest, a blue lake was in front of us. The dark timbers curved in the back, but the lake glistened under the moon.

"Whoa." I said breathlessly. When we all stood up, the dark gray mansion towered over us like heavy stone. Moss was spread over various parts of the castle with the brown-red roofs. Very few windows were seen.

We slowly walked over to the Brierwell Mansion.

"Well," Disha said, "This is it. Reeva Harvey should be here."

We reached the big wooden doors with metal clasps and metal handles. I gave a good four knocks.

Patiently waiting, I shifted my feet forward and back just past the time.

After nearly five minutes, someone replied, "Go away." Well, if I was a running fugitive, I definitely wouldn't reply. But I'm not complaining here.

"We're lost," Robert whined. "Can you…let us in?" He looked at us and shrugged.

The same voice yelled, "Go away! I haven't done anything wrong."

"We aren't accusing you!" I replied. I waited a minute to let the steam cool off. Disha shot me the you-just-blew-our-cover look. Patience is worth more than the consequences– Aunt Katelyn would always say. Worth more than the consequences.

Disha stepped forward, "I got this," she assured us. "We are just travelers, here to make the world a better place. And if you help, we can get you out of the mess you were in with Zecron. But if you don't want to, then I understand." She gestured to us, "C'mon guys let's go."

They turned and walked away.

"Wait." a head peeked out of the door. I guess reverse psychology works better here than it does at home. A young woman gripped onto the side of the door and creaked it back and forth, "Come in." she said with a heavy sigh.

"Works like a charm." Disha whispered in my ear.

Everything inside was covered in dust. Surprisingly, she wasn't.

The windows creaked and the entire place looked like it was infected with aliens or monsters. The infection was spreading everywhere but the furniture and nothing inside seemed to be a source of light.

Reeva Harvey gestured her hand for us to sit on a purple velvet couch with a black rim. She re-wrapped her shawl over her shoulders and prompted, "How are you going to help me?"

Disha said, "We'll need some more information first." She took out a miniature notebook and pen from her pocket. What doesn't she have?

"What knowledge do you have about Macladez Zecron?"

Reeva stiffened and she gripped her shawl harder, her knuckles whitening. She lowered her head and leaned it back.

"Leave."

"We will if you tell us." Disha said.

"I said *leave.*" Reeva asserted. She stood up from the sofa and started backing away from us, pointing her hand at the door. "I don't want to deal with any of your magical shenanigans."

Disha turned her head around, stalling the time and pretending that she didn't hear her. Reeva's face looked hot, like she was put on the stand.

"Okay, so rough start," Robert began, rubbing his hands together, "Why do you live in this haunted house in the first place?"

"Robert!" Disha yelled; she shot him a sharp look. Robert winced as the situation hit him, "Oh gosh…"

The face on Reeva grew hotter and hotter. She grabbed the rod that leaned against the dusty pillar and shouted, "Leave at once!"

"We will, we will!" I replied, grabbing both of their hands. Robert ran toward the door but Disha stood firm. That girl was just throwing herself into the fire at this point.

"C'mon Disha!" I desperately cried, "Before she turns us into dust with her reciprocal or something!"

Reeva clanked the rod onto the ground and let it echo for a moment.

The room became very silent.

Very silent.

I took my hand off of the door knob and wiped away the gray dust from my fingertips. The windows shook back and forth from the quiet wind, like the entire mansion was offended by Robert's words.

A sniffle broke the silence, "Bold of you to assume I still have the reciprocal."

"Bold of you to assume we have it." Robert said blandly. Disha kicked him in the shin. He lowered his head, "We don't."

"So, you don't know who I was, you don't know who I am, and you will never know who I will be." Reeva defended, she rolled the rod across the room and it collected enough dust to stop itself. "The Whislow Agency has achieved an all new low. How wonderful."

I tightened the leather jacket around my chest just to hide its icons. The Whislow Agency is supposed to be prestigious, right? Or not?

"Reeva," I began, her eyes widened at the hearing of her name. "One of our important councilwomen has disappeared and…we just need some more information. That's all."

"It wasn't me!" She yelled.

"Can you please at least tell us then," Disha started shushing her voice, "anything about your–past accusations?"

She wiped a tear from her cheek mumbling to herself, "They're only children." She stood up and leaned her head against the pillar, "I can show you."

She led us into a dark hallway, only the light of the torch helped everyone's eyes see through.

"So, you don't have magic within you?" Reeva asked us.

"No." Disha answered, rolling her eyes at Robert.

"At least it hasn't been taken from you." Reeva sighed, "Watch your step, only one thing can activate what I am about to show you. And that's a regret."

The hallways seemed to be endless and dark. There were no doors or anymore rooms, but just forks branching into more forks of hallways. The walls were blank. Maybe dust covered whatever paintings were here first, but other than that, it was just *gray*.

Reeva stopped at a door. It was bronze and had a heavy door wheel on its center.

Inside was a misty blue ball. Sitting on what seemed to be a cloud.

"The Zecron Orb!" Disha gasped.

"No, it's not the original one. This is simply the version Zecron forcibly gifted me" Reeva Harvey said, "Touch the orb and think in your heads, *I want to see the dreaded past of Reeva Harvey.*"

We three did.

Soon, we all began to float and we were in the scene of Reeva Harvey's past.

"Reeva Harvey, how are you still here? You said you had no magic?" I asked.

"Well, this orb is pretty complicated. You see, when I received this orb. It was only to see my past and learn from it. The only capability I have from it is seeing the past. And that's because Zecron never wanted me to forget about his success…and my past."

We were in Whislow Head-Quarters. Robert was standing in a walkway system and people were passing right *through* him.

Reeva chuckled, "Yes, they can pass right through us. They can't sense any of us. It's like we're air. Senseless air"

A young girl, about 18, seemed to be Reeva. There was a silver pin on the floor and she picked it up.

Reeva sighed. "I used to be quite the collector back then. The part of the whole reason why I'm in this mess." She said, shaking her head with a hand slapped against her forehead.

The girl walked out of sight and we four quickly followed her. The young Reeva stopped. She gave an eerie face and mysteriously walked toward the manager's room.

"Wait," Disha asked, "How can we hear that eerie sound if only you at age 18 heard it?"

"Well," Reeva explained, "This is my past. Whichever dimension the young me goes to, you go to, hear whatever I hear, and well, you get the idea."

Young Reeva opened the door of the room and there was the Geoport. She walked into it and disappeared. The whole surroundings changed for us too.

We all appeared in a forest that soaked in the violent waves crashing upon the shore.

"The Obsidian Harbor." Reeva said, "One of Zecron's lairs."

The sky was dark with only stormy clouds swirling above, and we followed Young Reeva walking into a huge wooden ship. It looked like it crashed at the dock and was later abandoned.

The ship was lit by a fired torch on each side of the walls. The voice was deep and hollow and directed Reeva into a room.

In the room was a man sitting in a chair. He neatly set the dozens of quills he had in a jar. It wasn't a ship, more like one big room disguised as one just so it could have the permission to dock at the harbor.

"Hello, Reeva Harvey. I have been waiting for you."

The young Reeva Harvey gulped. "Y-you have?"

"Oh yes. You seem to be the chosen one in the Whislow Agency. Keeper of the *clever element.*"

Young Reeva shook her head, "N-no. I'm just a regular agent like everyone else. I'm not a keeper of anything and I've never heard of being the chosen one."

"Well, I'll be! The agency has never disclosed this information?" the man said. After a moment he calmed down. "I'm Macladez Zecron. Pleased to meet you. Legend has it that whoever comes here by a call, is the chosen one and the new Keeper of the Clever Element."

Young Reeva nodded, "So, what is the Clever Element?"

"Someone who sacrifices, someone who endures, and someone who isn't what they seem. But right now, none of that matters anymore. Now, you are the powerful, Miss Harvey."

"I am?"

"Right," Macladez Zecron said, "You see, Miss Harvey, you are truly talented. Why be with an agency when you can be better? More Powerful?"

"Please give me some time to think about it." Young Reeva said.

Macladez Zecron looked impatient. "Oh yes. But you would be foolish to turn down this offer. With your gift, you could be my personal assistant, help me in countless escapades. But please try some of these magical items. We need to see what would be *best* for you to use."

Young Reeva bit her lip. "Well, um, okay."

Reeva slammed her hand against her forehead.

"What's wrong?" I asked her.

"Oh nothing, but only later did I figure Macladez Zecron hacked the magical items so when I touch it, it captures my identity."

"Guys!" Robert said, pointing at the two characters, "They're getting away!"

We quickly followed the two into another room where all the magical items were.

"No," Reeva said "Don't touch-" but it was already too late. Her eighteen-year-old self already touched the hacked magical items.

Soon, the four rapidly zipped forward as if they were traveling through light years.

"What's happening?" Disha asked Reeva.

"We're fast forwarding." She explained.

The next scene was in a room that seemed to be where young Reeva was sleeping.

An orb, the Zecron orb, came floating up beside Reeva. Her eyes opened and hypnotically came to the orb.

Reeva shook her head and slammed her hand against her forehead again. "Biggest mistake I ever made, touching it."

After young Reeva touched the orb, there was an explosion. Then, young Reeva awoke in a flower bed in the garden room.

"What happened?" she asked.

A woman walked into the garden room, with a stern face. "Don't fool me. We know what your tricks are."

Many objects, including the silver pin, were floating in the room.

"I don't understand. Why is my collection floating?" she said in bewilderment.

Macladez Zecron appeared with many others into the room.

"You have been stealing objects and making them powerful." Zecron said. "You used your magic to steal my orb!"

Everyone gasped.

"See?" Zecron showed, "I've watched her. She was conjuring dark magic to transfer into the objects! Reeva Harvey is using her magic and objects to gain power and to rule Philoxenia!"

Everyone gasped again, angry at Reeva Harvey. They left the room.

Zecron crossed his arms, leaning on a pillar, "How did you like my trick?" he said with a chuckle.

"You tried to frame me! You did this and proved that I did so!"

"You're right. And there is nothing you can do to stop me. I always saw your great talents and wanted to prevent that."

Reeva tried to pick up a spoon on the nearby table with her reciprocal. She concentrated, but it won't budge.

"You," Reeva said, infuriated, "You found a way to transfer all my magic into these objects. Now I'm wanted because of you."

"Yes indeed." Zecron said smiling, "I hacked the magic objects at the harbor so when you touch them, I can get your identity and reciprocal. Once that was settled, I transported my orb into your room and all you had to do was touch it. The *collector, they* say, was foolish enough to do so! All your magic was transported into it. I really should be thanking you, child." he then gave an evil laugh.

The whole scene faded away and we four were back at the Brierwell Mansion.

"You see, I am innocent." Reeva said.

We exchanged suspicious glances.

"But why did you collect so many things?" I asked her.

Reeva sighed, "It was just a hobby. I would never steal anything. It's just that I liked to compare objects; mostly objects. I don't know if this is a coincidence, but this same crime has *actually* been committed. Except he never got to finish the crime."

ZWEEP!

The three looked outside, there were a few flying objects in the air. It had flashing lights.

Robert opened a new curtain, "Wow, I've heard about UFO's, but this is the real deal. Who's in it?"

"Oh no," Reeva said, panicking, "The authorities found me. I have to hide."

She then took the keys off a counter, and quietly but rapidly ran into a hallway.

"Okay," I said, "Let's-"

A faint high pitch scream came from the hallway.

Our blood ran cold and we rushed there and found Reeva. She whisper-shouted, *"My scarf is in the pink closet."*

Reeva's eyes widened as she faded transparent into thin air.

I swiped my hand where Reeva was–feeling nothing but the wind.

"Oh no," Disha said, "Reeva Harvey, she's vanished too."

"That means, she isn't guilty." Robert said, "Wait, the vanisher must be nearby." He then gulped, "Wait, if the vanisher's here, we could vanish too .... just like Reeva." He breathed heavily. "When's is it time to panic?"

"It's fine," I said, "We're not magical yet, so there's no point in kidnapping us."

RINNNNNNG!

The sound was coming from a telephone.

"Should I answer it?" I gently pressed my fingertips against the phone.

"No." Disha said.

"Yes." Robert said.

The phone kept ringing and soon the ringtone made the same sound as the UFO's flying above the mansion.

"H-How?" Disha asked.

"Yeah, how is the ring tone the same as that?" Robert said, completing Disha's question and pointed his finger to the roof.

"You guys look around the mansion for any clues and keep a low profile on the UFO."

I couldn't help myself. She picked up the phone but didn't say hello.

"Where is Reeva Harvey?" The voice on the phone said.

I froze. Disha was on her tip-toes, she'll know what to say so I handed it to her.

"This is the Whislow Agency, we have her taken care of." Disha said, and quickly hung up, her breath racing.

I bit my lip and closed my eyes for a moment until the smooth zips of the UFO's faded away.

"Well," Disha began, "Now we know it's not Reeva Harvey who took Councilwoman Cordelia."

"No guys," I said, panting, "This case is much worse, there's literally someone out there working for Zecron to take *almost every* Philoxenian."

Robert shrugged, he swept the dust away from the ground with his shoe and sat, "You never know, Reeva could pretend to disappear just to throw us off."

He has a point. Whoever this *vanisher* is, has to be smart. But Reeva Harvey genuinely looked too hurt to do something that grave. No one can fake being that scarred. At least I don't think so.

"I don't get it." Disha admitted, "This vanisher would only take powerful people like Councilwoman Cordelia or magical objects. Reeva Harvey said she didn't have any magic. Why would the vanisher take her?"

We just shrugged, stumped at this dead end even though our case just began.

She does have a point. Yet, Reeva does know much more about Zecron than any of us three combined so, maybe someone needs that information. And because she knows so much about him, there has to be *something* around here to help.

"Why don't we just explore this place for a while?" I suggested.

Chapter Seventeen

They Hid It In A Hidden Passage

"What if Reeva made that entire scene up and she *does* have the reciprocal?" Robert suggested. The hour we spent searching around the mansion was the hour he kept brewing up his wild but logical theories.

The fact that there were barely any doors made this somewhat harder to find any information.... or easier. Depending on how you look at it.

"What did she say?" Disha tried recalling, "My scarf is in the pink closet?"

Robert shrugged, he sat down and took out a large blue paper. His blueprint. Disha groaned, "You're seriously going to work on your project right now?"

He took out a pin from his leather jacket and switched it on, it let out a small white light and he carefully shone it over the details on his paper.

Disha looked at me in hopelessness. There were barely any closets here, let alone a pink closet.

I decided to stroll around the mansion for some time, pacing through the hallways. So far, nothing. Sam just told us Zecron is dangerous, and the culprit should be related to Cordelia, and Reeva just added to the fact that Macladez Zecron was evil. This isn't getting us anywhere.

"What if Reeva Harvey was just upset that she wasn't as powerful as she thought she would be when she became Clever Element so she really did make at least *half* of the story up." I heard Robert say from behind the halls.

Ok, maybe Reeva Harvey did help a little with the Clever Element and the Obsidian Harbor and whatnot. But all we can say is that someone out there is ready to finish Zecron's plan and steal everything that is magical. Someone's going to become the most powerful being in the universe– oh boy– this is hard to wrap my head around. This isn't a kidnapping case anymore. *Gulp.*

I reached a dead end at the end of the hallway. Everything was so dark and quiet that I couldn't hear Robert's theories anymore. I turned towards the wall, how can this be called a mansions if it's just–

Wait.

The dust.

I swiped my finger across the wall and felt wooden ridges between my fingers. I blew the speckles of dust off of my fingers and it turned blue. The same kind of blue where I couldn't tell if it was teal or turquoise, like the dust leak back at Whislow. I took off my shoes and dug them into the wall until I found a doorknob. Well what do you know, there's rooms!

I went from hallway to hallway with one swipe, until something pink emerged from underneath. The closet. I used the bottom of my shoe and spread the dust out and kept digging and kept digging until I found the latch. When I knocked it open, there was nothing but empty shelves and her shawl.

Her shawl.

I swear I never saw her put it in the closet, but alright. I took out my shawl and it instantly crumbled into my arms. Oh gosh! It crumpled and crumbled until it smoothened into fine grains. The grains didn't stop there. They swirled away from my hands and formed a pink scarf.

Yes! I got it.

Maybe she wanted us to help her out and get rid of her curse? Or else she would've just told us to leave. Wait…what if it could help me out with the Path of Birds quest to make that wish? A little nail hit my chest thinking about how she just wants a curse-free life and I'm out here wishing for fame. But I guess if she really wanted it, she would go out and follow the Path of Birds herself. So, I'm not really in the wrong here. I gently tucked it back into my pocket in my leather jacket and I retraced my footprints on the old wooden floor to find myself back to the others.

Disha said, "A specific key. We need a specific key." There was no living room anymore. I could see her hair poking out from the bottom floor. The purple sofa was sitting on the side and half of the living room shifted into a downstairs basement. They probably figured out the whole dust situation too.

I approached the ledge of where the living room stooped and the basement appeared. Robert was clinging to a whole ring of keys.

"None of them work." Disha said, rotating the ring and trying each one. She eyed the keys all carefully. I jumped into the basement with them. "What'd you find?"

"Well, if you move the purple sofa just enough, you find this basement" Robert explained, "and there's this box with a latch."

"But the keys are too thin!" Disha exclaimed. I knelt down next to them, none of the keys seemed to be fitting.

The red one seemed to be exactly parallel to the gold one.

"What if I…" Robert said, he fidgeted to the red and gold keys. If you looked closely enough, they were almost identical. He connected the red one on top of the gold one. "It'll fit now."

Disha took the key and turned it in the lock, the box clicked.

"See guys, I have common sense."

The whole wall in which the box was attached spun around. But there was one problem, the entire room was covered with green lasers.

"My common sense also tells me that we shouldn't touch those lasers." Robert said, pointing at them.

"Wow, Robert, amazing observation." Disha added.

Disha pointed up at the wall inside, "Look, there's a button way up there. It probably turns it off."

A smile flickered on my face, "Aunt Katelyn didn't teach me gymnastics for no reason, I got you guys."

I turned my back to the lasers and arched over them into the next bit of safe space. From there, I decided on whether to jump and hopefully land under the next laser if I was quick enough or to just back tuck and use my arms to lower me below them. I chose the second option.

With each arch, split sit, sliding, and even handsprings at times, I finally found myself next to the button.

Yes.

"Wait, Sienna." Disha called from the front of the room.

"Yeah?" I called. She was holding the pink scarf in her hand and lightly waved it around, letting it touch the lasers. As soon as it touched the lasers, they faded away.

I shrugged, "Well…gotta put my gymnastics skills to use *somewhere.*"

In the room we were standing in, there was a silver round table. A light from an unidentifiable place gave an iridescent glow to another object on the table, a book. The book was written: **The Legend of the Sparrows by Macladez Zecron.**

"This is the book Estrella showed me. This has to be the original one."

"Imagine if this used to be Macladez's old house, and he's just some really self-absorbed guy with the whole mansion filled with his own things." Robert said.

"In that case," I smiled, "That would be great. We'd at least find out about his family–or someone who could potentially work for him. But there's no way that this could be his house, if the orb here isn't the original one. "

"And if we don't", Robert shrugged, "We'd at least beat everyone in escape rooms."

Disha shook her head in annoyance and opened the book to the part where those kids became stars. Her jaw dropped in disbelief while reading about the Obsidian Harbor. *Estrella's story.*

"Should we check the Obsidian Harbor?" Robert asked. Suddenly, a chill breeze stung in the air.

I looked at him, "That's where the kids got cursed, that's where Reeva–"

"You forget we're eleven." Disha butted in, but she had a point. She pointed at his blueprint, "You've been working on whatever that is for so long and–"

"It's a Cornuport." Robert said. He faced the blueprint towards us. Among the dark mansion, I could make out a vest and the contraption had two large, eagle-like wings extending until the end of the page. The more I narrowed my eyes, the more scribbles and notes and little sketches I could make out. The blueprint was previously crumbled and the folded lines were prominent. It was so close to ripping.

"It's like Geoport…but better. Someday, we'll be able to fly. Just like Mateo did."

Mateo Rivera.

"You knew him?" I asked.

He pressed his lips together and nodded, "Kind of."

If Estrella had a unicorn horn, would that mean that Mateo was part–pegasus? And I'm being told that some mystical guy with wings and all is being trapped into a swirling ball of mass? Or, *is* a swirling ball of mass? I scooted closer to see the blueprint, I could see the ridges of the wings, minor screws starting to piece the whole thing together.

"Honestly, it's harder to design it than it is to piece it together." Robert admitted.

Still, for a preteen, this is some serious talent…

"If we're not ready to go to the Obsidian Harbor, then what's the next best place?" Disha asked.

A place that's dangerous, but not too dangerous. A place where everything happens, but at the same time, nothing at all. I curled in my knees and thought. A place dangerous enough to need strong security but somewhere kids can go. Where's the place I got caught?

The train.

"Guys, we have to go to the train station."

They narrowed their eyebrows, even Robert gestured to his blueprint, "Did you not see what I'm working on right now?"

I shook my head, "No, not for transport. I mean, it's somewhere a lot of people go, even us kids. And who knows? Maybe the villain is…traditional?"

Disha pursed her lips and then they curled it into a smile, "It's where you got in trouble, isn't it?"

H-how does she know that? I could see it in her eyes, the satisfaction of reading my mind. Maybe she has a potion to do that or something. You never know.

"Okay," Disha concluded, "Sienna, you make sure the UFOs are cleared, I'll get the book, and Robert…you can just make sure you're intact."

We all scrambled through the mansion and ducked beneath the branches as we waited for the UFOs to clear the village. Strange form of patrol.

In the iridescent night, where the grass waved in and out from the breeze, shone on the Geoport. We rushed to it and stepped inside and the gate closed behind and closed the latch. We opened up the map on the Geoport, and the rails shook a little. The map triggered and zoomed through the landmasses of Philoxenia. Yet, nothing else happened after that.

"Well guys," Robert let out a sigh, "I guess the Vanisher zapped the magic out of this one."

Disha gestured to us with a solution, "It's fine, we'll walk." As we left the Geoport to sit there, motionless, another thing struck me. I had no money nor ticket again. I patted through the jacket, only finding the weird letter I found during my first trip on the Geoport. But nothing else.

"It's fine, Sienna." Disha assured, "Our uniform is enough for them to let us ride free."

I narrowed my eyes, "But didn't Reeva say the Whislow Agency has a terrible reputation?"

Robert laughed, "You see, the whole world thinks the Whislow Agency is some kind of–top agency or something. But once you get in, you realize it's literally garbage." He glanced at Disha, who narrowed her eyes into a scowl and he put his hands up, "Not saying that Whislow is garbage or anything just that it's not…as amazingly … promisingly … amazing."

She rolled her eyes and shook her head. This was going to be a long walk.

The grass disappeared and we were walking along the crumbly gravel. I let Disha lead us because I had absolutely no idea where the train station was. I run away from things, not go looking for them.

The clouds started to cover the moon and the trees shrunk into small bushes that just sat alongside the rows of houses. Now that I think about it, it's not too different from back home in Idallis. Me and Aunt Katelyn could live here.

"Do you think the Vanisher knows us?" Robert asked as we were walking, "It seems that they strike everywhere we go."

"True," I agreed with him, "But why wouldn't they take us there and then?"

"News flash, Sienna" Disha revealed, "We don't have the reciprocal."

"Then why did they take Reeva? After she claimed she had no magic?" I asked.

"That's the thing, why *her*?" Disha led on.

"I think that will be a mystery for us to solve." Robert said.

"You think?" Disha rolled her eyes. We went back and forth with our confusion the entire time we walked. It just didn't make sense. Councilwoman Cordelia disappeared, and Reeva, and those people in Samuel's shop. But not us.

The train is where I first got in trouble, maybe it'll help me find the trouble this time.

A line of tracks came into sight and so did a dim light from a small ticket booth.

I whispered in Disha's ear, "I swear if we get caught on the train for not pay—"

"Relax, I've done it multiple times." She smiled, scoffing my fear off. I looked over at Robert, gesturing to him how absurd this was. He stretched one side of his lips and raised his eyebrows, "Don't ask me."

We stood on the wooden platform among families and families of people.

A turquoise and transparent train came to a stop at the station. A cloud steamed out from the back of the train and people began boarding. My heart began pounding, but Disha grabbed my wrist and dragged me onto the train.

We found a booth in the back of the train, blue cushions and a wooden table between us. The train immediately began traveling on the tracks again and into the rest of Philoxenia.

I said, "Anyone on this train could be our suspect, just waiting to strike." I glanced around all of the other booths, "If someone disappears, we know we've found the right place."

"Are you serious?" Disha groaned, she slapped her forehead, "If someone disappeared from here, this would be the last place the Vanisher would be. Why would they be at the scene of the crime when they can commit it hidden?"

"She's got a point." Robert added.

I hate to admit it, but Disha is probably right. With this much power, there's a high chance they're kidnapping people and stealing magical objects in their *sleep*.

A Ticketmaster filed through, stamping tickets and clicking a counter. Disha simply showed her badge and the Ticketmaster nodded, continuing his count. I guess the Whislow privilege is real.

I folded my legs in and scooted against the window, watching the grass dance by. The sun was slowly setting into the sky and the purple stars were emerging. Philoxenia looked so different now, with lavender shadows casted over houses and blue lanterns racing through the streets nearby. The wind was brisking the tips of the grass blades now and small sprinkles of lights were twisting and twirling through the meadows. It was like the small section of spring in our little snow globe back home…

"Tighten your core, Sienna! Tighten!" Aunt Katelyn shouted from behind me. I had a bruised knee from falling off of the balance beam in our backyard.

"I'm sorry Auntie, but I don't have a core with me right now."

A small chuckle came out of her pink lips, "My little beanie, your core is in your stomach."

I narrowed my eyes, her words made no sense, "Well, that's sad, I don't have one."

Aunt Katelyn kneeled right next to me on our back lawn, a long balance beam was stretched out in front of us and she always set the beam on the lawn because I always fall.

She placed a hand on my stomach, "Just tighten your tummy, okay?" I sucked in my stomach and glanced up, "There." She said, "That's just part of it." She closed my hands into fists and brought them together in front of my chest. "Pretend this is our snow globe, okay?"

I nodded.

"Now, you could be soaring through the sky, flying over mountains, but you need to keep this snow globe in one piece. You need to hold yourself together in one strong form to keep this snow globe safe."

I nodded again.

"Think you got it?"

I nodded once more.

She lifted me up and set me at the beginning of the bar. I stepped one foot in front of the other and in front of the other and in front of the other and in front of the other. One foot in front, the other foot in front. Not too close. Not too close. Save the snow globe. Save the snow globe.

"Yes, beanie! You did it!" She caught me as I jumped off the end of the balance beam, she raised her palm for me to slap and her cheeks were filled with satisfaction.

I remember 5-year-old me being giddy with joy, feeling on top of the world, even if I just walked across a stick in a backyard. But at least I knew how to hold myself together…

…"Do you guys get the feeling that you're being watched?" Disha asked. Her face ran cold.

"I get that feeling all the time." Robert admitted. Disha slapped her forehead once more.

I unfolded my legs and glanced around, and it didn't feel like I was being watched. Everyone was just chatting amongst themselves in their little booths.

Disha squinted her eyes at me, "And can you not doze off? We're in the middle of a case, and Philoxenia depends on us."

I put my hands up defensively, "My bad. My bad." I looked at the notepad she was scribbling on. It just had notes of the cabin, one couple was whispering, one group of friends were playing cards, just casual notes.

"I swear if someone disappears on this train then–"

"Hey look!" Robert pointed out the window. We were slowing to another stop and behind the station was a large crowd of townspeople holding baskets upon baskets of produce.

There was a tall wooden building that stood out from the conventional country-side city with a large plated name:

The Hall of Unsuspecting Coincidences

"That's 123 Alphabet Avenue," Robert read out, "That's kinda funny."

Chapter Eighteen

Maybe Coincidences Aren't Coincidences

We got off of the train and headed into town, our leather dark jackets standing out among the pastel clothed townspeople.

If I'm being honest, our supposed plan is going nowhere. We went to their shoemaker, and people disappeared. We went to Reeva, and she disappeared. The train…well, at least no one disappeared. And the enchanting orb? What are we supposed to do with it? And the book, it only tells us stories. Past stories.

What if everything is just…a coincidence?

What if the orb disappearing has nothing to do with Cordelia disappearing. And if the orb isn't connected to the case, then how do we know that Zecron is?

Oh yeah, it is connected because Reeva told us he was responsible for stealing magical stuff a long time ago.

WHY IS THIS SO HARD?

HOW DID I GET MYSELF INTO THIS CASE?

WHY DID I GET MYSELF INTO THIS CASE?

WHY DID I GO TO THAT CONVENTION?

I hate this case so much. I just want to make that wish on the constellation and go home. I felt a tug on my wrist, "C'mon Sienna."

We headed inside the large, brick building. It seemed like clouds loomed over it, even though the entire sky was sunny. And what's even weirder was that there was a gap between the flow of the crowd, and the building stood in that gap. The bricks were on the edge of falling like a game of Jenga. One push and the whole building could break. The pit in my stomach dropped.

We stepped inside the building, the carpet was sandy, and every time we walked over it, we almost slipped.

"Alright guys," Disha alerted us, "Maybe a building pertaining to coincidences could help us with *our* coincidences."

Robert turned to me, "Everyone's been disappearing when you're around here, what if you're the secret vanisher?"

I narrowed my eyes, how could a chill guy like him turn against me? "Robert…what are you saying?"

He shrugged his shoulders, "I'm just *saying*."

"It's a good explanation." Disha said.

It is…but I don't even have magic in me. I mean, if I could accidentally retrieve all of this wealth from wherever this person may store it, then, it's not totally a bad thing for *me*, right?

Stop, Sienna, stop. You're not selfish. Be quiet.

"Right," Disha said, "If you see anything, anything at all, about an orb, or Zecron, then let me know."

"Well, what if Zecron has nothing to do with everyone disappearing?" I suggested.

Disha shrugged, "Why would the orb disappear right before Cordelia does?"

"Because the person stealing probably just wanted the orb too?"

She shook her head, "Then why didn't they steal anything else?"

My head spun in the pool of confusion. Just find the magic thief. Just find the magic thief. That's all we have to do. Simple enough, I delusionally convinced myself.

The narrow hallway dissolved into a large lobby, where a man leaned over his counter. A large, pearly white smile appeared on his face.

"Hello young ones." He gave us a thumbs up, "Excited to expand your horizons and vast knowledge?"

Robert and I exchanged glances.

The man opened up his gestures and jumped over his counter. "What brings you here today?"

"Well," Disha said, "It would be wonderful if we could learn why the building is called, the House Of Unsuspecting Coincidences."

He chuckled, his grin widening even more, "My dear, the name is rather self-explanatory. Coincidences that you'd least expect, you'll find it here."

Perfect. The answer to all of our questions.

He led us down a vast hall filled with glass displays of artifacts, pictures, records, and sometimes even just…anything.

"Our proud members…" The man began lecturing with that artificial grin on his face he just couldn't seem to rub off.

After him talking on and on about the members, he stepped into an even wider hall, flores laced with marble and walls bare enough to let the main pieces take lead, models, statues, vehicles.

"Before the ages of stone and nature, we made our sculptures with *zems*. But later, it was rediscovered as clay, coincidence, isn't it?"

We stared at him blankly. He kept smiling, "Well, you may ask…what's the difference? Well, there is none, it's just a coincidence clay was invented twice." He chuckled at his own, unfunny joke.

We kept walking down the marble, seeing his artificial smile through the transparent displays. Disha followed right behind him and Robert was tugging at the sculpture's arms behind me.

"Dude," I whispered, "What are you doing?"

He replied, "My sleeve got caught on–" he swooped his arm…and the sculpture's arm with it. My heart skipped a beat when the arm knocked the floor–triggering the man to turn his neck. I gulped.

The man rushed over, and locked the arm carefully in place again, "It's all right, no worries." I could feel the irritation even in Robert's eyes, the man was truly expressionless. As he went to clean up the clay debris, I swear I could've seen his hair turn into long, black, frizzy locks for a split second. I think I was going crazy.

We slowly strolled through the museum and each display ranged from small inventions to straight out models of homes.

My jaw dropped when I saw the next display.

There was a red caravan, with the orange and gold rims around the corners. Bright letters shouted, "The Harrison Circus."

No. It couldn't be. It can't be. Not here. Of all places.

I rubbed my eyes to try and awaken my tired mind. This has to be a dream. Those dreams where you feel like you're doing something but you really weren't.

Wake up.

Wake up.

W a k e u p…

"Beanie! I made lunch." The door of the caravan swung open, and out came Aunt Katelyn with her pink apron and a plate of sandwiches.

I rushed into her arms, she always smelled like the peach roses we grew inside of the caravan.

I wolfed down the sandwiches she made as she untied her apron, "Alright Sienna, it's time, auntie has to clean the caravan, do you want to be my little assistant?"

And just like that, little me sprung up, fetching a bucket of water to swirl bubbles all day long.

Aunt Katelyn would always hum a song to me, or joke about the craziest stunts done with her older students.

I was scrubbing the windows with a heavy sponge when she said, "We spend all of our time in the caravan, we might as well live in it." It was true, we grew flowers, painted, made sandwiches, you name it.

As the sun traveled west, I ran my fingers down the window panes, satisfied with the clean squeaks each swipe made. Aunt Katelyn had just stepped out with a duster in one hand, "All finished, beanie?"

"One last thing," I remember saying, I turned to the bucket of water left and scooped up as much water as I could, splashing her.

She giggled, "I see how it is…you better run!" And off she went, chasing me around the caravan until we were both drenched in soapy water.

As she dried me, she said, "Sienna, what would I do without you–"--

"Hello?" Disha waved her arm in front of my face, "You there?" My palms were sweaty, I forgot I was still in this weird museum. "Yeah, I'm here."

She pointed to a paper on the wall. A large document with brown lettering and small print covered the page.

MACLADEZ ZECRON'S WILL

I traced down the page until I saw where her finger was pointing,

To my son, Felix Zecron, the Enchanted Orb.

If I wasn't in this super complicated case, I would be asking why the museum had this document in the first case. But since it helped, I'm not complaining.

"We just need to find this Felix Zecron, it can't be too hard." I said. At least we have an objective now.

Disha's face lowered, she shook her head, "Sienna, _anyone_, can whip up a spell and disguise themselves in this world."

"So," Robert said, "They could literally be a lamp right now?"

"They could." Disha answered, she gave up reacting to his insane questions. "But since the orb's been acting up since people have been disappearing, I think Zecron passed down more than his orb to Felix."

"Felix needs to finish the very thing Zecron didn't" I added on, "to be the Vanisher."

Bingo.

It clicked.

As we exited the big museum room into another hall, my pocket rang. Inside, I found a small rectangle buzzing. A phone? How'd that get in there?

I picked it up when we started walking back into the statues room to head into the lobby, "Hello?"

"Hey, it's Estrella."

"Hey, what's new?"

"Have you checked the Obsidian Harbor yet?"

"No…" I responded. I wasn't even sure if I *could*. Knowing Zecron with the little information I had, there's no way that *anyone* could just enter his camp.

"Well, you should, and if you do, there's something you should see."

"Which is?"

"It's the Árbol de Agradecimientos, the Thank You Tree. It's where all the camp members wrote appreciation cards to Zecron. Last time when I was on my Path of Birds quest, I found a feather there."

My eyes widened, this is perfect. Any clues to find a feather will make this whole case and journey so much easier. "Thank you, Estrella, I'll keep a look out for it."

"Pero, the thing is, teleporting is kind of…broken at Whislow, so it'll be a long journey."

"Who is it?" Disha asked, intrigued from my other ear.

"It's okay Estrella, as long as we *can* there, that'll all that matters. Thanks." I hung up the phone and turned to Disha, telling her what Estrella had, but only fear erupted out of her eyes.

"Sienna, did you forget how…how…Sienna that's where people at that harbor literally became spheres of light. I don't think you'd—"

"I mean risk is inevitable." Robert butted in, "We can't avoid it."

As I watched the panic rise in her eyes, my mind scattered on what to do, the man came back, with a familiar looking instrument in his hand. A box with springs on the sides. Interesting.

"Children, allow me to perform for you." He began playing a small melancholy tune and it crescendoed into a loud symphony. All from one instrument.

What was it again? A mani…manipulating something. Manipulating Mertilda. My heart dropped, Mazie said those were dangerous. It's probably fine as long he doesn't–

He scooped out a large dollop of powdered chalk from his pocket and smeared it over the springs, "Stand still children, it's all *for* entertainment."

I looked at him, and around me and back at him. The statutes were a little too realistic. The veins on their arms, the blemishes on everyone's faces, different textures of shirts and skins, there's no way that an instrument can substitute for Medusa, can it? My heart started pounding in my throat and I grabbed the wrists of Disha and Robert and started to run.

"It's alright children, just hold still." he said with his obnoxious smile. Disha quickly caught on and she raced alongside me. Robert glared at him, and around the room, "If you didn't invent clay, then just say that." He rolled his eyes, and started running.

I could see the smile of the man slightly trembling, and a segment of satisfaction appeared in Robert's eyes.

"It's not clay, it's *zems*, they just have similar properties." He said, setting his hands on the springs.

His eyes flickered green and a feather appeared in front of me on the floor.

Three down, three to go.

"Plagiarist." Robert shouted from above my head. We raced even faster, the door was almost there. Almost there.

The man shouted, "COME BACK HERE!" his smile was gone, Robert broke him.

Fight or flight kicked in and I couldn't feel my legs but they were racing me through the halls and past all of the dedicated members who turned people to clay and all of the displays that make me think this world isn't real.

We escaped the building and ran faster and faster, afraid that the man was going to come after us. This was a real, *"those who enter never exit"* situation that I never want to experience. Maybe that's how Disha feels about the Obsidian Harbor.

We ran away from the town, away from the bricked grounds and people strolling around until we reached another, empty town that let us stop and catch our breath. A cold breeze braided in between us, the gray houses stood on each side and traveled down the alleys. The distance between each side became narrower and narrower, as the whole neighborhood was in the shape of a triangle. An equilateral triangle.

I took a step forward, letting the sand on the ground crumble underneath my shoes. It was loud enough to ring in my ear. All because of the silence in the town. This ghost town.

Chapter Nineteen

Caught in a Ghost Town

Tumbleweeds danced through the triangular neighborhood.

Every window was shut with velvet curtains, the doors rickety and old. They didn't even have doorknobs, just the opening circle where you could see barely anything, because everything was coated with lint. I looked behind me, the old-fashioned urban city was only a couple miles away, but the difference between this town and the one behind us was immense.

I guess Philoxenia can't make up its mind on what world it wants. Medieval kingdoms, industrial cities, haunted mansions, advanced agency headquarters, ghost towns…

The houses were built on wooden stilts, and the houses at each end of the triangle were the biggest. The roofs were pointy, except for the roofs on the big houses. They were broader and only their chimneys were emitting green smoke. Not the other houses.

"Maybe we should turn back…" I suggested, pivoting to the only opening in the neighborhood.

"And face the wrath of that museum guy?" Robert said, "No way!"

"Then, let's use your jetpack." I said. If we can't go back the other way, then the only other exit is up.

Robert said, "If I built it, Sienna, then it would be my first thought too."

"Then we can only go out that way--"

"I'm too young to turn into clay." He protested. He clasped his hands together, pleading that our last resort would be to go back in the direction of the museum man. He has a point, I don't want to turn into clay either.

I shoved my hands into my pockets, One, two, three feathers. Three down, three to go.

I scanned around the entire vicinity, there was nothing really *odd* about this neighborhood, but the small things threw the entire mood off. Like the missing doorknobs.

"What is this, a door knob protest?" Robert asked, shaking his head. He read my thoughts exactly.

"I mean, there has to be *something* here." Disha offered, she kicked her shoe into the dirt and eyed the rod fences around the houses.

Doors. Door knobs. That seems to be the main important thing in every place now…

Mail.

I rushed toward the nearest house and swiped my hand underneath the door gap. Nothing.

Disha giggled, "Hold on, I got this." She hurried over and kneeled next to me. "You need a source of ID." She took out a piece of paper from her jacket pocket and held out my thumb. The dirt was damp underneath us and she pressed my thumb into the ground, and later squeezed it onto her paper. She slid it underneath. "Okay, this should work." I looked back at my thumb, *it was Mazie's fingerprint.* I guess Disha must've forgotten. This should be interesting.

She slid the paper through the slit and waited. "C'mon," she murmured. After dusting off the dirt from my fingertips, stacks of envelopes finally came through.

The first envelope was sealed with a large sticker screaming MP. Mazie Polaris.

"Who's been sending you mail?" Disha asked, leaning over my shoulder.

"We'll see," I lead on. It's inevitable. I can't hide the mail.

A letter came out,

Dear Mazie,

2 days left. Don't forget.

Disha's jaw dropped, she looked at me in disbelief, "Sie…you…you identity thief!" Her heart was pounding through her throat, and her face was flushed red. She looked like she was going to stand right up, and find a way to turn me in. Some way or another.

And what got my heart pounding was when she really *did* stand up.

"Disha, Disha, Disha." I hushed, I held her hands, or else they would've conjured up her nonexistent powers in some way for her to report me. "Listen, just listen." The redness slowly faded. She stared at me blankly, waiting for me to go on.

I turned to Robert as well, but he was just standing there, looking back at the urban city in fear. His fingers trembled.

"Look, my aunt and I used to live in Idallis city. We had a nice house, nice community, I went to a nice school, nice friends, and she had a good job. But when she lost her job, we couldn't keep up with the prices of Idallis city, okay so we moved to Honeyville."

Her expression softened, her breath decrescendoing from sharp inhales to light ones.

I told her about how I got here, how Mazie helped, and why I was solving the case. I made up about the fact that the agency would give me "benefits" for solving the case, because I don't think it's a good idea to tell them about my plan with the wish in the Sparrow Constellation.

"Disha, I swear I'm not a thief--" before I could finish, she squeezed my hands and pulled me into a hug. I didn't know why, but my eyes were going to water if I didn't blink hard enough. Must've been the dust and dirt in the city.

"Aww, friendship." Robert smiled behind us, waiting for Disha's vexed reaction.

Disha looked at the other envelopes in the stash and said, "Is it rude to sift through the other mail?"

"Probably." I said.

"Hey man," Robert said, "She *gave* you her fingerprint, she's gotta deal with the consequences." He concluded and darted to the mail before we could even say anything.

It's definitely an invasion of privacy, and maybe illegal. But she *did* give me her fingerprint, and in a way, I'm helping her, because this person looks like they're pressuring her into something that's in two days.

Robert opened another envelop and glanced at Disha, "Dude I'm serious, I'm not gonna do anything illegal, it's just that the opportunity came up and--"

Disha raised an eyebrow, and crossed her arms, glaring at Robert. He didn't give in and turned the other way, tearing open the letter. Disha sighed.

The green smoke from the chimneys was fading into just small puffs from the large houses. An eerie feeling filled my stomach, so eerie that if all of the doors randomly opened, I wouldn't be surprised.

"No way. No way." Robert repeated over and over, "Oh there's no way, there's no way."

"What?" I asked, I leaned over his shoulder to read the letter:

A puzzle clinked into the picture. The lightbulbs finally turned on. The pieces are coming together. This case *isn't* impossible.

Your precious orb.

How many powerful orbs can there be out there? Tons, maybe. But the inference isn't a weak one.

"Felix Zecron," Disha said breathlessly, "Campbell, this man or woman in disguise is Felix Zecron, the one, the Vanisher," She turned to me, "Sie, you're practically sisters with Mazie, just take us to her, she'll tell us about this Cambell, and we'll get help to fight him, problem solved."

Satisfaction rushed through my veins, "Okay, okay, okay. We'll take the train to Edmonia, find Mazie, *if she's not already vanished,* and then find Campbell, reveal them, and boom. Case solved."

"Wait, how many *orbs* are in Philoxenia?" Robert asked, "Or are we just going with luck?"

"Just go with luck, Robert." Disha rolled her eyes.

As we turned to find a way to jump over the fence and go onto the other side of the town, the green puffs from the chimneys suddenly paused. They let out a large gush of steam and abruptly stopped.

I scooted closer to Robert and Disha, and we all watched the chimney like our lives depended on it. Well, it kind of did.

Large circular shadows zoomed over us, and above me were those UFO's from before. *Gulp.*

Every single door opened in the neighborhood, but no one was there. And the creatures from the UFO's slid down ladders, slowly forming a circle around us.

They had green manes and blue skin, almost resembling horses standing on two feet. They each slowly thrusted their hands behind them, summoning little phones that came flying through each door. Their eyes locked in on us, and each one was whispering in their phones. One large creature who summoned her phone from the large house on the corner shouted into her phone, "Disha Raj, Mazie Polaris, and Robert Wilgrinton, you three have been violating Philoxenian laws by trespassing through private properties."

So were they really after Reeva Harvey? Or were they after us?

They encircled us closer and closer, and now we're just two feet away from them instead of 2 yards.

Their deep blue eyes locked in with ours and they leaned forward. A series of whispers dominoed through their circle and they all faced their phones to us. This is it. There's no way out, we're going to get arrested.

"Mazie Polaris," They affirmed.

I gulped, fidgeting with my thumb.

"You are a suspect for the Vanisher vs Cordelia case." They turned to Disha and Robert, "and since you were in the vicinity of the disappearance, you two are also suspects."

I exchanged panicked looks with Disha and Robert, I kept looking for a way out. They're not too tall, maybe we could escape–

One of the large creatures was approaching us, a stiff green vest to match her mane and eyes as big as our three combined and they flickered green. She kneeled down to be our height and said, "The crimes you commit, you will pay for."

I couldn't help but notice her vest, it had something familiar on it–a feather. A purple feather. I took a breath the size of the ocean and leaned closer to her, "We're sorry." I whispered as I snatched the feather. She looked at me, bewildered.

"You will be sorry."

The UFO lowered and shot out a ramp that led to the entrance of the vehicle. The creatures blocking the ramp stepped aside, eyeing us three to take the ramp.

I can't go to jail. What about the wish? What about Aunt Katelyn? I have four feathers now, I can't give up. Just two more. Two more.

As we started walking down the dirt aisle to the ramp, the creatures made close lines parallel to us.

"It's okay, we're just suspects," Robert assured, "They can't put us in jail for being witnesses."

For once, he had a point. But there's no turning back now, even if we were the ones being arrested. This has to be the worst coincidence that I've ever been a part of.

The light in the UFO was blinding, but once the light faded away, all there was inside was a myriad of panels and controls. There weren't any seats or rooms.

And as soon as they ordered us to sit on the cold floor, the lights went out. Or maybe I was just exhausted.

When the lights flashed on, we were already at the large building that even more creatures were patrolling.

"Let's go, let's go." The large creature pushed, I looked back, and for a split second her blue eyes turned green, and her green mane turned into those long black locks. She grabbed us and we three slid down the large ramp, and into the entrance of the large building.

As we walked inside, it was nothing like I had imagined. Yes, there were cells, but there was a blue luminescence filling the rooms. There were no stairs, but platforms that took the creatures to different levels. Some of the cells were rusting with rods just like the ones in my world. And others had glass walls, and glass doors.

But inside every cell was a bed that went from one end of the wall to the other. And there was nothing else. Nothing.

We reached one of those rusting, traditional cells, and the creature threw us in there, muttering, "Stay here until further investigation."

I glanced at Disha, "The system here is just like the one at home."

She shrugged, "No one said Philoxenia is completely original and unique."

We both sat on the bed, and Robert chose to slump to the ground, leaning his head against the wall. We all had bits of everything on us. We all smelled like clay and antique mansions, dirt was all over us, and we definitely needed a shower.

Creatures came and went, I wanted to know *what* they were, but not even Disha knew. Hours passed by, and while I was exhausted, I couldn't get my eyes to close. It's like they were on alert mode this entire time, watching every detail of every situation.

I started at the ground reflecting that blue luminescence. There was a rectangular glass roof in the building, letting the stars be the other source of light. But other than the central part of the prison, all of the halls and jails were dark, our eyes depending on that blue light.

I'm already so deep into trouble, is there even a point continuing the Journey of the Sparrows? Or even solving this case? What am I going to actually get with it, a badge? And what would I do with that? And how can I go back home safely?

If I had the chance, would I go home? This late into the game? My hands and legs ached from all that flight or fight running and I wanted nothing more than to go into Aunt Katelyn's arms and feel her warmth. But that would mean leaving all of this progress we made. We just need to find Mazie.

I watched the moon shift across the sky as I thought about where Aunt Katelyn might be. A boulder of guilt crumbled in my stomach, did the circus camp notify her I was missing? Does she even know?

I just need to make this wish and everything will be fine. I just need her to see that constellation and bring success to us. And life will be as good as it can get.

"Come on. Come on." Robert murmured, he kept kicking the loose brick in the wall with his shoe, "Come on."

"Robert, what are you doing?" Disha asked. He didn't reply, he just kept kicking the brick until it loosened even more. And when it did, his eyes lit, straightening his posture to kick the brick at a better angle.

The brick scraped along the wall like chalk as it slid out, and to my surprise, laid a purple feather in the walls. He smiled from ear to ear, dusting off the feather and observing it like he discovered something new. "My fourth one, yes." I heard him say. My heart dropped to my stomach. So he really was collecting feathers.

"You're collecting feathers?" I asked, pretending I had no idea what they were.

"Kind of. If I get six, I'm going to make a wish for absolute intelligence so I can finally get stuff done. Like my Cornuport."

If I had four feathers, and he had four feathers, then how is this possible?

"How many feathers are there?" I asked. Disha explained.

"There's a lot out there," She explained, "But each person is only supposed to find six. The thing is, it's easy to find the first five, but the last one is impossible. And since every person's journey to finding the feather's is different, the sixth feather reflects that journey. There's like a pattern you're supposed to realize."

"Are you looking for them too?" Robert asked, she shook her head. "It's impossible, I told you."

"Robert," Disha began, "If you just study a lot, you'll be smart in no time."

"Yeah, but why would I work harder when I can work smarter? Then I can actually finish this project and maybe, everyone in my family wouldn't think I'm dumb."

"You're not dumb, Robert, if you're in this case. And look, you're almost done designing it!" I assured him.

He shook his head, "My dad's been on tons of cases, it's not that big of a deal to him."

I didn't know what to reply to him, so I just nodded my head, "It's alright, he'll realize your potential, if not now, then soon."

He gave a small smile, but silence filled the air and none of us talked for a while. We just watched the moon shift again.

What does the annoying auction guy, Samuel, the museum guy, and the creatures have to do with each other?

They were all different people, different jobs, different capabilities, and they had absolutely nothing to do with each other.

Are they all magical? Well, that's too broad, too easy of a pattern.

I kept wracking the four people in my brain back and forth, forcing a connection between them. There's nothing, I thought, nothing. Maybe I'll just wait for the fifth one and then I'll wait.

My head was slumped over Disha's shoulder, and she was counting the rust on every crevice of the walls. Robert was asleep.

To our surprise, an officer's footsteps approached us, and the gates opened, a numb expression on his face announcing, "Children, someone has bailed you out."

Chapter Twenty

The Obsidian Harbor, Obviously

A creature lined us up, one by one and had us walk out onto the elevator. The platform was almost shaking when I stood atop it but as soon as all three of us were on it, it dropped us to the first floor in just a split second.

The windows got bigger since we were now on the first floor, and the light was almost entirely from the stars outside, not from the eerie blue luminescence. Several large counters would emerge from the ground and go back into it too, serving as a desktop for all of the creatures. Whatever it is they were using the desks for.

A young man in a Whislow uniform was busy signing *onto* the counter at one of the desks. He had short brown hair with a red streak running through it, wait, was he at the convention with us?

He turned around and a smile approached his face, "There you three are." He turned back at the creatures eagerly waiting for him to finish singing the last thing. It was like the counter *was* a tablet.

"That should be enough," he told them, handing them a brown cloth bag that clanked when he tossed it onto the desk.

The doors in the front opened, letting in more starlight. And before we could say anything to him, ask him a question, the creatures holding the bag of money scurried over to us, and pushed us out the door. "No need for a trial!" they shouted from behind.

No trial? That's great news. But who are they suspecting then? Are they off our backs forever?

"You know that Shoemaker, Samuel Orion, he's been convicted. All signs point to him for this crime." the man said, turning his head toward me. It was like he read my mind.

But it makes sense, everyone disappearing but him, him knowing the ins and outs of Cordelia's council after being their designer.

Now, it was just us three, and the young man out in the breezy night filled with shadows, stars, and no shelter.

"I'm Rex Parson, by the way." He turned his neck back to look at each one of us.

"Disha."

"It's Robert."

"I'm…" I paused, should I go with Mazie? Or with Sienna? I mean all of the political places think I'm Mazie, but he literally bailed us out, so he would mind the truth, would he?

"Mazie."

I was half-expecting Disha to be uneasy with the lie, but she was immune to it.

"Mazie?"

"Yes." I gulped. He let out a gentle smile, "Nice to meet all of you."

We kept walking down a sandy path where I heard faint waves crashing along the shore. Meadows filled everything but the path and from here and there, the ocean thought it was a good idea to spray us with sea mist in this cold, cold, night.

"Why'd you bail us out?" Robert cut to the chase.

"Be grateful, it's not that hard." I heard Disha mutter in his ear.

"I was sent on this case too, as a witness of Cordelia's disappearance. I was at that open-for-all meeting, with you too." He pointed at Robert and I.

"And after discovering it was Samuel Orion, I heard they already found suspects, *you three*. It just didn't make sense, it was unjust. With the bail, they let you guys go home before having to wait for Samuel's trial to be over. "

"Well I thought it was Felix Zecron," Robert added, perplexed. We were outside in the cold meadows now, with the prison shrinking more and more as we walked into the wispy grass.

Rex slowly nodded, "That's what I thought, too. But he's been gone since Macladez Zecron passed, the orb was never in his possession, unlike what the will promised."

A part of me was glad, happy, that this case was over. Solved. That the Vanisher was finally sent to where they belong. But the rest of me feels regretful. I wasted all this time, trying to solve a case that's unsolvable by an eleven-year-old. I left Aunt Katelyn back home. Does she even know I'm not at camp? I only have four feathers, and the last one is *impossible* to find. But that's all I have left from this dimension, the wish.

There's no point going to Edmonia anymore. No point finding Campbell anymore.

The meadows rest into dirt trails, like dusts of flowers scattered over the road as if a second string to street lights.

"Where are we going?" Robert questioned.

Rex looked at him confused, "Back to the Whislow Agency, so you guys can go home."

Disha stopped, like bad news of the century has been dropped on her shoulders, "We're done? Just done?"

Rex nodded, "I thought you guys would be relieved."

It was clear in Disha's eyes, no case solved means no badge.

"We are." Robert answered, "What makes you think we're not?"

"No, 'Thank you' and the long faces, it's pretty clear."

"First of all, thank you, Rex. It's just…" I began, "We've wasted a lot of time on this."

"No time spent on a case is wasted, Mazie."

That's true. You'd have to learn *something*.

We kept walking along the sandy path, until Robert slowed his pace, with a concerned look. "I don't think I could go home from Whislow---my dad doesn't live here."

"Neither does my aunt." I agreed.

Rex paused, eyeing the ground, "We can always stay at my place for a little while before I take you all home."

And that's what we agreed on. He didn't live too far away.

It felt weird trusting a random stranger, but honestly *everyone's* a stranger in Philoxenia to me. And in just a few hours I'll be home, to my favorite non-stranger, Aunt Katelyn. Just a few hours until I'm back home, with no case solved, no wish made, and nothing gained from the world.

It was a sharp feeling.

The flat sandy path turned into small hills with a neighborhood of little huts, each one with different types of roofs, some made of traditional straw. Others had innovative tiles that turned into different colors as the breeze hit them.

Rex pointed to the far hut on the left, it was a mix of both. The walls were white tiles that chimed different colors but the roof was made of blue wood. And the door was just a velvet curtain.

He spread the curtains open, "Welcome to my cozy home."

Until this point, I've realized I've never seen a *home* before in Philoxenia. Yes, there's a bed, and multiple rooms. But there's no kitchen. Just a large Rubik's cube with each face a different color sitting in the corner. There was a sofa, luckily, and that was about it.

"Hungry?" He asked, he reached his arm out to the puzzle cube and rotated the top row down. A whole table filled with soup, noodles, pies, cakes, bread, curries, and sandwiches crowded the table. The cube he had was just like those bakeries back in Idallis. Weird.

Until this point, I've realized I haven't eaten in a while.

We wolfed down on almost everything, waiting for Rex to rotate another face to lend us water.

"Does everyone have that cube at home?" I asked, finishing my last bite of cake.

Rex laughed like I asked him a silly question, "Yes, obviously. Aren't you from here?"

The persona I created was a girl named Mazie who's been a part of the Whislow Agency for years, why'd I fumble with this one question?

"Yes, but I've seen different ones, I'm wondering if this *type is common.*" I gulped, trying to shoo his suspicions away.

"In this neighborhood, certainly. Some larger, some smaller." He chuckled again, "Ironically, Macladez Zecron's great, great, great grandparents created this invention ever since they discovered what electricity was in the other universe. You could just *switch* lights or a fan on. So why not other things?"

After dinner, Rex offered to lend us some entertainment, rotating another face to activate three-dimensional holographic motion pictures. Or in my case, a TV.

We sat down on the couch, absorbing whatever channels came on.

"Our most recent suspect, arrested just a few hours ago for the global crisis, Samuel Orion, has disappeared."

Our eyes widened as the news was delivered by a stressed news anchor, trembling in his seat, like he was next.

"Sitting in his cell before his court case, he, and almost every other being in the jail has disappeared. We've placed our most powerful reciprocal-restraining devices on him, and yet a mass disappearance has occurred. We shall continue this case further. Stay tuned"

"Do you know what this means?" Disha stood up, announcing. "This case isn't over. The Vanisher is still out *there*."

"But all signs pointed to Sam." Rex questioned, perplexed. "I've been solving cases for ten years, and not once have I incorrectly solved one."

Part of me lit up, my chance was back. But another part of me was confused, what now? We barely have any clues. I'm not as knowledgeable as Mazie–

That's it.

"Hey Rex," I asked, "Do you think you could take us to the Kingdom of Edmonia, there's someone I think who could help us."

"Almost everyone in Edmonia has disappeared." Rex said with a sigh, "Whislow's been taken down too."

Disha said, "Then where–"

"The Obsidian Harbor, obviously." He replied.

I anticipated the panic to set in for Disha, but instead, she looked numb. Maybe after everything that's happened, nothing fazes her anymore.

I asked Rex, "Is that where Felix is?" He shook his head and kept walking down the sandy path.

"It will be impossible to find where he is. He is Macladez's *son* after all. So, it's important to find the Clever Element instead."

Robert glanced at me, "The Reeva Harvey thing?" he whispered in my ear. Well, she's gone, so I don't know what Rex is going to do about it.

As we headed out of the huts and followed Rex, Rex repeated, "It's someone who sacrifices, someone who endures, and someone who isn't what they seem." He grabbed a large stick from the dry marshes and used it to climb as our sandy path turned into hills. "The Clever Element is the key factor for this whole plan the Vanisher is doing. Once they've collected every bit of magic, they activate the Clever Element to tie all of the magic together. If we find that person, and wait long enough, we'll find Felix, too."

Oh. Now this all made sense. The satisfaction was getting closer and closer. If we solve this case, and maybe get *some* kind of reward, then that should be enough.

Rex snapped his fingers in the air and craned his neck to the sky. A large Geoport came crashing down, almost hitting us before we jumped out of the way into the crisp marshes.

The Geoport landed on its sides, its bars full of rust and the little pad inside was completely shut.

"That is not something my reciprocal powers can fix." Rex admitted. He slowly took a hold of the bars and thrusted it back up, "A little help?" He grunted. We reached one corner each and pushed it right-side-up.

Rex tried surprising himself by hovering his hands over the pad inside, the pad vibrated an inch but nothing else happened. He kept forcing and grounding his hand, "Work…work, …work." The pad vibrated more and more, until the little lights switched on. Rex kept pushing until the rods shook and now, the Geoport was hovering a foot off of the ground.

"Let's go guys." He said.

We hopped in and the Geoport and it set off, occasionally dipping a couple yards below as Rex took pauses when holding his hand over the pad.

"Macladez Zecron's office is there. He has files and everything, if we can find out *who* it is with that information, we'll be set." He said, holding a pen and paper in the other hand, drawing from what I could see, comets.

Robert took his blueprint out again and was busy sketching that too. I remembered what he said earlier and kneeled down next to him, "You know Robert…all inventors are geniuses."

He looked up from his project and rolled his eyes, "Be quiet, Sienna, you don't understand."

It was the first time he looked absolutely angry, his face slightly red and his sketches getting even more aggressive, "Your aunt seems really nice, okay? She probably believes in you in everything. You don't have family members who always dismiss you, or believe you have no future."

Disha overheard the conversion and knelt down too, "Look, Robert, just because you're absolutely unhinged, doesn't mean you're not smart."

He replied, "Disha, all you want from this case is a badge, okay? You have a brain, so take care of it." He brushed it off and didn't say anything afterward. "And I'll get back to you once I've made that wish. Or finished this project."

So he stayed true to his words and kept sketching until I saw the other end of the sea crashing waves onto a harbor. We were getting close.

Overhead the rods, the Sparrow Constellation was glistening above the waters. The stars were so bright their reflection in the ocean was just blasts of purple radiance.

I took a deep breath, "Thanks, once again, for bailing us out, I don't think I would've survived out there."

He smiled again, not looking up from his drawing, "Consider it the favor of a new friend."

Suddenly, a purple flower glistened underneath the pad, and I grabbed out to reach for it, and inch away from another hand. Robert's hand.

"You're collecting them?" Robert asked.

I nodded, "Yes…I know, I know…"

He shook his head softly, "It's fine, Sienna, really."

I gave a sigh of relief, it was my fifth one, which meant I only needed one more. And I couldn't deal with any conflict now.

"What are you going to wish for?" He asked, erasing some lines from his blueprint.

We were already so far into the case, far into everything, that I couldn't lie now.

"Well, I've seen the Sparrow Constellation from back home, but my aunt couldn't. And if I could get *everyone* to see it, having them thinking I discovered it, it would launch my astronomical career and get my family out of a bad situation." Now that I said it out loud, yes, it did sound a little corrupt. A little greedy.

"But you don't need to, if your aunt already believes in you." Robert said.

I guess that was somewhat true, but it wasn't to prove myself to her, but to *us,* that we were capable enough to be successful.

I said out loud, "My aunt used to be in a circus, and she's probably faced this many times. Trying to prove her competence. But once she had to take care of me, there's more to it. "

Disha didn't respond, but I could tell through the slight irritation on her face she didn't like my idea of the wish. But she did steal the idea of the reciprocal for *her* newspaper article.

"*Mazie*, you always have to prove yourself to people, don't you? You don't care about anyone, not even yourself, except that stupid validation!" Disha yelled. It came out of nowhere.

Rex glanced at me, my eyes widened and my veins were boiling but I could barely muster out a sentence.

"I do care about people. I really do. I'm doing this for my aunt."

"Then why do you always have to preach about Aunt Katelyn's eminent role in a circus? Every time! To everyone! Back at the circus camp, here, the ghost town. And what's next, you telling everyone you can see purple stars?"

My face grew hot and my blood boiled in my veins. I don't brag, and what does she know? I thought she cared for me, that hug meant nothing. "Then what are you on this case for? The badge, right? You don't have a loved one to save. You're not doing this for the better future of the community. You're just on this mission to prove yourself, too. "

Disha looked down at her shoes and fidgeted, "Well at least I don't live in the past like and brag about something so irrelevant."

"My goals aren't irrelevant!"

"Think about it, when you make the purple stars visible, there will be people with the Reciprocal of our world. People who knew about these stars for a long time, but kept it a secret because that's just the norms of Philoxenia."

"They won't be mad when the rest of the world can see the stars. They'll be proud they can share a piece of their culture. At least I'm not following everyone else and getting a common badge."

"But don't you get it? You didn't discover the constellation! They've known about it longer than you have, and when they realize you took advantage of their world, you'll drive them insane!"

"Like you did with your theory on the "reciprocal" in the newspaper?"

Silence.

The Geoport started lowering and the salty scent was all around us. Even though I had an insight of the harbor from Reeva's past, the feeling just didn't sit right with me: the sea crashing into the abandoned ship, the forest filled with redwood that didn't promise a definitive answer of what was to come, and a grumpy Disha. I guess, it's going to be an interesting investigation here.

Chapter Twenty-One

The Legend of the Sparrows is Not A Legend

I held out the letters we got from Mazie's mail to show to Rex, "Look, this Felix or Campbell" is asking Mazie to meet her at the Platform Portal. We should just go there."

"But she seems very skeptical in these letters, Sienna. Why would she come to the Platform Portal?"

He's got a point.

When we landed, the evergreen trees danced restlessly in the wind. There was an ocean softly crashing on the rocks, syncopating with the music the trees made. The grass was damp and all was left was a wooden board with broken, almost rubbed off letters announcing:

My eyes widened and backed away from the sign, I'm not turning into a star. No way. Not today.

Disha grabbed Robert's jacket's collar, "T-that's…"

Rex sighed, "Yes, it's the camp site." He gestured with his arm for us to follow him, "C'mon, we have to find Zecron's office."

"He has an office?" I asked. Rex turned back and nodded, he took out his watch and shone a light on the path he was walking toward.

Above us, shone the Sparrow Constellation, its purple stars reflecting in the ocean. Aunt Katelyn will see them soon. Soon.

The tug of Disha didn't soften, I glanced at her, "You good, Disha?"

She shook her head, her heart was pounding so loud that even I could hear it.

Robert narrowed his eyes, "Okay, I'm creeped out too but not to the point where I'm–"

"Enough, Robert." She said, her voice solid.

Rex paused in his tracks, exchanging a concerned look with Disha, "What's going on?"

We took Disha's arms and stabilized her on her feet. She took a deep breath, "When Mazie used to work at the Agency, she let me volunteer at the Orb Preservation room."

She let go of his jacket, "There was this orb she just made called the Pseudo-Orb, which could disguise itself as any orb she wanted."

She took another deep breath, "So when I went to do my weekly orb dusting, I thought it was the real Zecron Orb I was dusting, which doesn't activate that often. But no, it was the Pseudo-orb, and when I touched it. It brought me here."

She gestured her hand around the Obsidian Harbor,

"I was coming here and I saw Macladez Zecron turning my family over. From Honeyville into his henchmen."

She closed her eyes, "His descendants and ancestors flying around saying stuff like, Disha, take us home. Stay with us Disha…" Her hands were trembling immensely, her gaze vigilant around the harbor.

Rex shook his head, "Whislow's responsible for the most fraudulent inventions, it's just trying to get into your head, none of it is actually real."

"You sure?"

"I promise."

Her stiffened gaze didn't soften and his promise didn't help her feel any more secure. But she was ready to keep walking. I glanced at her, my fists still hot from her words back at the Geoport.

We began walking to Zecron's office again. It was a dim cabin with red shutters swallowing the tide.

Rex opened the door and switched on candles by the desk that dominated the room. There was a rocking chair in the corner, an open window, and most of all, a desk cluttered with numerous files. I expected the room to look at least somewhat modern, but there were no galactic walls or thirtieth century tablet tables. Instead, the office, or cabin, had wall simply constructed with wooden planks that creaked with the minuscule movement of the air.

"Start reading, folks." Robert said, and began to dive into the files.

For the first hour, we spent time reading manifestos and lists of items that definitely weren't in English. I couldn't shake the feeling that something was lurking in the office. Like those ghost-hunting movies always airing after a kid's nursery rhyme show back in Idallis City. My spine tingled; the room definitely had some secrets hiding in the walls. I could feel it.

Robert found a picture and lifted it up above the candle, "Check this out!"

It was a sketch of that instrument back at the Hall of Unsuspecting Coincidences. The instrument that Mazie had. The Manipulating Mertilda.

"But what does that have anything to do with Zecron?" I asked.

Rex shook his head, "Beats me…" He took a deep breath, "I mean I used to have a friend who was a musician and was my partner back at Whislow a very, very long time ago. You could say—musicians get powerful and so independent, that you're shunned away. Maybe that's what Zecron did. Perhaps he was a musician."

We looked at Rex, the corners of his eyes becoming misty from the thought of his long-lost friend who left him.

The Manipulating Mertilda. I thought again. Speaking of the Hall of Unsuspecting Coincidences, it still puzzled me how they had our *exact* caravan.

Maybe that auction guy knew the museum director? I mean both of their eyes were flickering green, and I found feathers along them.

And they're both annoying, maybe that's the pattern?

Rex glanced at me, then glanced back at Zecron's files, and then back at me again, perplexed. "Something wrong?" He asked.

I twitched my lips, "It's just weird how I saw my aunt's trailer back at the Hall of Unsuspecting Coincidences."

"Well, she must be famous here."

I shook my head, "No, she's from the Tech world."

Rex narrowed his eyes; I can't tell if it's because of this case or because of my aunt's situation.

"Has she done anything…associated with the reciprocal?"

I shook my head again, "No."

"Well what about your parents?"

The question numbed me, "She's never mentioned them. I just know she's my dad's little sister. "

Rex softly dropped the papers back onto the desk and turned to me, "Do you want answers?"

"Of course I do, of my aunt's, especially."

He picked the papers back up, and I peeked through under his arm, they're just Zecron's manifestos. Manifestos that combining all magic entities into one, the benefits of his authority, the nuisance of children with magic, and tons of other problematic ideologies.

Robert was in the corner, flipping through notebooks filled with indecipherable words, and Disha was sifting through the other drawers, pretending not to listen. But her face showed it clearly, her eyebrows narrowing at every question Rex asked, and then dissatisfied at every answer I gave.

"I've always wanted to know more about my father, and do the things he's done. But my mother never cared to finish what he started. So, as soon as we've cracked this case, we'll get answers, okay Mazie?"

Maybe he has his own questions he needs answers to, too. Mentioning his absent father, there's probably a census bank here somewhere, filled with citizens of Philoxenia. Who knows? What if Aunt Katelyn is one of them?

I nodded, "Alright."

"So," Disha began, changing the topic back to the case, "Are we still suspecting it's Felix?"

Everyone nodded, "Find anything about him?" Robert asked, she shook her head.

She pointed up to the Sparrow Constellation, "Could that help in any way?"

"That last wish the constellation has." Rex added, "it's really powerful. And Felix could use it to manipulate the magic even further."

"Then one of us should make that wish before he does," I implied. I should probably *volunteer* to make that wish, you know, since it'll be convenient.

"No, we need to destroy that last wish." Rex concluded.

Those words hit me like our old circus trailer at full speed.

"*Can* you even destroy one?" Disha asked, disturbed by his comment as well. I'm sure she'd *volunteer* to make that wish.

Rex fidgeted with the lamp on Zecron's desk in a thought. Everything in the room felt like it was flickering. Sometimes files would be on the desk and for a split second they'd be gone. The pens and lamps would do the same.

"If Sam reappeared, would they re-arrest him?" Robert asked, changing the subject again.

"Yes, of course he would." Rex answered, he narrowed his eyes at Robert, "Why do you ask?"

"I don't know…he was just a poor little guy trying to make some shoes. What if he got sent back so the real Vanisher could still keep their cover?"

Robert had a good point, if you committed a crime, and someone else got arrested, why would you make them look innocent?

"Well, *when* we find the actual Vanisher, we'll replace Sam with him. Or would you prefer that *you* were in jail right now?" Rex questioned.

Disha's eyes widened, "No we would not prefer that, Rex."

"A bail does not come cheap, you know." He said with a sigh.

Disha looked sick to her stomach, "And you're sure no one is tracking us three? No UFOs or creatures on our trail?"

"That I don't know. But that bail should keep you guys safe for at least a while."

My stomach started making somersaults and it felt like nervous fireworks were exploding in my chest, "We were pretty much the only ones in that council room, and after my proposal—she." A lump formed in my throat and suffocated any words wanting to escape.

Rex patted my head, "It's alright Mazie, I'm keeping you guys safe. You all are guilty of nothing and even the Vanisher can't attack you. Your lack of reciprocity is really benefiting you here."

Disha calmed down, "Okay. Okay."

I felt the ruffles of feathers underneath my fingertips in my pocket. Just two more. Just two more.

I sifted again through the files on the tables, finding a list in *English*.

1. *Reeva Harvey*

2. *Mazie Polaris*

3. *Disha Raj*

"Hey Disha," I called, "You might want to look at this."

She came over and as soon as she saw the list, she fell back, almost fainting.

"What's it about?" Robert asked. I shook my head in confusion, trying to talk myself through the puzzle, I said, "Well Reeva's connection with Zecron is that she's the Clever Element. So you and Mazie–Mazie Polaris"

Someone who endures, someone who sacrifices, someone who isn't what they seem.

"The Clever Element," Rex began, "Is what's going to activate Felix's Zecron orb."

I turned to Disha, her face was pale and she was sitting on the floor, rocking herself back and forth and back and forth and back and forth.

I signed, kneeling down to her, trying to disregard all the things she said back in the Geoport, "If it makes you feel better, you don't have the reciprocal yet, so it's more likely that it's Mazie."

Her face relaxed just a little, "Okay, okay, yeah, you're right. It *has* to be Mazie Polaris."

285

Rex smirked, "It's funny how you and Mazie Polaris have the same name."

I got it, changing the subject for once in for all, "Well if Mazie is the missing piece. And if Felix doesn't have that, then he can't activate *all* of the magic yet. We just need to somehow get that element out of Mazie in time."

"The orb. The orb!" Rex shouted, scurrying around Zecron's desk through all of the papers and files. "That's the single most important thing to activate and deactivate anything of Zecron's power."

"The Enchanted Orb could be anywhere." I said, "How are we supposed to find it, go to Mazie Polaris, all before Felix comes there?"

"We'll split up." Rex added.

"Mazie, you go back to the Whislow Agency, Robert, you go to Edmonia, and Disha, go back to Reeva Harvey's mansion just in case it's still Reeva who's the Clever Element."

Rex paused, "But we can't take the Geoport or any magical transport, it'll be too obvious in front of Felix."

He turned to Robert, who was scanning his blueprint while we were discussing. Rex snapped his fingers, "Perfect!"

Robert looked up from his blueprint, "May I help you?" Unable to comprehend the grin on Rex's face.

"Start building the–"

"Cornuport?" Robert finished his sentence, his eyes widened, "No you don't understand, I *can't* build this. I'm not ready."

Rex shook his head, stretching his arms out, "We're in Zecron's office, you can probably find anything you need for your engineering project, right here."

With much persuading, Robert gave in and finally began to assemble his Cornuport, or as the Tech World states, the ultimate jetpack.

Disha, Rex, and I strolled around the office, only to find no other pieces of evidence. We have to be sure that it's Mazie, not Disha, or anyone else, or else this entire plan to keep Mazie from being the Clever Element could go haywire.

"We need to cover more ground," Rex began, "There are cabins from the camp a couple of blocks away."

We all backed up, "No, there's no way we're going near anything that has to do with camps."

Rex proposed, "Robert should keep working, and someone should keep him company, and the other one of you two and I should cover more ground."

Disha pinned her finger to the tip of her nose, "I'm staying here. I'm not going there."

Oh great.

We began walking through the meadow patches again to meet the Obsidian Harbor Camp sign.

"Do you know if Mazie Polaris or Reeva Harvey ever came to this camp?" I asked him.

He shook his head, "Not that I know of."

A wolf howled in the distance; I jolted as it scattered my thoughts everywhere.

This place was creepy.

There were wooden cabins that lined up alongside the trees, some large, some small.

A large circle of grass was found further back.

"Probably it's where the camp kids went to play. " Rex hypothesized.

He stepped towards the nearest cabin, and creaked open the door, gesturing for me to follow.

"No way am I going in there." I responded. I was willing to wait outside while he briefly scanned it, concluding, "I don't think the cabins have anything to do with this case."

We kept strolling around for more clues. Other than the cabins and the first sign we saw indicating of the camp's location, there was nothing else here. Only trees stretched for miles, with branches wrapped in colorful yarn holding what seemed to be Thank You notes to Zecron.

This was where Estrella found one of her feathers. I slowly stepped toward the tree, with Rex cautiously pacing behind me. As I reached my tip-toes and let my fingers fly through the thins notes that waved in the wind, no two notes were alike. I couldn't find Mateos, or any of the other stars', but all of them were some form of *We appreciate you, Mr.Zecron"* or *"You're the best, Mr.Zecron!"*

"C'mon Mazie, we gotta keep going."

It seemed to me like Rex was a sole agent, no group or partner in solving anything. Except for that musician friend he had a while back.

"Do you play an instrument, too?" I asked. He shook his head in response, not keeping his eyes off of the pathway between the cabins and the small walkways in the crevices of each cabin. He stopped between ever cabin, took out his flashlight and scanned every nook.

"No, why do you ask?"

"Well since your friend was one, and I thought maybe you'd know a thing or two about the Manipulating Mertilda— you know, from the picture we found back in the cabin."

He shrugged, "I mean sure, my friend might've taught me a thing or two, but they'd always play for the children. Not much of a teacher. I'd say that instrument was probably just Zecron's hobby, but if you find any special chalk that goes with it, then it's serious."

The chalk is what makes the music dangerous, I remembered. And I can't tell if it's a good thing or bad thing that Felix or even Macladez Zecron himself would use it. Most likely bad.

When we got to the end line of all the cabins, we realized we found nothing in the span of two hours.

"Did Macladez Zecron ever teach his students here anything about their magic?" I asked.

He responded, dryly, "I've never been to his camps before but—" He thought, "It would probably be simple tricks, he would probably never share his projects with anyone."

I mean that made sense, this Zecron guy definitely did like power, and so does his son, Felix, picking up after him.

Probably conscious of the fact that he has an eleven-year-old girl next to him, Rex decided not to investigate the camp any further.

"Everything here is so…so *dry*." Rex concluded, "There's nothing. Nothing at all."

We began our way back to the dimly lit cabin and when I opened the door,

Disha was rocking on her back, looking paler than ever. Robert's project was almost done, to my greatest surprise, but he dropped all the tools to comfort Disha, who looked like she saw a ghost.

I kneeled next to her freaked out face, "Disha, what happened?"

She shook her head, trembling, not saying a word. Robert took a swallow and responded, "Well, I was working on my Cornuport, and it's coming along not too bad. And just a couple of minutes ago, we both heard these whispers saying, *Disha, Disha, Disha*."

The news sent chills down my spine. There was something lurking nearby.

"Then are you the Clever Element?" I asked her, she bit her lip and shrugged nervously. "Oh I hope not."

"Why don't" Rex began, "We all stay quiet and help Robert finish his Cornuport to see if the sound comes back."

So that's what we did. Robert took advantage of the wood and screws from Zecron's furniture and started assembling together his Cornuport.

"It's now or never," Robert said, "I'm making this now or never." He was trying to talk himself through the process, so he could actually *finish* this thing.

"I'm never working in that Orb Preservation room again." Disha concluded, handing him a couple of bolts she could find.

Robert nodded, "Yeah I don't think that energy in there is good for you."

I nodded in agreement.

Robert narrowed his eyes, "Anyone have any thread?"

Rex grinned, "There's plenty of yarn thread outside on the trees. I'll fetch it for you." He sprinted out with a gust of wind following behind him.

"Disha, Disha. Are you there, Disha?" Disha jumped, creaking the floor underneath us. "You heard that, Sienna, right? You heard that?"

I nodded, terrified, "Yes I did." The voice was monotone and soft, unlike any voice I've heard before.

"I come in peace." Disha said, breathing heavily. "Who are you?"

Silence.

"I asked, who are you?"

The same voice replied, "You don't need to know, my dear. But my son, Felix, has a present for you all."

It was Macladez.

"Holy moly," Robert whined, "It's that creepy legend guy."

His present sure enough appeared. A large piece of green twine appeared before our eyes.

"Hey, can you give me my last couple of feathers?" Robert screamed, "I appreciate it!"

No response.

Robert took the twine, "No worries! Thanks for the twine, I could really use it!"

He then used that to tie a couple of pillars on the bottom of the Cornuport in place.

And a while later, Rex swung in through the door, leaves ruffled in his hair along the red stripe.

"I got some yarn, man," He said, out of breath, "Those kids tied the string to the branches extremely tight."

And no more than two hours later, the Cornuport was finished. A gray, jetpack looking device with two straps and a screen behind it.

"Alright," Rex said, rearranging the files back on Zecron's desk and pushing the unscrewed drawers back in place, "The Cornuport's loaded, we all know what to do."

Robert said, "There's only one."

Rex scoffed, "Nonsense," He stretched out his hand and quadrupled the Cornuport into four, "Felix can't stop us if we have transportation due to plain science, now let's go."

Like before, I was assigned to go to the Whislow Agency. Maybe the orb would be there, and then I can bring it back to Edmonia where Robert will go to find Mazie.

We stood outside in the pitch-black darkness that was brightening into daylight. As per Robert's instructions, we switched on the flips and the engine was starting. After much instability and wobbling of the engine, my feet rose into the air. The mist from the sky was soaking in my face and there I was, off, to Whislow.

Chapter Twenty-Two

The Enchanted Orb Knows Everything

The Whislow Agency was absolute chaos, and the Orb Preservation Room looked absolutely demolished, there was *nothing* in there. Nothing but crumbling shelves and glitching walls.

I ran from hallway to hallway to find absolutely no one.

Time is running out. Time is running out. Felix could be there by now.

I found a room as I was running through one of the hallways with bright doors, through one of them, I heard chattering. It said, "Nurse's Clinic".

I opened the door and saw Estrella coughing inside, a bandage wrapped around her unicorn horn.

"Mazie." She said, coughing in between the syllables, "I'm so glad someone's still here."

I ran up to her bed and held her hand, "What's wrong, Estrella? What happened?"

"I was hurt and…pyrexia." She said, I could feel her hands trembling in my palm.

A nurse walked in, holding a tray of some yellow drink to serve to Estrella, "Take small sips." She instructed.

I have a concerned look at the nurse, glancing at Estrella and back. The nurse informed, "Pyrexia is a medical term for a fever, she's been feeling *extremely* warm. But she shall be well in a week or so."

I needed to get back to Mazie or at least I had find the orb. But I couldn't just leave Estrella, not after her being sick and hurt. Aunt Katelyn wouldn't leave me if I was sick, she just wouldn't.

I rocked back and forth on my feet.

She struggled out a couple words, "Mazie, is my brother okay?"

A pit dropped into my stomach, "Yes." I softly said, looking up at the ceiling. I stuffed my hands in my pockets and dug out one of the crumpled letters. It hit me.

If it's anything dangerous, just know you won't see your precious orb again.

Mazie knows where the orb is.

She *has* the orb.

How did we not see that?

"Go."

"What?" I looked down at her, a smile tugging on the corners of her blue lips.

"That look in your eyes, you solved something. Go. Go! Make sure my brother is okay. The nurse is here, don't worry."

I sprung up from the squeaky-clean tiles, "I will, Estrella. I'll be back!" I announced as I slid out of the clinic and initiated the jetpack again.

It was rocky, but fast enough to get me where I needed. My legs were breezing through the wind as the train swooshed past me underneath my feet. The large, red-brick colored castle was emerging from the hills in front of me.

Edmonia.

When I arrived at Mazie's home, Disha had sunk to her knees and Robert was pacing the floor.

"Guys, Mazie has the orb! She has the orb!" I repeated.

"We know."

The entire place was a mess. Instruments were broken, their strings found all over the floor. All of the curtains were open, every book was anywhere but on the shelves. And the orb sat in front of us, dim and dark.

"It's right here." Robert informed me, "But we're too late, she's gone."

I turned to Disha, the girl who always perseveres, and wouldn't stop until she got what she wanted, no matter how stubborn or arrogant she got. But when I looked into her eyes, the dark brown eyes transitioned into that glowish green. The green like that Auction guy, Samuel, that creature who arrested us, and now Disha.

"Disha, I know you were always uneasy with me here, and I get it, I wouldn't trust someone with another person's fingerprint. But please–"

"People are disappearing, there is no point in continuing this any further, Sienna. Or Mazie? I guess you've finally replaced her."

Disha took off her jacket and wrapped it over her arms. She stepped over the debris. "Where are you going?" I asked her.

"Back to Whislow."

"But–"

She shook her head, "Mazie's already been taken, the key piece to ruling the dimension. We can't stop that. We failed, Sienna. We failed this case."

"How do we know she's gone, though?" I asked. "What if she's running errands or–"

"She's gone, Sienna." Disha said, her eyes flickering. A sharp feeling hit my stomach. Like the annoying auction guy, Samuel Orion, the Hall of Unsuspecting Coincidences guy, the creature, and now her. Her brown eyes flickered green again as she said, "Mazie has vanished."

And flickering green eyes meant–

A feather.

A blue and orange feather emerged on her shoulder and I snatched it as she was monotonously speaking, her gaze erect.

Five down, one to go.

"End of discussion." Disha concluded.

She kept walking, until her shadows became smaller and smaller, and then they disappeared.

"I have to admit, Sie, I don't know what to do." Robert said. "I guess we all got our hopes up too high when the puzzles kicked. Because no matter how smart we could be, we're still slow."

I said, "But how could we fail so badly?"

Robert shrugged, "Beat's me, Sie."

I sighed, "I mean it makes sense. How are a few eleven-year olds' goanna stop *the Vanisher?*"

"Maybe it's time I tell you the truth, Sienna." Robert said, "People say that I have zero common sense, and that I can't keep serious during important events. And when I couldn't keep it in anymore, I'm sorry I broke down in the Geoport. But we can't blame each other. Look what this case does to us all. We're a mess. So, I'm sorry for making assumptions about your family life."

I nodded, "Don't listen to them. And don't worry about it Robert. It's alright. We'll just—"

Robert said, "Look, I should probably go home. Nice working with you."

I knew he would bail out of this case, but I mean it was worth a shot—somewhat.

I said, "Ok. If Disha left, why wouldn't--" But just a second later, Robert was gone, on his way to whoever knows.

I sighed. I should probably go home too.

So, I found my way walking back to the nearest train station I could find.

A Train hopper. That's who I was when I came here. That's who I still am, I guess. But a train hopper with a uniform, this time.

That's still not mine.

I got on the train, indicated the Whislow logo to the ticketmaster when he came to verify. He didn't even look at it, just brisked by everyone's tickets.

And by everyone, I meant four people sitting dispersed around the train. There were no families like last time, no groups, just a few people.

"Where to, miss?" The ticket master asked, perplexed at my empty hands, empty of a ticket.

"Platform Portal, sir."

"That'll be the last stop."

It didn't matter, I sat next to the window seat, my eyes tracing the running trees and the misty oceans that I was once in love with. Before failing so hard.

All I could think about was what I'm going to say to Aunt Katelyn. How I'm going to explain my attendance.

The manager was sitting down at the edge of the platform, gazing into the galaxy.

"Hello."

"Rex, you're back again?" The manager replied. He was swaying his feet over the infinite galaxies.

I narrowed my eyes, "No, it's me, the *vibrant mumbler*. Can I go back to the Tech World?"

"No. There's a glitch. And Philoxenians, or those with the reciprocal, can't go to the other dimensions during a crisis."

My jaw dropped, "Please, sir, I have to. I have to go back home, our case is over, and I don't even know if there's a chance of me finding the last feather—"

"The answer is no."

"You don't understand, it's urgent."

"No."

"Who created this rule?"

"I did." He said, a moment of silence followed.

"I'm sorry, but you know how hard it is to prove something? To prove something to my aunt. To finally bring happiness into our lives. I can't let her down."

The Platform manager breathed silently, "Well, I'm not sure. I have forgotten what it's like to be in a family."

I glanced up, my throat tightening with regret of what I just said, "What do you mean?"

"It's really not the time for backstory. I'm not scavenging for sympathy, but it's just how it is. Philoxenia is not that all perfect."

"I'm so sorry about that. Maybe I could talk to the agency about it." I said, like I had a long running relationship with Whislow.

"No, there's not much to be done. Many, many years ago, when I was your age, I made a decision. I traveled dimensions, and once, I was offered a choice. I could have all the riches I wanted, but with the cost of living here forever. It was permanent, it was the worst choice I ever made. I left my family for this. And every day, ever since then, I yonder into the stars--waiting for something, for another chance. For another chance of love and joy. But it never came. Look at me." The manager spread his hands through piles of diamonds, fingers touched gold, boots squeaked over the shiny jewel floor. "Look at me. I have so much. I have more riches than you can count. I-" He lifted his magical staff--, "I have the ability to control dimensions, Enter, leave, command. I manage the format of our voyages. But--without a feeling of love" His voice broke, "Just don't make the same mistake, kid."

Someone who sacrifices, someone who endures, and someone who isn't what they seem.

This old man sacrificed his life for this job. Enduring it every day. The deal he made for this job is permanent, may seem powerful, but is mentally vulnerable. He wasn't who he seemed. He seems grumpy, but he's not. He's *hurt*.

It hit me.

He's the Clever Element.

I gave a small nod, "I don't know what to say." I wiped a tear sliding down my cheek. I clasped his hands together, "You don't know how much I needed to hear that, sir."

He gruffed sarcastically, "Yes, I'm *sure* you did."

He gazed back into oblivion, calm and quiet. I don't know how he's going to feel about being the Clever Element. Or being involved in this crisis. Or if he's even willing to contribute.

"Have you ever thought about the Clever Element?" I brought up.

"I've never cared for Zecron's philosophies."

Just the response I expected. "Well…this case kind of regards Zecron…and" I stammered, carefully harvesting words to say, "You may be the Clever Element."

He sat there, reactionless and a blank slate for an emotion.

"All I'm saying is, you have the power to stop this crisis, to stop the Vanisher–"

"You found the Vanisher?" The manager asked, "Well who is it?"

I lowered my head, "I thought it was Zecron's son, but I really don't know…"

"Zecron's son was just here, that's why I wondered why he was back again."

"No, you said Rex was here–"

"Exactly."

Oh.

Oh.

Oh.

Oh no.

It can't be him, not after me info-dumping my entire life.

Too much is at stake.

Maybe that's why he got the Geoport to work. That's why he was so relaxed, so confident. Confident that he wasn't going to be kidnapped.

He made us three run to different places so he could vanish Mazie in the meantime.

He took us three, who were on the case, off track so he wouldn't have us, non-vanishable forces against him.

"What was he doing?" I asked.

The manager replied, "I wasn't paying much attention, but I did see a storm of Whislow agents."

Whislow agents.

Was Estrella with them? No, she had pyrexia. Wait—

Estrella never said she was hurt… by pyrexia? Pyrex? She must have meant she was hurt by Rex. By Rex.

"Where'd Rex go?" I asked him.

The manager briskly whispered, "I don't know if I'm allowed to disclose that due to location privacy."

Impatience was settling in.

"But, for the world's sake, he had special access to the Realm."

Even if I go there, I don't know if I can stop him, not when he's surrounded by the most powerful objects and people, and I don't have an ounce of the reciprocal in me.

But he's nothing without the Platform Manager, is he?

If only I had the orb with me, then I'd be somewhat fightable.

It's back in Edmonia, though. And is it still there? It can't be, Rex's, or should I say, Felix's plan is going into its last phase of motion.

"Can you help me?" I asked him.

The manager turned, "I'd rather not stake my career."

I groaned, the grumpiness was still a part of him.

"Could you at least give me some advice?"

"Find the Zecron Orb, it knows everything." He replied and gestured back to me on the blue light to get back to Philoxenia.

As I began walking, it still felt weird leaving him to just sit there all day, transporting people as he needs to. No one to really have a conversation with. At least I have my Aunt Katelyn.

I paused, "And maybe, you can experience that loving joy again, sir. I'll be the one." I gestured. "A friend, if that's what you want to call it. You deserve it, everyone does."

A smile, a genuine smile, glistened across his face. "Thank you, my vibrant mumbler."

"No," I said, "Thank you." I made my way to the blue ray waning into the railway. "I gotta catch that orb, since it knows everything."

Chapter Twenty-Three

The Realm

I took the same path back to Mazie's home in Edmonia.

Still that empty, music-less, Mazie-less house as Rex left it.

To my disbelief, I found the orb still sitting where I left it. Too heavy to lift, I tried looking around for carts or rugs to drag it alongside me with.

"Hello, Mazie." My heart dropped.

The man with the red streak across his brunette hair, Rex, Felix, Campbell, stood just a couple inches away from me.

"Rex…" I muttered.

"I see you have something of mine." He said with an innocent smile smothered over his face. Guilt is what hides inside of the smile. That's what.

"Actually," I interrupted, "Chief Faryyan wants it back in the Orb Preservation room." I said, "It's the safest option, he said."

I debated on whether I should confront him now, or pretend I still trust him. But then again, my powers are zero compared to his.

"Chief Faryyan has disappeared, Mazie. What in the world are you talking about?"

A stone sunk in my throat.

"But thank you for safe-guarding it, Mazie." He said.

He kept repeating my pseudonym, in that cadence after every sentence, it was unsettling.

I stood in front of the orb, my heels tapping the outer shell.

And to my surprise, Rex picked it up like it was the lightest feather in the universe. He set a couple of books aside as he walked out of the house. The only card left I could play was the "innocent child."

"Can I come with you?" I asked. "Pretty, pretty, please?"

Rex gave a frustrated sigh, "If you want to."

He found a large open area in the middle of Edmonia and drew a circle in the air with his hands.

A large vertical tunnel appeared in the air and he stepped into it, leading me to follow.

And before a split second passed, we were standing in the Platform Portal, with the Manager polishing his golden staff.

"Realm. Now." Rex ordered. I looked up at him, with him just responding to me in a straight, blank, but occupied expression.

"As you wish." The Manager responded, tapping the golden staff and following through with the same procedure, having us standing on the table to the Realm.

As the Manager began; a large and large wisps of blue light to form the passage started emerging. he whispered in my ear, "The orb is all you have."

I nodded, fully noting in my head that I couldn't even carry it. And before I could finish thinking about how I'm going to keep control of the orb, we were already standing in another room.

The room was the biggest room I've ever seen in my life, ever. The walls were a reddish orange made out of gems and stones, with huge windows peeking into the universe. Almost everyone I've seen throughout Philoxenia was there. *Everyone.*

The Realm.

Before seconds, I saw Mazie, standing in the corner, angry, frustrated as she punched as hard as she could through the bubble she was trapped in.

"Rex, where are we?" I asked, keeping that oblivious character in mind.

Rex turned to smile at me, making it appear as welcoming as possible, "Oh my dear–"

My hands wrapped behind my back and a cylindrical cage dropped on top of me.

"Stop the act, Sienna." Rex said.

He caught me. He knows me. He knows my *name*. My head spun into a dizzy, I felt like I was about to faint in this crisis.

"And you stop the act, Felix." It was all I could say right then, thinking I was bold.

Felix gave a playful look, as if he was trying to look offended but the smile just made the confidence diminish that offense, "Oh my act? Why don't you sit there, child, while I mind my own business, alright?"

He tapped a pattern on his wrist and the bubble over Mazie crumbled away. She took those very few seconds to run, but was unsuccessful.

"Don't do this, Felix." She begged, "Let everyone go home, please."

He tugged on the reciprocal from Mazie's hands, and she was wincing, trying to hold onto it like a mother holding onto her child.

He kept tugging on it and took that reciprocal to surround the magic orb like a protective membrane. It was like Reeva, her reciprocal taken from her.

"*Evensenuct.*" He ordered.

My heart was pounding in my chest. Felix is more powerful than I would've imagined, my hunch on the Clever Element is more likely to be wrong on his hypothesis that it's Mazie—

Nothing happened. Not a single Philoxenian budged and every single object stayed in place.

"Evensenuct!" He ordered, his impatience growing.

"EVENSENUCT!" He yelled with every single breath he had.

He was wrong.

He was *wrong*.

My heart beat started to slow, it turned out to be true.

Mazie isn't the Clever Element. It's the Platform Manager.

I turned around, Whislow agents banging on the indestructible bubbles, villagers using the items they had on them to carve their way out–inevitably failing.

I saw Samuel Orion, sitting in his bubble, grabbing bits of the bubble and trying to rip it apart.

That annoying Auction guy, looking like he was losing hope, dropped his jaw when he saw me. So he *did* have the reciprocal.

"Harvey!" Felix shouted in the middle of the Realm, and spread out his fingers to pull Reeva into the light.

"You were my father's old apprentice, weren't you?"

"Clever Element." She corrected him softly.

"Doesn't matter," He gruffed, "You know him better than I did, what was his method with the orb?" He asked.

She lowered her head, "I don't know."

"What?"

"I don't know!" She repeated, "Let us go, Felix. Let us go."

He began to pace our side of the Realm, eyeing everyone in sight down, with a cold and cruel gaze.

Felix tossed the orb onto one hand and used the others to pull on the magical objects stacked on the other side of the Realm that was miles and miles away.

Just the gravity of all the reciprocal in this Realm had me overwhelmed, let alone when it's all activated into one large force.

Well without the Clever Element, he resorted to pulling together everything with his own powers.

All of the objects, cages and bubbles floated to the center of the Realm beside Felix and he began tugging on the reciprocal from many of their hands, one by one. Then two by two, then three by three.

Everyone was losing their magic little by little, but the entire population of Philoxenia was too much for Felix to bear. He would be here for months.

"You can take all of our reciprocal," Reeva panted, "But you can't combine them."

He tugged on Reeva's reciprocal, a red cloud emerging from her hands and surrounding the orb as another protective membrane, "*Evensenect!*"

Silence.

Frustration was growing on Felix's face, his anger enraging in the walls of the Realm, the gemstones darkening to a deep read.

A bubble clashed behind me, a stressed girl with brown eyes and black hair doing her best to tap on my cage with her bubble.

Disha.

"Pst." She whispered.

"Hey," I called, "Felix took you here, too?"

"*That's Felix?*"

I nodded, "Anyways, how'd he find you?"

"I…don't know. Last place I was, was at Mazie's house."

"And you were walking to Whislow." I added.

She scrunched her nose, confused. Maybe her green eyes meant she was entranced, or her mind seized, or something along those lines.

And if she appeared here, then it *has* to do something with Felix.

"But you don't have the reciprocal, why are *you* here?" I whispered.

"Cogsworth!" Felix screamed. "Hold the orb."

He handed me the orb through the cage, and loosened my cuffs a little.

To my surprise it was much lighter than I was expecting and I could hold it with just my fingertips…

… "Be safe." A man said, handing over a baby to another girl…

A girl who looked like Aunt Katelyn.

I was covered in dried leaves from the tree above and there I stood, in front of a large train with so many circus caravans extending from the engine to the caboose. Each its own design, mottos, advertisements, and animals painted on.

And right in front of me was the red caravan.

Our caravan.

"I will, Rupert." She said,

Rupert. So he *is* related to me? Who's Princess Victoria from that newspaper?

Aunt Katelyn grabbed ahold of the baby and held it in her arms, stretching a reddish-brown beanie over my head. "Hello, my darling. My little beanie."

Beanie.

That's not just any baby.

That's *me.*

I stepped a little closer so I could hear the conversion. But with the rumbling of the elephants practicing on arena grounds not too far ahead, it wasn't easy.

A woman was standing next to Rupert, her hair red just like mine. Rupert's eyes were icy blue–just like mine.

She held the bottom of the baby as Aunt Katelyn gained a stable grip.

"We'll be back, Katie." The woman said, "It's going to be alright."

What's going to be alright? Where are they going?

"Are you sure you can handle," She lowered her voice, "*Zecron?*"

"We will handle it just fine, sister." Rupert condoned.

He's my father.

"But you don't have to take responsibility," Aunt Katelyn assured.

"Katie," Dad said, "It was my fault, I opened the portal to Tori's kingdom, and Zecron found his way in, thinking he could just…take over."

Tori. Victoria. Princess Victoria. Mom?

"You don't have to fight though, can't you leave it to Tori's father?"

"I have to help," Dad asserted.

"But we're not even magical," Aunt Katelyn said, "And Tori *is*. Rupert, when will you understand that we're just simple acrobats, who are safer off not toying with Philoxenia?"

"I completely understand," Dad said, "But you understand, when your heart is with a Philoxenian, you can't just leave the world."

Aunt Katelyn looked back down at me, cradling me among the reddish-brown blanket I was wrapped in and swaying me side to side, softly.

Mom placed a hand on Aunt Katelyn's shoulder, "Katie, you may be only eighteen, but you are the most mature woman I have ever met. And I know you will do a wonderful job taking care of my daughter."

"What should I call her?"

I guess I haven't been named yet.

I found a tear streaming down my cheek, I rushed faster than my legs could carry me to embrace my mom and dad, but all that happened was my arms fell right through.

That hit hard.

"Her sapphire eyes certainly do stand out." Mom proposed.

"Especially from the color of her little beret," Dad added.

"The color's burnt sienna." Aunt Katelyn explained, wrapping the ends of the bonnet around my head, "Sienna, how about that?"

"It's perfect." Mom agreed.

Aunt Katelyn even *named* me.

I found all of their eyes to be streaming with tears as Aunt Katelyn was overwhelmed with them leaving and her responsibility to take care of a whole new child while my parents were overwhelmed with leaving both of us.

Aunt Katelyn nodded, "I can take care of Sienna, my little beanie."

Dad exchanged a tearful smile with her, which then led into a long embrace. Even though I was really *there*, I did my best to embrace them. The sounds of the animals and screaming performers fading away from this precious moment.

"One last thing," Mom said, taking out a weird gadget from her pocket, her face looked almost completely like mine, and even had the same ginger hair. She wasn't wearing a gown here, but every word she spoke, every moment she made truly showed her royalty. And my dad, he looked just like Aunt Katleyn, his muscles built and strong from the acrobatics, his hair still kept neat, and his blue eyes just like mine.

Mom pressed the gadget on, "I don't want my daughter living during the times of Zecron, so it's best you take care of her in 2007 rather than 1907. When all of this is over."

Aunt Katelyn nodded, understandably, "Of course, I wouldn't want anything to happen to her. It's best I don't introduce her to this past, and raise her starting anew. Until you both come back."

"Yes, that's perfect. Once we help with Tori's kingdom and decimate Zecron's rule of terror, we will come back."

They embraced in one whole hug again, and this time I stood in the middle of it, gazing at my infant self. She looked nothing like me, but almost everything like me at the same time.

They parted, and Aunt Katelyn stood inside our caravan, anticipating the moment Mom would press the button.

"Bye Mom!" I shouted, as if it was the last thing I could say, "Bye Dad!"

And with the press of a button, the caravan disappeared, leaving a large gap gazing into the horizon where tons of cast members repetitively practiced their stun ts.

I wasn't gone. Aunt Katelyn was transported to 2007 but I was still standing here.

Mom and Dad turned to me, my heart started pounding faster and faster. But they were probably just looking in my direction.

"Rupert, do you really think we'll be able to see them again?" Mom asked, her face washed up in tears.

"Let's hope so, Tori. Zecron is unpredictable."

"Don't say that, we *will* see them again."

Dad nodded, "Yes darling, we will."

Mom sighed, resting her head on Dad's shoulders, he said, "It may take months. It may take days. Even years. Even a decade, but we *will* see Katie and Sienna again."

Mom smiled as much as she could, "If you were to go back to both of them, after this is over, and saw Sienna, all grown up, what would you say?" She asked, curiously.

"Well," Dad began, wrapping an arm around Mom's shoulders, "We've missed you so much. Sienna, I hoped you reached for nothing but the stars when we were gone. Look at you, you're so much taller."

My tears became waterfalls, as I stood there, my hands wrapped in front of me. I wanted to hug them so bad. It was like they were talking to me.

"You've grown into a beautiful girl, just like your mother. And I hope your auntie is doing just fine. Remember darling, it doesn't matter where you are, what you are, but *who* you are. And I'm sure Katie has raised you well, and don't forget, diamonds are found in your heart, not in the mines."

Mom smiled, "That was beautiful darling. Whether or not she knows about us, I hope she'll grow up knowing we love her." She concluded and they brisked away back to the bushes and the blue ray shone–blasting them back to Philoxenia.

"And I love you." I replied—

— "Cogsworth!" Felix screamed, "I said hold it—properly now!"

I woke up, drenched in tears from the scene and took a large breath to start breathing normally. My fingertips were still holding the orb, and I was still in the Realm.

Everything felt okay inside me. But externally, it wasn't. Zecron's reign lived on. So much for living a hundred years in the future. From one Zecron to the next, I guess I'm dealing with the latest descendant.

I gained some of my strength back and obeyed Felix's orders, there was no fighting back now.

As I was holding it, I saw a familiar shadow emerge in the crevice of the Realm.

"Sienna! Disha!" Robert shouted,

I shook my head rapidly. *No, no, be quiet, Robert. He'll see you.*

"I went to the portal and then the Manager told me everything–" He stopped, her expression dropped at the sight of me and Disha seized by Felix.

Disha was making gestures beneath her chin to silence him, "Shush" She mouthed.

It was too late.

"Useless child!" Felix announced, trapping Robert in a cage.

We were stuck here, along with everyone else. It's not like Felix is going to find the true Clever Element soon, and if he does, he'll be so powerful that he probably won't let anyone out. So, either way, we're trapped.

Disha and I looked over at Robert, surprised to see that he was *smiling*. Across the Realm, he gave a thumbs up and nodded when Felix was preoccupied with the orb, trying to figure out why it wasn't working.

After Robert gave the thumbs up, A large figure came quietly in the room behind Felix.

The Platform Manager.

"Hello, sir." Felix said, his eyes squinted, perhaps perplexed by the idea he wasn't powerful enough to bring the Manager here with his own powers.

"Enough." The Manager said calmly.

Felix shook his head and threw a large wisp of force at the Manager who crumpled it with his fingertips like it were just some dried leaves. Following that, the Manager blasted him against the wall.

The duel went on. With Felix blasting his reciprocal in the air and the Manager responded just by standing in one place and collecting his magic.

The frustrated Felix didn't give up, and reached out his hands to keep tugging on the Manager's reciprocal, struggling immensely.

"The Zecron line will end." the Manager said, "Enough."

And one by one, the Manager opened the gates and cages to let the people loose.

The cage lifted up, off of me and the cuffs loosened enough to let my hands loose. At last, we were free.

Felix was blasted onto the floor, starting breathing heavily. He took out the orb from his left hand, "Fine–take it."

The Manager gruffed, reaching out his hand to grab it.

"No!" I scrambled. One touch and his powers would be consumed by the orb.

"Just take it!" Felix yelled.

It was too late; the Manager grabbed the orb.

Nothing happened.

Was my hypothesis wrong? Then who's the Clever Element?

A second later the orb cracked and crumbled into pieces in the Manager's hands. He backed away to avoid the glass, leading Felix to crawl toward it in desperation.

"The orb! My orb!" He screamed, trying to piece it back together. He paused, "The clarity of this orb, the textures on the inside it–it's. It's…" He stood up, furious. "This isn't my orb."

I found it in Mazie's house, it had to be her orb. She said that Felix would never see his orb again if he–

Oh.

It was the Pseudo Orb.

That's why it told me my past history.

Felix started limping towards me, "What did you do with my orb?"

I leaned back, whimpering, "I don't know, Felix."

While he was busy growling in my face, Robert called behind him, "Manager, I have it here! But don't touch it!"

The manager grabbed the Zecron orb with a shield of his reciprocal behind the back of Felix.

The Manager gestured to us all to step in and encircle Felix. As he made an effort to blast people in the air, the Manager stopped them from hitting the floor.

The Manager stood right next to me, and held up his staff.

Felix looked Robert directly in the eyes, "You will not get away with this." He muttered.

He used all his might to grab the orb and it inched slowly and slowly in his direction. The orb lighted up, running past him and toward Mazie. Felix was still convinced it was her.

The Manager let loose of the orb and Disha screamed, "What are you doing, sir?"

The Manager lifted his hand up just slightly toward Disha to suggest to her it was going to be alright.

The Manager had to get the upper hand in this game, and with the expression of preparedness on his face, I could tell he was truly going to fool Felix.

"The power is mine!" The Manager screamed, directing the orb at Mazie. "I will possess all of this. Nothing can stop me."

"No, you won't." protested a voice.

The Manager raised an eyebrow, "What did you say" he said in a sarcastic voice.

"No, you won't." The voice came from Mazie, she forced herself forward as much as she could.

"Is that so?" The Manager cackled, and he started walking towards her slowly. "Just like they say, a troublemaker. You're nothing but a person who finds benefits for everyone. Now, what shall I do with you?"

"Let her go." someone ordered.

The Manager laughed, he was having too much fun playing this game.. The Manager let go of her staff and dropped the orb on the floor. "Easy, so easy. Why bother using the bound if you all fear me anyway?"

The crowd started looking at each other with confused looks. The Manager was trying to release them a minute ago, and now he's trying to retain all of this power. What is going on?

"Let her go." the same voice ordered.

"Oh come out already for whoever you are." The Manager said, impatiently.

Felix stepped forward again, using his shortcoming strength to lift him off of the floors of the Realm.

"Campbell?" Mazie gasped, conflicted. It's been so long since she saw Felix *as* Campbell, she couldn't be sure how he changed so quickly.

The Manager grinned, his plan was falling into place. He waved her hand which made the orb go back into his blue wisp. He couldn't stop smiling.

"Let. Her. Go." Felix repeated.

"See if I care." The Manager replied.

The wind was getting colder and the sky turned cloudless and gray. Mazie couldn't recall how happy she had been since she had last seen him. As each look Felix gave the Manager, the weather got dark.

Silence.

Mazie's emotions couldn't match the situation at the Realm. "Campbell! I'm so glad to see you. I knew it was you, of course you wouldn't do such a thing. I am so sorry I couldn't--"

Felix paused her, "I'm not on your side, Mazie."

Mazie Polaris gasped. Campbell was never like this to her. She couldn't believe that her best friend could do such a thing. "I-I I don't understand."

Felix ignored her comment. "Platform Manager, is that what they call you?," he said with a slight grin, "I'm impressed. Over all these years, I thought you just transport people wherever they need. But you, you are so much more than that. I would be more than happy to become your ally."

The Manager rolled his eyes and blasted Felix into the air. The Manager cackled again.

"You think I would become your ally? Well I don't think so!"

Tears filled Mazie's eyes. "What made you do such a thing? Campbell, what is going on?"

Felix was brought down to the ground. The manager was finally letting him explain himself. Maybe it's because this is the only time he would explain himself, or it's just a part of his master plan.

"You probably think my life is so happy and fun, don't you?" he explained. Mazie opened her mouth to speak but no words came out.

"Well you're wrong! The reason I was so optimistic in our friendship is because it's best to leave the past and be positive. The reason I left was to go on an expedition to find answers. Find answers for you. I was going but I wasn't going anywhere near my destination. It was then until I realized that I was a fool. You think about finding one's benefits but not people's true self. Why was I searching for your answers? Well, only for my best friend. I wanted you to feel like a part of the community so I tried to bring happiness to you. You always think no one understands about you but don't care to take the time and know what others are going through. No one's life is perfect, Mazie. Yet why do you get all the respect when others have done more? Who knows?"

Mazie was frazzled by what he said, "I think you're going about this the wrong way. So-"

"The world is limited. Care for only yourself I say. Should've known this sooner but I guess I learned it the hard way. I want to join with someone who is like me. Like the Platform Manager. " He said.

"Alright, Felix." The Manager gruffed, "We can be allies."

That was the only cue he needed. Felix stretched his hands toward the Manager willingly. Keyword: willingly.

The Manager held out his hands too, raising the anticipation in Felix but then froze Felix's arms, his eyes seemed more green than usual and were flickering.

"I will never swoop down to your level, Felix." He said.

Mazie's eyes were darting everywhere, her thoughts running a million miles per second, "Manager what–"

"Your *friend,* Miss Polaris, was just Felix Zecron going by the name of Campbell. Now he as Campbell may have fooled you but Felix has done far worse than fake his name."

"It is a crime to impersonate others," Disha said, looking at me, "*Without* their will."

"What is it to you?" Felix responded.

Disha gasped, "You were that creature from the UFO, that's how you knew which jail we were in." Her eyes widened in disbelief.

"And I was *you,* too." He announced, "But it doesn't do either of us any good, does it?" He said coyly. He started shaking his shoulders front and back, "Let me go!" He screamed at the Manager.

"It does you no good to hurt young children like Estrella!" I screamed, "Or to disrupt lives."

Felix scoffed, still straining from his frozen arms.

"On three," the Manager announced, "Everyone close to the orb, touch it and push with all of your reciprocity. It'll be enough to penetrate it."

He glanced at Robert, Disha, and me, "You guys too,"

"One…Two…"

Chapter Twenty-Four

The Last Feather

"Three." The orb shattered into a bazillion pieces, reflecting all sorts of light from the stars out the windows.

"No!" Felix screamed from the top of his lungs, only serving as a contribution to the shattering of the orb.

His eyes were flickering brighter than ever, which meant—

The last feather.

It didn't just appear in my hand, but emerged as an outline of a feather and the inside design slowly started to fill in.

It was soft and brown, just like the feather of a sparrow. Simple but perfect.

Everyone was breathing heavily, as the Manager was directing everyone into a line to exit back home.

But Felix was the first to go, as the Manager stated he would send him to a faraway place of punishment.

"So, we solved it?" Robert asked, we were inching up very slowly in the line.

"I guess so." I replied. It was still surreal knowing that I completed the quest for the feathers. All of them were just impersonations of Felix. And it was surreal knowing this case was *actually* over.

We may have been trapped and have had to be saved by the Manager, but without knowing *he* was the clever element, I don't think we'd be standing safely here right now.

I looked behind us and it turned out that we were the last in line, and the process of going home was actually going by quickly. Considering the fact that he had to send almost the entire population back home in Philoxenia.

After hours of waiting, we finally reached the Manager.

One, two, three, four, five, six feathers I counted. Perfect, all the feathers I need to make the wish—which is what I came here for.

"Sir, may I please borrow your staff to make my wish?" I asked.

Robert and Disha's jaw dropped, "You found all six?"

I nodded.

"Only with my supervision." The Manager answered.

Above through the open windows of the Realm, flew the Sparrow Constellation—with its distinct purple stars. All I had to do was hold the feathers above the staff and make the wish.

I still remember the first time I saw the constellation, in our old caravan, with my birthday telescope.

What was my sentence again? Oh right, that I wished to let everyone see the constellation in regards that I discovered it.

I held the feathers over the staff, ready to make my wish.

I looked at each individual star—some were grandchildren, some were brothers of another.

They all had a loved one out here, they all deserve love, of course.

For a second, it felt weird, taking advantage of held-hostage kids for fame. It felt wrong.

But it's what I came here for, for the fame that Aunt Katelyn and I finally deserved after such struggle. It's all we need.

I closed my eyes and held the feathers over the staff, tightening my grip and said, "I wish to release the six children from the Sparrow Constellation."

A feeling enveloped over me like a warm hug, Disha ran over and embraced me, "You did the right thing," and Robert joined in.

Every swing Aunt Katelyn pushed me on. Every cake she baked me. Every hug she gave me. Every kiss on the cheek. Every gymnastics lesson. Every laugh we shared. Every late night we joke about nothing. Every new life lesson she taught me. Every gift. Every smile. Every light. Every piece of joy.

I already had it all. I already had a life to share with others. I guess it's not meant to be rich and famous, but it's meant to share with someone I love. And these kids have been deprived of that.

The six purple stars twinkled one last time and floated to the ground of the realm, emerging as six silhouettes. Some were wearing their muddy clothes from camp. One had Pegasus wings. Another looking like that picture in Norma's rooms. A duplicate of Chief Faryyan, but much younger. They were all there.

When the luminescent purple light stopped illuminating them, the kids all fell to the floor, leading Robert, Disha, and me to help them up.

You can't blame them, they've been trapped as stars for years.

"Thank you, Thank you, thank you!" One of the girls screamed while hugging us.

I patted her back, "You're welcome, you're welcome."

Robert said, "We're delighted to be your heroes." He placed one hand behind his back like a nobleman.

Disha chuckled, "Glad you guys are safe."

An emotion of happiness surfed inside me. All of their faces were stressed and clothes were torn, but in their eyes, they've never been anymore grateful.

Which makes me feel grateful.

The Manager tapped his staff, "Alright, enough of that—let's go home."

He was back to his little grumpy self, I assumed, but at least there was a twinkle in his eye that wasn't there before.

We headed back to the Whislow Agency, taking the six stars—or children now, behind us.

"Father!" The first girl screamed at the sight of Chief Faryyan. "Wow, you have gotten so much older."

He dropped the binders in his hands at the top of the staircase, "Kaya!" Tears filled his misty eyes as she ran into his arms

I felt a tap on my shoulder and a gust of wind behind me, "Hello Mateo." I said, a teenager with large pearl wings fluttering

"Do you know where my sister is?" he asked, looking around curiously.

I nodded, "She should be healing in the nurses room."

"Gracias, heroína."

Heroína. It was mainly the Manager, but sure, I was a hero, somewhat.

Robert and Disha seemed to have helped everyone else find their way around Whislow. And I watched Norma's grandson strolling around the lobby like his eyes were opened to a whole new world.

The Agency was still building itself back up, the stairs were broken, the glass almost everywhere was shattered. Desks were unaligned, and the debris in the hallways were immense. But more than anything, the Orb Preservation room was completely demolished.

"Guys, she's back." Robert pointed toward the Council Room. I could still see bits and pieces of the Council Convention flier around the entrance. But there she was, Councilwoman Cordelia with gray shiny hair, bruises here and there, sitting comfortably at the head of her table.

"We brought her back," Disha restarted, smiling, "Good job to us."

She turned to me, "Girl, if you never told the Manager–" she began stammering, "You literally saved us."

I blushed, "Oh well–it was the Manager, I just made the wish."

Her jaw dropped, "What happened to "I discovered the Sparrow Constellation Sienna? Who's this humble one now?""

I giggled, "Same old me," I pointed to my head, "Just a little bit smarter of a girl."

"A *whole* lot smarter." Robert emphasized, "You know how bad that would've backfired if you took credibility for a constellation that held six minors captive?"

I burst out laughing, "That's a whole lot worse.'

Disha said, "You know Sienna, it takes guts to give away a wish of yours for them. And I–" She hesitated, "I'm glad Mazie sent you to us."

"I'm glad too." I responded, "You know Disha, you sure know a lot about–pretty much everything. Be grateful for that brain of yours."

"I will be," She smiled.

We were standing in the middle of the Whislow Agency, right under the glass dome–or the open-air dome now.

I turned to Robert, "Dude–you finished that never ending project of yours, congrats."

He brushed it off, "Well, not without Felix's pressure, I couldn't. But I'll take it."

"What is up with you guys? When did y'all become so humble?" Disha questioned, confused, but had a large smile on her face. She turned to me, "Remember those fortune cookies back at the Circus Camp?"

I nodded slowly, *You will not get what you currently desire.*

That was somewhat true. I wanted the Constellation to bring me and Aunt Katelyn fame or wealth, or any of the above. But that didn't happen because I changed that wish. Who knows, maybe they are something to believe in.

"Mine was, you will remember who gave you the most important gift."

"And what about it?" Robert asked, intrigued, leaning forward in our circle.

Disha grinned larger than she ever could, "Look, I know I gave you a hard time Sienna during the journey, or for calling out the stupidity of your questions, Robert, every single time…"

"Don't worry about it." Robert said, with a hand up.

She continued, "What I mean is, more than that scholarship, you guys gave me something I couldn't get for a long time, and that was *friendship*. So, thank you."

Robert laughed, "Who's the cheesy one now?"

We all laughed it off and brought in one, large hug.

I went to the nurse's room to check on Estrella, she wasn't there. So, I dashed through the broken golden sideways elevator and into the Creature Sanctuary.

I saw her, still with a bandage on her horn, feeding a couple of birds sitting in a small pink nest among tons of other little trees by the shiny waters.

"Hola!" She waved, as I came closer, she said, "You kept your promise." She pointed to her brother sitting on the bench a couple of yards away, petting fire-breathing cats, it seemed like.

I scratched my head, "Of course, Estrella. It took me long enough."

"Are you kidding, Mazie? You brought my brother back—that's all that matters." Estrella said. She straightened her pigtails to align with the roses bordering her horn. The sun awakened from the hills, exposing the plants and stealing their shade. I turned to Estrella, the rims on her horn glimmered in the morning.

"Call me Sienna," I admitted, "That's my real name." She glanced up at me, with a cheeky smile.

She set aside the birds resting on her shoulders and let them outside of the greenhouse into the sanctuary.

There was a small box placed in the corner of the nook. Estrella teared open the tape and smiled, "It's probably from my tío. I've been waiting to open it."

She clutched a glass globe in her two small hands, letting the light shine through. It was sectioned into four parts, each representing a season. The orange aura of autumn intervened its way into the white wonderland of winter. Spring's green and summer's yellow blended its way into the center–all making the separation of the parts seem unnoticeable.

I gasped, it couldn't have been the same one from our yard sale. I raised an eyebrow, "Did you ever go to the Circus Camp?"

Estrella giggled, "Me? No, but my father wanted me to go. But you know I can't leave the animals unattended. He gave me this to remember that half of my magic will always be from the Tech World."

"And he's allowed to know y-you're, magical?"

Estrella shook her head in laughter, "You're really new to this, huh?"

I shrugged, "Just…afraid to unleash another Felix into the world I guess." I laughed.

"As long as he doesn't tell anyone else, then it's alright."

If I told Aunt Katelyn, would she freak out? Would she want a part of it? After everything that happened one hundred and eleven years ago? *Could* I give her a part of it? A better, non-Zecron part of it?

Maybe I can.

Chief Faryyan knocked on the glass of the greenhouse, "Miss Cogsworth." He peered into the glass, with Kaya standing right next to him.

I stepped outside, blinded by the sun, "Yes, Chief?" He said my name. My last name. My heart began pounding in my throat. Oh no, oh no.

The silence in that pause was deafening.

Kaya answered, holding a large book in her hand, "Miss Cogsworth, that was phenomenal work."

I blushed, "I had some help—" My heart slowly went back to its original rate, and my head cleared itself of anxiety.

"No, the Sparrow Constellation, how did you—how did you?" She asked, "The feather, how…"

"I figured out in the end that Felix impersonated people and their eyes always flickered green. Feathers kept showing up during then so when Felix's eyes flickered the most—I knew it was because of him." I answered.

Kaya took a long, deep nod, astonished. "Wow." She took herself out of that trance and peered open the book, signifying Chief Faryyan.

"Sienna, you may not be the clever element, but you have proven yourself to be someone far more special. Macladez Zecron wasn't clever nor kind enough like you to finish the book, it is your chance to do so. You have inspired many people along the way on the case, one including me." said Chief Faryyan.

I was at a loss for words, "Oh my goodness, thank you, Chief. But that infamous Zecron novel…?"

Chief smiled slightly, "Yes, I know it may not have the highest reviews in Philoxenia, but it was never finished. It's your turn now. It is your turn to finish it."

Faryyan handed me the book and had me press the book with my hand at the heart of the cover. The book flipped its page to the end and a new page appeared. Amazing.

Words appeared, writing:

One's life is based on their mark. Their deeds. Magic

I picked up the pen that Kaya was holding out, and thought of the last word, *Magic.*

"Magic." I said, still thinking. What helped me on this whole journey? Reeva Harvey's passion brought out her magic. Disha never compared a pure diamond and her friends, her friends were worth more. Robert's positiveness made his life positive no matter how dark things got, that brought out his magic. It all connected to their personality. But what was true magic? I thought about someone back *home.* Someone who had the most magic in my life. Someone, even if they didn't reciprocate, they still had the greatest powers of all. Finally, I knew what to write.

One's life is based on their mark. Their deeds. Magic is in everyone. It isn't always supernatural, but in our spirit. Our mark is our purpose,

everyone has it. Our actions change our mark, creating the future. It's our hope and good will that will bring the light out to fix the problems. Everyone has their goal. It's not their destination that matters, but the journey there itself. Magic, it will always be within us. It will only activate when one does. Always believe in yourself.

I set down the pen on the bench in the greenhouse and the book closed. The title cover changed, when I glanced at it again. The colors were different, no longer a plain redwood color, but a mix of hues from the shades of purple and blue. It looked *lighter*.

The Legend of the Sparrows
A True Guide To Magic
By Macladez Zecorn
Finished By Sienna Cogsworth

Faryyan took the book and waved his hand from side to side around it. And just like that, the book floated away, out the door of the greenhouse and further into the Sanctuary, finding its way to the library.

"Fall will end soon enough, it will be great to see you again, Cogsworth."

I smiled, "Thanks, Chief Faryyan, I'll do my best to be back."

Back.

"Is Felix…is he….?" I trailed off.

He sighed, "For now he's been imprisoned, but I won't deny he is unpredictable. But there's something inside you that I know you'll be okay. Your mark indeed has changed, no one knows what the future holds, Cogsworth, but yours will be something special."

Disha called me up to her office, saying she had a package waiting for me.

I went up the golden elevator, in the crowd of agents older and younger. It feels a lot better now the Agency is back to normal but better, rather than empty.

The elevator paused at the office floor and I made my way through the crowd to her neat and tidy office.

"Sienna." Her eyes brightened. My eyes went directed to her jacket---it was dominated by a badge in the shape of a parrot.

She noticed me glancing at her badge, "Pretty, right? I didn't think the bird I'd be was a *kea parrot,* but the Chief said it's the intelligent one."

"Well, you certainly deserved it, after all the work for all these years." I acknowledged.

She straightened the badge upright on her leather jacket and said, "Thank you."

There was a brown box sitting on her white desk that was soaking in much of the light in her room. What used to be scraps of clues and notes on her walls were all gone. I guess she's starting fresh now.

"Is that the package?" I asked, and she nodded, scooting it to my end of the table for me to open.

As soon as I opened the box, wisps of air grabbed my finger and my thumb was throbbing. I checked it, the prominent ridges were gone and the fingerprint was back to the normal curvature it always was.

Mazie Polaris.

Dearest Sienna,

Don't worry, you're not in trouble. I told the Chief all about my actions, about giving you my identity. He's more angry at me than he ever will be at you, so you are fine.

I wanted to address that you may be confused why I trusted you so much and put so much faith in you. It's because I knew your mother, Victoria.

I wasn't sure if you already knew about her back when I first met you, and I didn't want to be the one to disclose it if it wasn't the right time and place. But I think I can tell you now.

Your mother was a kind, gentle, caring, and generous princess. She deeply cared about her people and nothing went out of control on her watch.

Until she met your father. I worked as a musician under her father's reign, and when she met your father, many more doors opened for her. Like the Tech World...and of course, Zecron.

None of us know how far along she and your father are in the battle between them and Zecron's forces. But she is out there.

And when she left, she wanted you to have this Sienna. I wish I could give this to you in person, but it's better this way than never.

Please come back and visit,

Mazie.

I set the intense note to the side, my heart slowed and I caught my tears from falling onto the note and smearing the ink. Peered into the box with my foggy eyes, I was speechless.

There stood a silver tiara with three amethyst gemstones in the shape of spears in the front. The rest of the tiara was decorated with smaller crystals. Each gem, though, shined at every angle I turned it and my eyes widened as my fingertips felt the royal and rich minerals in my hands.

"Quite the gift." Disha said softly, her hands resting on the chair.

I slowly placed the gift in my ginger hair. My heartbeat synced with the instance of me securing it on my head. A swarm of emotions rushed into my veins and I was in awe. I've never worn anything this special, ever. And it coming from my mother, made it priceless. I stared at my reflection in Disha's table, "How does it look?" I asked while rotating my head side to side.

"Like you stole a princess's identity."

I shot a look at her.

"I'm kidding. I'm kidding."

I slowly took the tiara off my head and placed it back in the box like I was stacking fine china. Then, I laid the note on top. It all made so much sense now, a random girl wouldn't just give me her fingerprint if I wanted it. *I* wouldn't give her my fingerprint to a stranger if they wanted it.

I closed the lid of the box and looked up at Disha, "Do you have more cases or…."

She shook her head happily, "Nope, I'm going home."

Disha did a double check of all of her drawers and led us both back down in the golden elevator, packed with busy agents, as always.

I couldn't wait to go home. I wanted to hug Aunt Katelyn and never let go. I wanted to walk around the ending streets and smell that nostalgic fresh bread every morning. I wanted to drink tea with Norma and hear her savage comments.

Norma.

Wait.

"We need to grab Norma Huxley's grandson, he lives in Honeyville, too." I said.

"Well where is he?" Disha asked, looking around.

And sure enough, when we got to the lobby floor, he was still strolling around, curiously and cautiously.

"Mr. Huxley!" Disha waved. His attention was immediately snatched and he started making his way toward us. His hair was all ruffled and his hands were in his pockets, in the clothes he had back at camp. With Macladez Zecron. Man, that was still hard to wrap my head around.

"Yes?" He called.

I answered, "We're going to take you home, alright. Back to your grandmother."

"I don't want to go back there." He said, taking his hands out of his pockets and backing away.

"Alright, fine." Disha said with a mischievous smile, she grabbed my hand and we started making our way to the entrance, "We'll go home, because we certainly don't want to get trapped in a constellation this time."

"On second thought." He put his finger up, and Disha turned back with a satisfied smile at his expected reaction.

We ventured way back to the train station, not with a ticket, but simply our reputation for being a Whislow Agent.

And now that Disha has her badge, our seat on the train is fully locked in.

We picked one of the seats in the back, and right in front of us sat the family that I saw on my way to Edmonia…

"Enjoyed Edmonia, kids?" The mother asked, putting the ticket in her pocket.

The children nodded eagerly, pressing their hands against the window as the grass danced by, "I don't want to go home, Mama."

"Well, it's safer now, so we can do so much more you kids want to do, alright?"

The children frowned, turning their heads back to their parents, "All that happened was you two disappeared, and then you came back, like you always do. What was there to worry about?"

The parents exchanged uncomfortable glances. Their eyes were communicating a million words a second, trying to carefully choose which words to use to explain the concept of *risk*.

But no matter how many modified ways the parents tried, the children were still skeptical, until the father cut straight to the chase.

"What if we didn't come back?"

"But you did."

"Because of miracles, children. Now, are you going to complain about the past or look forward to the new activities we will do when we get home."

They're eyes clicked and exclaimed, "The second one! The second one!"

The dad gave a thoughtful nod, "That's right."

I turned my head back out the window to see the top of the shining turquoise ocean rise and dive into the deep blue sea, giving another wave of the deep blue sea a chance to become turquoise.

When we landed at the train station that is a walking distance away from the Platform Portal, we couldn't spot it anywhere.

"The location must have changed." Disha proposed and we found ourselves walking a whole another mile until finding a Geoport.

The Geoport gate closed us in and floated up into the misty air. The fresh warmth of it gave a sensation of returning home. It floated up to the brilliant blue sky above, rising higher than the clouds and faded the light above. Norma's grandson was still looking curious and uneasy at everything around. Peering into every device, fidgeting with every little thing inside.

At last, we were walking into the Platform Portal. Although our prior need was to go home from the portal, I began looking for *someone* else. I began searching around the golden dome room, until I spotted the Platform Manager sitting on a disk table. His hair appeared grayer than usual and more wrinkles had seemed to crease in. But other than his features, I was more concerned about his wellbeing.

I approached the disk table, yet my footsteps became louder. The Platform Manager was in deep thought, though he got startled by my footsteps.

"How long have you been here?" He asked, concerned. He turned his head completely around, eyes widening at the sight of more of us.

"Not very long, just wanted to stop by before we go home." I replied.

He stood up and gazed out into space. "Well make your hellos and goodbyes quick."

Same old Platform Manager.

"Hello." Disha said, following his directions.

"Hello." He said back in a low tone.

"Is everything okay?" I asked him, sitting down right next to him.

He shrugged, "Why do you care?"

"Because you saved everyone." I explained.

His wrinkles became more apparent and he massaged his temples, "That's the thing, even after such deed, I'm restricted here."

"But you can control where everyone can go and move." Disha explained, concerned. The Platform Manager did not reply. He only turned away back to let his thoughts seep into the depths of the galaxies.

Disha figured it out for herself just seconds later, "Oh…you're like a Genie, trapped in a bottle. I'm…so sorry, sir."

He gestured for her to sit down, too. And she did, "Don't be sorry, child. It was my idea many, many years ago."

The Platform manager's face turned down and gave a sigh, "I don't know what it feels like to be home. But," he smiled, "I'm happy for you."

That was the first time I saw him as a well-wisher. "Can't you, I don't know, at least go on vacation?"

He shook his head, "I can only stay here to guard each dimension."

"But can't you leave a security system, you know, one with magic?"

"Still, who will send people throughout the universe?"

I went into deep thought, "How do you sleep?"

"I don't, it's an ability I have, almost a curse."

I stared through the open galaxy side, "Don't worry. I'll try to think of something. If you could think of ways to crush the Zecron Orb, I'm sure we can all develop a technology set to maintain the portals for you."

"The Whislow Agency was already considering that. But the proposition is that it's better if an actual being maintains the portals, full of intention and free of technological or magical error." He explained.

He shook his hands in the air, "But don't feel bad, I will one day get to explore other places. One day."

The Platform Manager and I shared a warm smile. He then placed his staff in the golden liquid. "Well then, problem solver, it may be the last time you head through the platform."

"Right." I said with a wink.

We three stepped into the transparent blue column. The Platform Manager tilted his staff and the green emerald on his staff glowed. "Until next time, my vibrant mumbler!" He exclaimed.

"Until next time!" We repeated with a salute. The blue dome fizzed and Disha, Norma's grandson, and I appeared in a water air void. I had only been on the water air void twice, but it was easy to get used to. This time, I just had to be careful holding onto the precious box.

Chapter Twenty-Five

Now I Know What's Priceless

We landed on the soft, sandy ground. The sun was almost setting outside and we were right outside of the large Circus Camp. The tent was still up and even though it was probably dinner time, the children were still practicing their stunts even more intensively.

The unicycles no longer had their training wheels and Disha's group was juggling more than five clubs. The improvement was insane.

Disha walked behind Norma's grandson and me as we trudged through the camp grounds.

"Don't let him see—"

Disha winced as the ringmaster was scanning the grounds meticulously.

"C'mon folks, we have a performance tomorrow!" He screamed.

The children hula hooping were slowing down the rate of their movement and started panting. "Can we–" breath "take-" breath "a–" breath "break?"

The ring master enraged, "No! You will not be cowards like those two young ladies!"

Disha's cheeks crimsoned and her heart was pounding, "Coward, huh?"

I grabbed her at the shoulders, "Shh, it's okay. Just don't let him see us."

We crouched behind the bushes; they outlined the rim of the circus ground with the hazy horizon projecting over us.

The grandson said, "Why are we crouching–"

"Shush." Disha said, placing a finger on her lips. "I'd like to keep my bones intact, thanks."

"Your bones–"

"Quiet!" She whispered.

The grandson was startled and he bumped into me, almost causing my box of the tiara to drop.

I'm lucky to say we made it past the camp without getting spotted by a single child, performer, or worst of all— the ringmaster.

As soon as we left the grounds, our backs thanked us and we started sprinting through the soft, long grass meadow. It felt more like heavy floating than running, as the sun was slowly inching down and the wind was letting the grass feud against us, having the mucky dirt on their side.

But my heart stopped after seeing the trailer park.

No two trailers were aligned and there was no pattern to the way they were parked, but everything looked intentional. The crooked lining of the outer trailers, and some trailers taking more space than others. It all felt right. It felt like…it felt like home.

Aunt Katelyn's trailer lights were turned off. And yet, the trailer seemed to be the brightest one in the park. It was different this time. With paintings on it of animals, large stripes in orange and yellow. The designs felt so familiar.

I was out of breath, one hand shaking with the heavy tiara and the other one knocking on the door. She wasn't at home.

The grandson pointed to the other trailer a block away, with a drape over the window with the design of daisies and a couple lawn chairs out front.

"Is that my grandmother's?" He asked, pointing at it. His eyes widened and his jaw was dropping slowly.

I nodded, "Yes, Norma Huxley's trailer is right there. That's the one."

He inched slowly toward the door of the trailer, with everything smelling like mint.

Before he knocked, he traced his fingertips to the etched blue painting of the trailer, like he was rediscovering his home. "Well, I'll be." He muttered, "I haven't….I haven't…I haven't been home in so long."

He then took a large swallow and gave the door a knock a good two times.

"Can't you tell I'm taking my post dinner nap!" Norma screamed from inside. She opened the drapes and turned on the porch fairy lights she hung just under the rim of the front trailer.

She swung the door open while removing her eye mask and abruptly stopped.

"Well count the stars and prove me wrong," She said, her voice lowering, "My grandson came back."

She blinked several times to truly believe he was standing right there, saying, "You came back?"

The grandson nodded, "I guess I did, Nana."

"Oh…" She muttered wrapping her hands around him, and he slowly sunk into her hug and replied, "I didn't know how much I missed home…until now."

She stopped hugging him and squeezed his cheeks between her delicate fingers, "Don't you ever run away, alright?"

"I won't, Nana. I promise."

She nodded, laughing, "I'm kidding! If you run away, take me with you. I can't stand Barry next door."

All of us erupted into laughter and my heart swelled from my toes to my head. A feeling of warmth exploded in me, like I was given a thousand hugs.

"Say, Norma?"

"Hmm?"

"Have you seen Aunt Katelyn anywhere?"

Norma frowned, shaking her head, "No, girly, I told ya, I was taking my post-dinner nap. How am I supposed to know?"

Classic Norma. You gotta love her.

"Well where was she all day?"

"I don't know, I had to take my pre-breakfast nap, and then cook breakfast, and then argue with Barry…it takes a lot of energy and attention."

Aunt Katelyn wasn't home? Then where was she?

"Miss Raj." A stern voice vibrated in our ears.

Disha gulped, turning her head around, frightened to see the very ringmaster behind us.

"Don't think I didn't see you back there." He said, each word with a pause in between.

Disha was lowering her head, "Sorry, sir."

He shook his head, his grip tightening on his baton, "You are coming back to camp and you are performing the trapeze act as you said you would."

"I've changed my mind–"

"No! I will not accept this."

And without a single word later, he was forcing us to come back to camp to prepare and practice.

He pointed at Norma, "Do you–"

"Nope! This is none of my business!" She yanked her eye mask back over, brought her grandson inside, and slammed the door closed. But the lock felt even louder.

We were walking back to the Circus Camp, joining the other kids who were practicing strenuously hard all week.

He grew incredibly angry at us, "Volunteer girl, go prepare the nets!"

"Yes, sir." I said, lowering my head and walking inside the large tent.

He threw a finger at Disha, "Well? Go practice!"

Disha lowered her head, "Yes sir…"

"No!" A voice screamed from the back. A familiar, silky, and sweet voice who was furious.

I turned, it was the one and only Aunt Katelyn.

Aunt Katelyn.

Aunt Katelyn.

"You have done too much to these innocent children." She protested. She was covered in splotches of paint, was wearing an apron, and had her hair tied up in a messy bun behind her.

The ringmaster simply said, "Ma'am, the show doesn't start until tomorrow, please come–"

She pointed a finger at him, "*None* of the parents and guardians of these children are coming. You hear me? This show is *not* happening."

The ringmaster shook his head, "Yes, they must. They have worked so hard that this show isn't even about their talents, it's about *you*."

The ring master took a step back, and then a step forward, fidgeting, "Nonsense, this camp has been nothing but an incredible opportunity for them."

Aunt Katelyn crossed her arms, "I will not tolerate your abhorrent attitude and from the looks of your personality, you have no respect for these children. No words of respect for my niece. If her friend changes her mind about a risky stunt, you have the right to let her."

My eyes started watering and I darted towards Aunt Katelyn, "Auntie! I missed you!" I dug my face into her apron and she hugged me with her arms wrapping all around me, "I missed you too, beanie."

"The children love it here." The ringmaster defended.

She placed one hand up, "Let's let them speak, shall we?"

One kid raised his hand, "The first days were fun, with good food, recess, fortune cookies, and learning the tricks. But after him forcing us to do tricks upside down, and barely feeding us, physically trying to make us contortionists, it was no fun."

Aunt Katelyn gave the I-told-you-so look to him and said, "Then it's settled, you have been violating the laws here and strenuously exerting these children. Their parents will be here shortly. Feed them, if you haven't."

"B-but–" he stammered.

"Everyone learns to win quietly and lose loudly, it's just that your loss is known all over town." She said, with a smile and held my hand, "Oh what's in this box?" She crouched down, "Now c'mon, Sienna, let's go home."

Then, we started walking our way to the trailer park, Aunt Katelyn smiled at me, "Don't worry, Disha's parents will pick her up too."

As we strolled through the meadow, she asked with a heavy sigh, "How was camp?"

I shrugged one shoulder, "It was fine–, but a lot more happened."

Her expression grew concerned and I told her everything. About Philoxenia, Edmonia, Mazie, Felix, the case, Whislow Agency, everything. Even that simulation the Zecron Pseudo orb gave me.

When I turned back to Aunt Katelyn, her eyes were streaming with tears, "Oh my goodness. I didn't think you'd ever discover that place."

I thought she would be upset, furious even for running away from camp without leaving a word. Yet instead, she seemed empathetic and almost guilty that I ended up having to face the traces of Zecron.

"Yeah, it's magical, but not all that perfect, Aunt Katelyn."

She nodded, her eyes streaming tears even more, "Oh Sienna. I'm proud of you for making that wish. It's not always easy to get out of desire, sometimes."

I nodded, "Yes, it wasn't easy."

She blinked her tears away and hugged me as hard as she could, an embrace never felt so much like home before. But it does now. Because Aunt Katelyn is my home.

She wiped one of her tears with her sleeve and said, "I didn't think you'd find out about your parents this way but I'm…I'm so sorry."

"It's alright, I guess it's kinda funny knowing I'm a kid of the 1900s."

She laughed, her tears muffling her voice, "Yes it is…and I also want you to know that your parents are still out there. *Somewhere.*"

I nodded, "I know, but I'm proud of dad."

"You are?"

"Yes, for raising the best little sister he could…because I couldn't ask for a better aunt."

Her face swelled and I put my ear close to her heart to hear her heartbeat when we hugged.

We finally reached the trailer park and Aunt Katelyn gestured a hand toward our house. "I tried making it look like a caravan…somewhat."

A grin tugged at my lips, "It's beautiful. And I like this one even more."

"I'm glad."

I finally set the brown box down and a memory flashed into my mind…

…"The clock, it's 11:11." Aunt Katelyn exclaimed, pointing at her clock she had since the circus that hung next to the oven. "Make a wish."

I closed my eyes and whispered out loud, "I wish Aunt Katelyn will wear a magical tiara for me."

Aunt Katelyn giggled, "Now don't tell me, or else it won't come true." She picked me off of the counter and carried me to bed…

…I opened the lid of the box and took out the tiara.

Aunt Katelyn gasped, her tears vanishing, "Tori's tiara…"

I lifted it up even higher, letting it shine with every bit of sunlight racing through the amethysts.

"You remember that 11:11clock?" I asked her.

She nodded, "Of course, how could I forget?"

"Well, my wish was that you would wear a magical tiara for me."

Her jaw dropped, "Sienna Cogsworth, your wish has come true." She slowly took a hold of the tiara and placed it in her beautiful brunette hair.

A pang of happiness stung my heart. It never felt so good to be home again.

I looked at the trailer, it wasn't the house in Idallis, it wasn't a mansion, but it was my perfect home. Because Aunt Katelyn is here.

I hugged her again, "I don't care how famous or not famous we are. How successful or not successful we are. As long as I am with you, Auntie, everything will be okay."

"Aww, you will always be my sweet home, little beanie. Because you are *priceless*. You know that?"

"What I do know is that I love you."

"I love you too."

The lights of the trailers were turning off and the sun was making its finale before running backstage for the night.

I stared at the sky where the sun was perched on top of the hills and the sky shades of pink and orange blended seamlessly. "I can't believe that's how a circus is, Auntie."

She shook her head, "A circus environment is based on the ringmaster. I've had so many co-performers with kind and caring directors, Sienna. If only I knew sooner–"

I paused her from the unnecessary guilt, "It's alright, I'm glad I got to go there. And find Philoxenia. And learn about life. And discover that I've always been happy, I don't need the boost of fame. I don't need you to undergo pressure to move us back to Idallis City. I want us to be where we can be comfortable."

Aunt Katelyn smiled. She patted Sienna back gently, "Well, Honeyville isn't anything like Idallis, but we can certainly make it phenomenal. Turn me into a lawyer, and you become an astronomer and we'll have an advanced town? Now, why don't we cherish a beautiful moment by the lake watching the sunset? And" She winked, whispering, "And we can go home and make a dessert together."

I grinned and nodded. "I think I'd love that."

We both strolled to the lake side and sat on the lake on the green, grassy hill.

The sun had dove into the lake and the vast night sky had appeared. Letting the shooting stars finally have their performance they were waiting for.

But it wasn't anything like the first time I gazed at the stars. It held promise, a painstaking yet satisfying reward that the promise held. That the universe held. The first time I looked up in the sky, I wondered why every star looked the same. Why they all decided to live in the sky and not anywhere else. But none of that was true. Because the greatest star of all was sitting right beside me. And she was priceless.

"The stars are beautiful tonight, aren't they, Sienna?" Aunt Katelyn said, stroking my ginger hair.

I nodded, "Yes. They truly are magical."

The End
(for now)

Acknowledgements

Oh, my goodness, I never though I'd finally get to write this page. I am filled with gratitude that you have made it to this page, for making it this far. For years, I've always kept my author dreams close, and now they're becoming true, all thanks to these people.

I want to first thank my Dad, who's helped me so much through the editing and publishing journey. For all the uphill battles and for never giving up, this book would not have been possible without you. I'll never forget the memories we've made on this project. You are always there to help me and support me, which is a very special thing I will never take for granted. Thank you to infinity for teaching me how to persevere, Dad.

To my mom, for always encouraging me to reach for the stars. I would have never have learned all of these valuable lessons if they weren't for you. Thank you for teaching me where home will always be and the true meaning of love. You are the true Clever Element, Mom.

To Sanvi, my little sister, for listening to all of my stories late at night even when it's time to sleep. I cannot wait for you to chase your dreams, whatever they may be. Don't you ever forget where our home will always be, no matter what.

As a current highschooler, I can not write this page without thanking *all* of my teachers. Even if you taught the opposite of English, you have still made your way into this book. For educating me and preparing me for the real world, I am forever grateful.

To my middle-school best-friend, for being the best writing buddy anyone could ask for. To all those Zoom and Google Meets meetings during the pandemic where we would chat about our stories, film our own T.V. shows, and fantasize about what our future holds. And thank you for listening to all of my ravings and rantings about my book. You brought light during times when there wasn't.

Thank you to all of my friends, for always being there for me. You never fail to put a smile on my face and I am so lucky to have you all. You girls are incredible.

And finally, thank *you*, reader. You have no idea how much you mean to me. Thank you for picking this book up and for making my dreams possible.

Until next time,
Aditi

About The Author

Aditi Bagul is a current high-school student who began her writing journey at the age of 11. From short stories to poems to full-sized novels, her author dreams emerged in middle school. When she's not crafting an elaborate fantasy universe, she loves playing the violin, the piano, golfing, and spending time with her family in California. You can often catch her volunteering at her local American Cancer Society Discovery Shop or playing the piano for retirement communities and hospitals.

www.ingramcontent.com/pod-product-compliance
Lightning Source LLC
Chambersburg PA
CBHW030112310726
48970CB00004B/1247